MURDER IN PORTOFINO

T. A. WILLIAMS

Boldwood

First published in Great Britain in 2024 by Boldwood Books Ltd.

Copyright © T. A. Williams, 2024

Cover Design by JD Design Ltd.

Cover Photography: Shutterstock

A CIP catalogue record for this book is available from the British Library.

Paperback ISBN 978-1-83518-762-3

Large Print ISBN 978-1-83518-763-0

Hardback ISBN 978-1-83518-761-6

Ebook ISBN 978-1-83518-764-7

Kindle ISBN 978-1-83518-765-4

Audio CD ISBN 978-1-83518-756-2

MP3 CD ISBN 978-1-83518-757-9

Digital audio download ISBN 978-1-83518-760-9

Boldwood Books Ltd
23 Bowerdean Street
London SW6 3TN
www.boldwoodbooks.com

To Mariangela and Christina with love as always

1

WEDNESDAY AFTERNOON

'You want to know something?'

Oscar looked up from the stick he'd been assiduously tearing apart with his teeth and I saw the end of his tail give a lazy wag. Taking this to be a sign of interest, I let him in on the secret.

'I was crazy to worry about Anna moving in with me. It's working out fine.'

I got no response but, in fairness, I wasn't expecting any. Labradors aren't renowned for their conversation skills, but Oscar makes up for it by being a very good listener. I continued my one-sided conversation with him. 'It's been almost a month now and we haven't had so much as a hint of an argument.'

My girlfriend, Anna, had moved into my little house in the hills outside Florence with me at the beginning of June and, in spite of my initial fears, being in close proximity all day every day hadn't made things weird between us – very much the opposite, in fact. Living with her felt increasingly natural and, as far as Oscar was concerned, he appeared riotously happy to have her in the house, not least as she still hadn't quite learnt to harden her heart when he put on his 'I'm starving' look.

I leant back against the rocky outcrop, stretched my legs and gave a contented sigh. The hot July sun here in Tuscany had almost completely dried me by now after my swim – well, more of a gentle paddle in the barely waist-deep water of the nearby stream – and I was a happy man.

My blissful state of relaxation was interrupted by my phone. As I scrambled for it on the ground alongside me, it occurred to me not for the first time that since settling here in Tuscany two years ago, I had now become remarkably relaxed about receiving phone calls. Back in the days when I had been DCI Armstrong of Scotland Yard, being constantly on call had taken its toll, not only on me and my happiness, but also on my already failing marriage. That had come to an end with divorce the previous year and, since then, my life had definitely been on an upward trajectory, even though I had just had my fifty-seventh birthday and I knew that sixty was right around the corner. Still, on a wonderful day like this in such a spectacular rural setting, I didn't feel too decrepit yet and I knew a phone call was no longer to be dreaded.

'Hi, Lina, what have you got for me?'

'How would you feel about taking on a case in Lucca?' Almost a year ago now, I set up my own investigation agency here in Florence and Lina is my personal assistant, receptionist, researcher, occasional dog-walker and friend. She's also the wife of my best friend over here – Inspector Virgilio Pisano of the Florence murder squad.

'What sort of case?'

'A missing person. A woman in her twenties has been missing for weeks and the parents are very worried.'

I gave it a bit of thought. Lucca is just over an hour's drive from my home and in fact, I was going there in two days' time to an open-air concert by no less a figure than Bob Dylan, appearing as one of the star acts at the annual Lucca Music Festival. I'd been to the pretty little city on a couple of occasions before and, although I didn't know it as well as Florence, I was reasonably familiar with it and I liked it as a place. As for the missing person, it wouldn't be the first time a twenty-something had decided to up sticks and go off somewhere, so I didn't get too excited – yet.

'Have you spoken to the parents?'

'The woman's sister. She was on the phone a few moments ago. She's taking a train to Florence in a few minutes and she's desperate for help. I told her I'd see if I could locate you and get back to her. I know you're supposed to be on holiday this week, but she really did sound in a bad way.'

I gave it some thought. Anna had gone into the university to do some work this afternoon so I had no particular commitments. 'What's the name of the woman you spoke to?'

'Diana Greensleeves.'

'That doesn't sound a very Italian name.'

'No, she's English... sorry, British.'

'And presumably, she's contacting us because she doesn't speak Italian?'

'Hardly a word. We didn't talk much – and you know what my English is like. To be honest, Dan, she was sounding worried. It would be nice to help her.'

I could tell from Lina's tone that the woman had made a strong impression on her so it didn't take me long to make up my mind. I glanced at my watch. 'Okay, it's almost two o'clock so give me a chance to get changed and I'll be with you by three. Give her a call and say I'll be happy to lend a hand – as long as she doesn't mind the smell of damp Labrador.'

I drove into Florence in my new VW van, still savouring the new car smell – although in fact, I had bought it second-hand and it was already two years old – but by the time I reached the office, even with the windows open, it was smelling less new and more of wet dog. I squeezed in through the narrow gateway and parked in my usual spot in the internal courtyard. It had taken me time and perseverance but after a lot of horse-trading with the owners of the five-hundred-year-old building where I had my office, I had been able to do a deal that gave me that most precious of things: a parking space just inside Florence's *centro storico*. Leaving the van there, Oscar and I hurried up the fine old stair-case to the first floor and went in through the door marked *Dan Armstrong, Private Investigations*.

While Lina made a fuss of my four-legged friend – now almost completely dry again – she explained that Diana Greensleeves was due to arrive at Florence Santa Maria Novella station as we spoke and that she hoped to be with us shortly afterwards. I queried whether the woman had given any more information about the missing person but all that Lina could add was that she had described her as her 'little sister'. I went through to my office, where it was stiflingly hot, and threw open the windows, pausing for a few moments, as always, to take in the view out over the roofs of this historic part of Florence. In spite of working here for almost a year now, I still hadn't tired of the over-whelming sense of history this city inspires in me.

Diana Greensleeves arrived at three-fifteen. She was wearing a formal, dark-blue, two-piece suit and it was immediately clear that she wasn't dressed for July temperatures here in Tuscany. Today, Florence was in the mid-thirties. She looked positively sweltering and I wasn't the only one to notice. After ushering the woman into my office, Lina returned less than a minute later with a bottle of cold mineral water and two glasses. I filled one and passed it across to my guest.

'A bit warmer here than Lucca?'

She took the glass from me willingly and gave me a grateful

smile. 'Yes, and a *lot* warmer than Guildford.' She looked as though she was around my daughter's age, probably in her late twenties or early thirties, and she had an educated English accent.

'You've come from England today?'

'I flew over last night and I've spent this morning in Lucca, trying to see if I could find any trace of Heather.'

'That's your sister who's gone missing?' She nodded and I continued. 'How old is she?'

'Twenty-three, almost twenty-four.'

'And when you were in Lucca this morning, did you find out anything?'

'A complete waste of time, I'm afraid. There was no answer at her flat and the school was all locked up. I speak no Italian so I haven't even been able to ask around. Hopefully, that's where you come in.'

'You mentioned a school?'

'The school of English where Heather was working. She did an "English as a foreign language" teaching course after finishing university and then she came straight over here. This is her first real job.'

'So she was teaching English?'

'Yes, mostly to adults. She's been living in Lucca for two years now. She's never been great at keeping in touch, but my parents haven't heard from her for a month or more now and she's not replying to her phone. Mum and Dad are very worried, so they asked me to come over and take a look.'

I was interested by her choice of vocabulary. 'Your mum and dad are very worried, but maybe *you* aren't so concerned?'

She looked up and caught my eye. 'To be quite honest, Heather's always been a bit of a tearaway. Although she's four years younger than me, when I was still doing my A levels, she was already running around with boys. After I'd gone off to uni, she was quite out of control for a few years and that's why we were all so pleased when she finally got her act together and got herself a degree and then this job.'

'So you maybe think this might just be your sister being a bit thoughtless, doing her own thing?'

She nodded. 'It wouldn't be the first time. I'm here because Mum and Dad asked me to come. I'm worried, but I'm nothing like as worried as they are.'

'I see. And the last time any of you heard from her was over a month ago?'

'Mum's been phoning her most weeks just to check that she's doing all right, but since late May, Heather hasn't been answering her phone. That's almost six weeks now.' She gave me a helpless look. 'I feel pretty sure this is going to turn out to be a wild goose chase but I owed it to Mum and Dad to come over. The trouble is that I don't speak Italian, and Mum and Dad don't speak a word of it either. It's been almost impossible to talk to anybody. Heather's phone doesn't even ring any more so it's either broken or the battery's run out. There's nothing from her on social media, no emails, nothing.' Her expression became a bit more concerned. 'She did everything with her phone and she carried it everywhere with her so it's weird that there's no response – although she's never been great at remembering to charge the battery.'

'But surely the other staff at the school must speak English.'

'It's high summer. As far as I could see, the school's closed and I haven't been able to find a soul to talk to.'

'Have you notified the Italian police?'

She shook her head. 'That's the next thing on my list – if she really has disappeared. I was rather hoping you might be able to come with me to do that. I imagine that you speak Italian.'

'I do indeed. Tell me, what made you come to me?'

'I looked up private investigators on the Internet and I chose the one with the English-sounding name.'

'Fair enough.' I paused for thought. I had a feeling that Diana was right and this probably was a wild goose chase but, for Lina's sake, I felt I had to offer to help. 'What are your plans tonight? Do you have a hotel room booked somewhere?'

'Yes, in Lucca. It's right in the centre of town, not far from the school. I'm planning on taking the train back there again after I finish speaking to you.'

I did a bit of calculation. Anna had said she wasn't going to be home until a lot later this evening because she would be at a hen party for one of her colleagues in the Medieval and Renaissance History department where she worked. If I set off now, I should hopefully be in Lucca by half past four or just after. A couple of hours to check things out and, if necessary, notify the police and I could still be back home well before Anna returned. I had been doing my best to spend as much time as possible with her recently, to prove to her – and myself – that she was more important to me than my job. As a start, this week off had been just about my first real 'holiday' since setting up the agency the previous year.

'If you like, I could drive to Lucca with you now and spend a couple of hours looking around. Hopefully, that way we can find out a bit more and, if necessary, go to the police.'

Diana looked massively relieved. 'Thank you so much, but shouldn't we sort out your remuneration first?' She caught my eye and gave me a little smile. 'I'm a lawyer so I like to keep everything above board.'

I gave her a copy of my terms and conditions and then added a practical suggestion. 'Why don't I come with you now so I can see what's what, and then the two of us can sit down and talk about money later on? I've no idea at this stage what's involved or how long it might take me to find your sister – if, indeed, she really has disappeared in suspicious circumstances.'

I saw her eyes run down the sheet of paper without any appreciable reaction. My rates aren't cheap but they compare pretty favourably with many of the other Italian investigative agencies. Finally, she looked back up again and nodded. 'This all seems fine and that sounds like a very sensible suggestion, Mr Armstrong. Thank you.'

'I've got the van outside. Why don't we head off straight away?'

2

WEDNESDAY AFTERNOON

It took a bit longer than expected to fight my way out of the Florentine traffic, made worse by flotillas of campervans and tourist vehicles from all over Europe. Florence in the summer months becomes overrun with visitors from around the globe and I had already discovered that even just walking from my office to the station could be a real challenge. However, by now I knew a few shortcuts to avoid the worst of the traffic jams and we arrived in Lucca as church bells were chiming five o'clock. A Spanish-registered Mercedes reversed out of a parking space just as we came along and I was able to park barely a hundred metres from the Porta San Pietro, one of the half-dozen gates through the massive red brick and stone defensive walls that surround the old town.

Although not as well known today as Florence to the east or Pisa to the west, Lucca is a real gem. The old town had its origins in pre-Roman times, and during the medieval and Renaissance period, the city was one of the most powerful and one of the wealthiest in Italy, if not the whole of Europe. Because of the rich variety of historic buildings within the walls, the city has quite rightly been named a major player in Italy's artistic and cultural heritage. The last time I had been here had been with Anna, and having my own Renaissance expert to point out places of historic interest had been fascinating.

But today, I wasn't a tourist.

I asked Diana to lead me to the school where her sister had been working, after which we would try visiting Heather's home address. We walked past the entrance to the Piazza Grande where a huge stage with batteries of lighting and sound equipment had been erected for the festival events. The square itself was filled with rows of seats, and technicians were working on stage getting things ready for Robbie Williams, who would be performing this evening. Lucca Festival attracts big-name acts.

The school occupied the first floor of a building in the *centro storico*, within the defensive walls, set a short distance from the main historical sights. As Diana had already discovered that morning, the place looked closed, and pressing the bell marked *Lucca English Centre* on the intercom by the door to the street brought no response. Unperturbed, I started pressing all of the other bells one by one until I got a response. There was a crackling sound and then a voice answered.

'*Chi è?*' It was a male voice and it sounded as though it didn't belong to a young man.

I switched to Italian. 'I'm sorry to bother you but I'm trying to speak to somebody from the English language school and there's no reply from them. I don't suppose you know how we could get in touch, do you?'

'They're closed for the summer. If it's like last year, they won't open again until the end of August.'

'Is there a caretaker here who might have a contact phone number?'

I heard the man give a little snort of derision. 'There is, but he's on holiday as well. He and his family have gone back to Romania for a month. Try the top-floor apartment. One of the teachers has been living there, but I'm not sure if he's still around now.'

I thanked the man and checked the top button on the intercom. It was marked *Smith*. This looked hopeful so I pressed it and waited. About ten seconds later, I was delighted to hear a buzzing sound and the front door clicked open. I turned to Diana.

'Let's go up and see what Mr Smith has to say.'

There was no lift in the old building and we had to climb four flights of stairs. Needless to say, Oscar got to the top before we did. There were two doors on the landing and the right-hand bell push was marked *Smith*. I pressed it and thirty seconds later, the door was opened by a lanky man, probably in his early forties, with a ponytail. He was barefoot and wearing the baggiest pair of shorts I had ever seen, accompanied by a scruffy, black T-shirt marked *Lucca Summer Festival 2018*.

'Mr Smith?'

'Yes... *sì.*' He sounded a bit vague.

I introduced Diana and outlined why we were here. In view of his surname, I spoke English and it was clear that he understood. He nodded a few times and replied, still sounding very woolly.

'What day is it today?' He spoke with just the vaguest hint of a Northern Irish accent – presumably, he had been living over here for some considerable time and his original accent had mellowed as a result.

'Wednesday.'

'Wednesday... I see.' There was a pause long enough for Diana and me to exchange sceptical looks before the man continued. 'And you're looking for Heather, you say?'

'That's right. There's been no word from her for over a month now and her family are getting worried. Have you any idea might have happened to her?'

The man ran his hands across his face, clearly doing his best to stimulate his brain. As he did so, Oscar started sneezing and I recognised the familiar smell percolating through the door behind the man. I've had enough experience over my years in the Metropolitan Police to recognise the unmistakable smell of cannabis. This explained this guy's clueless state. I was no longer on the force, so how he spent his free time was nothing to do with me, but I needed information so I did my best to walk him through my dilemma.

'One of your neighbours downstairs said that you work as a teacher at the school. Is that right?'

'Yes, sort of. I don't teach much these days. I'm the director of studies.'

'And you know Heather well?'

There was still a distant air about him, but he did at least nod immediately. 'Yes, she's been working here for a couple of years now.'

'Has she been in to work recently?'

He managed to shake some sense out of his befuddled brain. 'We close down over the months of July and August. I haven't seen her for a couple of weeks.'

'But she was here then?' I glanced at Diana. At least it would appear that Heather hadn't been missing for six weeks after all.

He nodded slowly. 'Right till the end of June. She didn't miss any lessons. She's always been pretty reliable, but, like I say, the school's closed now. I imagine she's gone on holiday.'

'Have you any idea where she might have gone? Do you think she might have stayed here or gone off somewhere?'

He shrugged. 'I've no idea, I'm afraid.'

'Is there anybody who might know? A boyfriend maybe?'

'Not that I know of, but we have half a dozen teachers and I'm not too clued up about their private lives.' From the look of him, he probably wasn't too clued up about anything right now.

'What about any of the other teachers? Would any of them know?'

There was a brief pause. 'You could try Rose.'

'Rose?'

'Rose Alighieri, she's one of the teachers.'

'And how do I contact her?'

It was like getting blood out of a stone, but I finally managed to get the phone number of this other teacher and confirmation that Mr Smith hadn't got a clue what might have happened to Heather. In fairness, from the state of him, he probably couldn't remember what he had had for breakfast, and it was painfully obvious that I wasn't going to get much more information here. I thanked him and, before leaving, gave him a little bit of advice.

'We may have to report Heather's disappearance to the police, so you might be getting a visit from a police officer some time soon. It might be a good idea to open your windows and let some fresh air in.'

A look of concern now flooded across his face and he hastily retired into his flat. Diana and I went back downstairs again and headed for a shady spot on the other side of the stone-paved street. I turned towards her.

'That's encouraging, isn't it? At least she was here and working only two weeks ago.'

'Yes, indeed.' Diana was sounding less concerned – and to be honest, she hadn't sounded that concerned in the first place. 'What now?'

'Do you know your way from here to Heather's apartment? Why don't we go there first and I'll see if I can speak to the landlord, her flatmates or a neighbour and then, if we draw a blank, we can try phoning this other teacher.'

Our walk to Heather's apartment didn't take long. This was barely ten minutes on foot from the school, just on the other side of the historic Piazza dell'Anfiteatro, originally the site of a two-thousand-year-old Roman amphitheatre. It came as a surprise to see that the apartment was located in a block of four apartments created in a beautifully restored Renaissance building with a videophone entry system. It looked as though considerable money had been spent on renovating the ancient structure and I found myself wondering how a humble EFL teacher could afford to live in such luxurious surroundings.

I pressed the bell marked *H. Greensleeves*, interested to see that this probably meant that she wasn't sharing with other people. I glanced sideways at her well-turned-out sister in her smart suit, beginning to think that maybe the Greensleeves family were wealthy and subsidising Heather's teaching salary. Alternatively, maybe Heather had a second job. I waited ten seconds and then pressed the bell again, harder. After a wait of half a minute, it became quite clear that there was nobody home.

I checked out the other three bells and saw that only two of them had names alongside the buttons: Schaffhausen and Chieti. I tried pressing all three bells, including the anonymous one, but there was no response from any of them. Finally, I turned and looked around, searching for any signs of life in this quiet side street. Apart from a handful of tourists in shorts and T-shirts walking along, hugging the shade, there was just one open doorway, diagonally opposite, so I crossed the road and tapped on the door. Seconds later, an elderly woman appeared, carrying an old-fashioned witch's broomstick. She looked down suspiciously towards Oscar.

'Please don't let your dog pee on my doorstep. I've only just finished cleaning up.'

Oscar looked mildly offended and I answered for him. 'I promise he's on his best behaviour. I was just wondering if you could tell me anything about the house on the other side of the road.'

'What sort of thing?' She was probably well into her eighties but her eyes were bright and she looked alert. I had a feeling nothing much escaped this lady.

'I'm looking for an Englishwoman who lives in one of the flats. This is her sister but I'm afraid she doesn't speak Italian.'

A distinct look of disapproval appeared on the old lady's face. 'That would be the blonde girl with the short skirts.'

Diana had brown hair but, of course, that proved nothing. Still, I checked with her. 'Does Heather have blonde hair?'

She nodded. 'Almost certainly. It changes every now and then, but she's tended to be more blonde than anything else over the last year or two.' She gave me a little smile. 'She says Italian men like blondes.'

'And does she like Italian men?'

Diana shrugged. 'She likes all men… and they like her.'

I could see the old lady attentively following our conversation and I wondered how much she had understood, so I turned back to her and gave her an apologetic look. 'Sorry, I was just checking to see if the woman we're looking for is indeed blonde.'

The old lady smiled. 'That sounds like her and I definitely get the impression she likes the men.'

'You speak English?'

'I don't speak it much these days as I don't have the opportunity. I worked in the Grand Hotel for thirty-seven years and the lingua franca for most of our guests was English so I picked up a good bit. What's the problem? Has something happened to the girl?'

'That's what we're trying to find out. I don't suppose you know where she might have gone? Have you seen her recently?'

She paused for a few moments' reflection. 'Not for a few days. I think the last time I saw her was, let me think, Friday night. Yes, last Friday night. She and one of her paramours came home at two o'clock in the morning and woke me up. I looked out of the window and saw them canoodling in the street before going indoors. She can be quite inconsiderate sometimes, although she's pleasant enough if you meet her and chat to her in the street.'

I relayed the information to Diana that her sister had been seen as recently as just five days ago and I saw her nod a couple of times.

'I told Mum and Dad not to worry. Anyway, that's very good news.'

I checked with the observant neighbour but she was unable to offer any suggestions about where Heather might have gone except for repeating what the director of studies had said. 'She's probably gone off for a few days' holiday. It gets so manic here during festival time, I don't blame her.'

Diana and I thanked her for her help and set off along the street until we came to a gelateria with tables outside in the shade. We sat down and both ordered mineral water and ice creams and I put in a plea for some water for Oscar as well. After the waiter had gone off, I turned towards Diana.

'What do you think? That all sounded very positive. Do you think your mum and dad will still be worried after they've heard this?'

She shook her head. 'As far as I'm concerned, this means everything's okay and I'm sure Mum and Dad will agree. It sounds as if Heather's got a boyfriend – and that comes as no surprise, knowing her – so I bet they've just gone off somewhere together and she couldn't be bothered to tell any of us. I certainly don't think we need to involve the police now, do we?'

'I think I'll just give this Rose woman a call. You never know, Heather may have said something to her about where she was going.'

I waited until the waiter had brought me a mixture of peach, apricot and vanilla ice cream and what had been described on the menu as a 'Chocolate Mountain' for Diana. This was a pyramid of white and dark chocolate ice cream liberally smothered in Chantilly cream. I caught her eye and grinned. 'That should keep you out of trouble for a while.'

She grinned back and that grin was repeated by Oscar when he saw that the waiter had very kindly brought him, not only a bowl of cool water, but also a handful of those fan-shaped biscuits you find on an ice-cream sundae. Needless to say, these were consumed before we even had time to pick up our spoons. Oscar likes his food but he doesn't exactly linger over it and savour it.

The ice cream was predictably excellent and from the speed with which Diana started devouring hers – not quite in the same league as Oscar but pretty fast all the same – it looked as though she shared my opinion. After a few delicious mouthfuls, I picked up my phone and called Heather's fellow teacher. It was answered almost immediately.

'*Pronto.*'

I spoke to her in English. 'Is that Rose Alighieri?'

'Yes, who's speaking?' In spite of her surname, she sounded distinctly Scottish.

'Sorry to disturb you, my name's Dan Armstrong. I'm here in Lucca with Diana Greensleeves, Heather's sister, and we're looking for her. Mr Smith at the English school gave us your number. We were wondering if you might know where she's gone.'

After a momentary pause for thought, Rose answered. 'She's on holiday. She told me last week she was going off on a cruise, but I'm not sure where.'

'Thanks for that. We wondered if she'd maybe gone off on holiday. Any idea if she's on her own?'

I heard a little laugh. 'Knowing Heather, I think the answer to that one is almost certainly no. You can be sure she's gone off with one of her men and I bet I know which one.'

'And he might be...?'

'Mario, or maybe it's Mauro, I forget. He's the one with the Ferrari and the yacht. I bet she's with him.'

'A Ferrari and a yacht? Who is this guy: a professional football player?'

'Search me. I didn't know there were such rich men here in Lucca. Me, I ended up with a pharmacist as a husband.'

I tried pushing her to discover the surname or address of Heather's holiday companion but it became clear that Heather's love life consisted of a panoply of men and Rose was unable to produce any more details. As for the cruise, she had no idea except that it was almost certainly here in local waters. I heard a little child begin to cry in the background and hastily thanked Rose for her help and rang off. I recounted what she had said and Diana gave me a long-suffering look.

'That's our Heather! I would have laid money on her having gone off somewhere with some random man – mind you, a Ferrari and a yacht is a bit OTT even for her.' Before resuming her ice cream, she confirmed that she was feeling the same way as I was. 'I think on the basis of what we've heard, we can take it that Heather's alive and well, don't you?'

I nodded in agreement. 'Definitely, and I certainly don't think there's any need to involve the police.'

She picked up her spoon again. 'Thank you for all your help. I'm sorry to have troubled you. I told Mum and Dad they were worrying about nothing, but they insisted.'

'No problem. I'll give you my phone number just in case you need me, but I think you should be able to relax now.' It occurred to me that this had to be one of the easiest cases I'd ever handled. Presumably, Heather Greensleeves was away sunning herself with her well-heeled boyfriend and this was the last I would hear of her. As for her sister, she had at least had a few hours in a beautiful city. 'What are your plans? Are you staying on to see Bob Dylan on Friday?'

She shuddered. 'Not if you paid me. I sing better in the bath than he does. Besides, I'm flying home tomorrow.' She shot me an enquiring look. 'Are you going to the concert?' Seeing me nod, she asked the obvious question. 'Are you a Dylan fan?'

I gave her a wink. 'I'll know better after I've seen him.'

3
_____

FRIDAY EVENING

'Well, what did you think of Bob Dylan?'

Anna and I had just collected Oscar from the very obliging owner of our bed & breakfast who had offered to look after him while we went to the concert, and we were taking him for a walk through the darkened streets of Lucca en route to our after-concert dinner. Dark didn't mean cool – it was still twenty-eight degrees although the time on the illuminated display outside a chemist's shop ahead of us indicated that it would be eleven o'clock in just a few minutes.

I had to wait a few moments while Anna chose her words carefully. 'I thought it was interesting, and Dylan's certainly an amazing performer considering he's now in his eighties, but to be perfectly honest, the music didn't do a lot for me.'

This came as no surprise for several reasons. For as long as I'd been with Anna, I'd never known her to be particularly interested in modern music – if something written and sung by an octogenarian can be qualified as 'modern'. The other reason it didn't surprise me was that I felt exactly the same way about the concert we had just attended.

I was very grateful to Virginia, Anna's daughter, who had gifted us the tickets to the Dylan concert at the end of a very pleasant week she had spent with us in June. Hedging her bets, she had also very kindly given us a pair of tickets for an opera at the Arena in Verona next month as well. Opera is definitely more Anna's thing than mine. Personally, I can take it or leave it – and some of it I can definitely leave – but we were both looking forward to visiting Verona in August. We would see whether the performance in the historic setting of the Arena might stir my blood.

I spotted the restaurant just a bit further down the road and glanced at Anna. 'That's it there. Are you sure they'll still serve us at this time of night?'

'Yes, it's all booked. They're doing a special after-show serving.' She laid a comforting hand on my arm. 'Don't worry, *carissimo*, you won't go hungry, I promise.'

As usual, we were speaking English together, which she speaks a whole lot better than I speak Italian. I smiled back at her. 'I knew you'd have everything under control. Anyway, I know what you mean about Dylan. It was to promote his new album, but I'm afraid I would have much preferred some of his old classics like "Blowin' in the Wind" or "Like a Rolling Stone". Still, it isn't every day we can listen to a living legend, is it?'

We were shown to a table in the courtyard behind the restaurant where Oscar was able to sprawl at our feet on the cool cobbles. The only problem with the cobbles was that I had to spend a minute or so fiddling around with the table until it was reasonably steady on its four legs on the uneven surface. As it was late, the restaurant was offering a fixed menu consisting of mixed antipasti followed by a choice of either cold prawn and scallop salad or grilled steak and fries. We both opted for the fish, although I'm sure if Oscar had been given a vote, he would have chosen steak any day.

It was a delightful evening, only slightly marred by a very noisy group inside the restaurant. The uproarious laughter, shouts and screams coming out through the open windows even caused Oscar to raise his head in disapproval a few times but they certainly didn't spoil our meal. From what I could hear, the group inside was made up of my fellow countrymen and women and I almost felt like apologising to the other diners on their behalf. Some people on holiday do have a tendency to overdo the booze.

The food was excellent and it was good to relax with Anna alongside me. We chatted about her work and I told her a bit more about my brief visit to Lucca two days earlier. She shook her head sadly. 'Children can be a real worry sometimes: so inconsiderate.'

'The missing woman is twenty-three, going on twenty-four, hardly a child.'

'Yes, but I still can't help thinking about my Virgina as an eleven-year-old.' She gave me a little grin. 'I know she's almost thirty and you probably think I'm crazy, but that's just the way I'm made and I'm sure a lot of mothers feel the same way. I can empathise with the parents of your missing girl. Anyway, it's good to hear she's all right. I wonder where she's gone for her cruise.'

'Wherever it is, she's got perfect weather for it – at least so far.'

After panna cotta with a caramel sauce followed by an espresso, I left Oscar snoozing at Anna's feet and went inside to the cash desk to pay. As I passed the room where all the noisy diners were still making a terrible racket, I noticed a sign on the door marked *Private Party*. At that moment the door itself opened and a waitress came out. She was looking a bit flustered and a wave of raucous laughter followed her. Glancing over her shoulder, I caught sight of three or four of the revellers sitting around a big table and, to my surprise, immediately recognised two of them as household names as far as British television viewers were concerned, although they were probably totally unknown to a European audience.

I struggled for a moment for the names and then they came to me: Martin Grey and Susie Upton, well-known comic actors who regularly appeared in sitcoms and satirical shows. I don't watch a lot of TV, particularly since settling here in Italy, but even I recognised them. I wondered whether they were here on business or for pleasure. From the look of them, I settled on the latter. Both were red in the face and looked slightly the worse for wear, probably as a result of overindulgence in food and wine. I just had time to notice that Susie Upton was wearing a far more revealing dress than her usual TV attire before the door closed again – but presumably she was on holiday, after all.

After queuing up to pay the bill, I headed for the door marked *Servizi*. This consisted of three cubicles with a couple of wash-basins outside. I went into the last cubicle in the line and as I was answering the call of nature, I heard two voices from outside by the washbasins and they immediately drew my attention.

'I'm going to bloody strangle him!' It was a man with a fairly neutral Home Counties accent and he sounded furious.

'Not if I get to him first.' This was another man. His accent was harder to place – maybe originally Welsh, but now overlaid with a liberal helping of London – and he sounded angry but maybe not equally enraged. I listened, fascinated, as the first man carried on cursing, no doubt unaware that they were being overheard.

'How could he do that? Lying, cheating bastard! Wait till I get my hands on him, I'll do for him!' There was the sound of rushing water as one of them washed his hands. Moments later, I heard the entrance door being opened and I just caught the other man's voice as he left the room.

'If I haven't already done it for you!'

By the time I emerged back into the main part of the restaurant, the two conspirators had disappeared but I spotted the door to the private party room closing behind somebody, maybe the two of them, but it was impossible to say. I went back to the table where Oscar was still stretched out on the ground looking as though he was settled for the night, and I sat down beside Anna to finish the last of the wine in my glass. I told her about the two famous faces I had just identified in the private dining room and recounted the conversation I had overheard in the loo. Her reaction was to give me a wry smile.

'And of course Dan the detective is now convinced he's just heard two men conspiring to commit murder. Am I right?'

'No, not necessarily.' In fact, she had read my mind – not for the first time – but I felt I should protest all the same. 'They were probably just letting off steam, but I wonder who they were talking about.'

'And you think they might be part of that group of British comics in the private dining room making all the noise?'

'I think they might be, but I couldn't swear to it. They were definitely British though.'

She gave me a gentle pat on the arm. 'Well, don't worry, you aren't going to have to swear to anything. This isn't a court of law and I'm prepared to wager that it was nothing more than alcohol-fuelled belligerence. By tomorrow, they'll probably have forgotten they were even talking to each other.'

'I wonder...'

A couple of minutes later, we roused Oscar and went back into the restaurant, heading for the exit. Just as we were approaching the door to the private dining room, it was flung open and we stepped back to let the occupants out. One of the first to emerge was an animated-looking Susie Upton. As soon as she caught sight of Oscar, she came over and immediately squatted down to make a fuss of him and, as she did so, her low-cut dress opened even more and I found myself faced with a totally new view of the famous comedienne, one that I felt sure UK television viewers were unlikely to ever be shown. Unaware of or unconcerned by her exposed state, she gave Oscar a big hug and he was only too happy to reciprocate by attempting to lick her ear. A moment or two later, a large man with an even redder face appeared behind her, grabbed her by the arm and hauled her to her feet without ceremony and gave Oscar and, by extension, me a filthy look as he started to drag her away.

Oscar glanced towards me with an expression on his face that quite clearly translated as, *What's his problem?*

I didn't recognise this man and I wondered what his connection to Susie might be. Might this even be her husband? If so, I assumed she had married him for his money, influence or some hidden talents because, as my gran used to say, he had clearly been behind the door when they had been handing out the good looks. Just to add insult to injury – literally – he was sporting a piratical black eyepatch over his left eye. Apart from having a face like the dark side of the moon and nostrils like the entrance to the Channel Tunnel, he looked as if he was a good fifteen or twenty years older than Susie Upton, almost completely bald apart from a lone tuft of hair marooned bizarrely above his forehead, and he was sporting the kind of pot belly that defies any attempt by a belt to control it.

To my surprise, Susie didn't respond angrily to being manhandled like this but just nodded obediently and let herself be led towards the exit. This struck me as strange but I don't have a lot of experience with TV stars. Maybe being manhandled about is par for the course for them. They were accompanied by fifteen or twenty other people who filed out of the private dining room, half a dozen of whose faces I recognised from UK television even if I couldn't remember their names. I found myself checking them all out as they went past, wondering whether two of these might be the pair I had overheard in the loo, but it was impossible to judge. Almost all of them were in high spirits and they were still making a hell of a racket as they finally left the building and peace settled in the restaurant behind them.

Anna and I took our time before following them out, hoping to give them the chance to disperse, but when we emerged from the restaurant, we found the noisy crowd still standing around, disturbing the whole street with their cackling laughter and hoots of approval or derision. My natural curiosity would have kept me there checking them out and trying to identify any other well-known faces – or maybe even recognising the voices I had overheard – but Anna had other ideas. She grabbed me by the arm and drew me away from the crowd.

'Leave them to it, Dan, before somebody calls the police and we get arrested along with them.'

She was right, of course, so I meekly obeyed and we headed back along the street so as to distance ourselves from the group. We turned the corner at the end and came out directly opposite the beautiful Basilica of San Frediano with its stunning golden mosaic façade. Even now in just the orange glow of the street lights, it was magnificent. I turned towards Anna and gave her a happy smile.

'You're right. I'm on holiday this week. No detective work.'

Little did I know…

4

SATURDAY

Breakfast in the B&B was unusually copious. Italian breakfasts rarely consist of more than coffee and a croissant but this morning, we were served fresh fruit salad with yoghurt, toast, butter and a choice of home-made jams, followed by peach tart still warm from the oven. This was accompanied by an excellent cappuccino for me and a pot of none other than English breakfast tea for Anna, and we had a wide-screen TV on the wall so we could watch the morning news. Even Oscar was catered for with his very own dish of dog biscuits, which he hoovered up in next to no time.

As Anna and I chatted over our leisurely breakfast, my eyes were repeatedly drawn to the TV screen and part of me – the annoying detective part – kept checking just in case there might be mention of the violent death of a Brit on holiday in Lucca, murdered by the two men I had overheard at the restaurant. Fortunately for my digestion – and my relationship – there were no reports of suspicious deaths hereabouts and we were able to enjoy a leisurely meal while we discussed our plans for the rest of the day. I started by asking Anna for her opinion.

'Is there anywhere you'd like to stop off on the way to Rapallo or shall we just drive straight there?'

As Anna had treated me to a weekend in Alassio on the Riviera coast for my birthday a few weeks earlier, I had decided to return the favour by taking her to a place she had long wanted to visit – Portofino. A quick scan of the few hotels in this resort of the rich and famous had confirmed my worst fears that the cheapest rooms still available in July were nudging a thousand euros for one night – without breakfast! In consequence, I had opted for three nights in a dog-friendly hotel in nearby Rapallo, still at a steep price, but a lot less than that. Rapallo is a seaside resort in its own right with a little ferry linking the town with Portofino in less than half an hour, and on a fine day like today, the mini cruise promised to be scenic in its own right.

Anna shook her head. 'Nowhere special. Everywhere on the coast is going to be packed, so why don't we just go straight to Rapallo, dump the van and take the ferry across to Portofino?'

It took an hour and a half on the motorway to get to Rapallo, mainly due to the traffic and the host of tunnels we encountered as the autostrada ran parallel to the rocky coastline. From time to time, we had tantalising glimpses of the brilliant blue of the Mediterranean – or more correctly here, the Ligurian Sea – dotted with yachts. I wondered idly if one of these belonged to Heather Greensleeves' Ferrari-owning paramour – as her elderly neighbour had named him. If so, then lucky her. It looked idyllic out there and a whole lot less frenetic than it was here on dry land.

We reached Rapallo around half past twelve and located the hotel without too much difficulty. I had deliberately chosen one with its own car park, although it was a bit of a squeeze to get the van into one of the tight spaces. Finally, I managed it and went in to inform them of our arrival. I was pleasantly surprised to be told that we could check in straight away, even though we had arrived so early. They gave us a comfortable room at the back of the hotel, which, although it didn't offer a sea view, was away from the direct sunlight and pleasantly cool even without the air conditioning. In fact, there was a charming view from the window up the steep tree-clad hillside behind and I could see a cable car linking the town with the hilltop high above. In Britain, we would probably have called something this high a mountain, although this was just one of the foothills of the Apennines that rise to over two thousand metres only a few kilometres inland from the coast.

We dumped our things, smothered ourselves with sun cream and headed down into the town. The first ten minutes of our walk involved risking life and limb on a precariously narrow pavement alongside a road with nose-to-tail – but thankfully slow-moving – traffic. For once, I kept Oscar on a lead as I had no desire to see him knocked down by a passing car, and I was relieved when we reached the pedestrian area. The little town was humming with holidaymakers and there appeared to be a café or restaurant on almost every street corner, as well as any number of shops selling seaside essentials ranging from buckets and spades to sun hats and bikinis. The seafront itself was typically Mediterranean, with a broad promenade shaded by huge palm trees and overlooking a fine sandy beach below. A busy road ran parallel to it and here there were numerous restaurants with tables outside, shaded by awnings and parasols. The sun beat down relentlessly from a cloudless sky and we took full advantage of the shade as we made our way to the little jetty from where the ferry would leave for Portofino.

Rapallo is situated in a sheltered bay with a harbour and a thriving marina, full of yachts. These ranged in size from little more than rubber dinghies to fine sailing yachts with masts twice the height of telegraph poles. Among these were assorted motor yachts ranging from the basic to the seriously expensive. Further out in the bay, there were several far bigger vessels, some of them with two or three decks and no doubt luxury accommodation for numerous passengers, and I spotted another, even larger one approaching from the south. Some had dropped anchor outside the marina, presumably because of their size. I wondered how far the budget of Heather Greensleeves' boyfriend might stretch. If he owned one of those monsters, he was doing really well – whatever it was he did.

We had the chance to see one of these private yachts at close quarters from the passenger ferry as we headed past the end of the breakwater into the open waters of the bay. Anna and I had opted to sit inside on the lower deck rather than outside in the direct sunlight, as much for our own sake as for my dog's. Black Labradors and baking-hot sun don't mix. It was also a bit less crowded down there as most passengers – almost exclusively tourists – had chosen to be up on the top deck in the open.

The motor yacht we passed towered over us. It was a sleek, stylish vessel with no fewer than three decks, not counting the captain's bridge and a sun platform above that, as well as a swimming pool at the rear with a couple of figures splashing around in it. It occurred to me that, with water all around, surely a swimming pool on a boat was a bit unnecessary unless the waters were shark infested, but maybe that was just me being cynical. Moored at the rear was a beautiful, glossy, wooden launch for ferrying the passengers to and from the shore if they so chose. I wondered who the owner of something like this might be. The flag at the rear gave little clue, although at first sight, it looked like a Red Ensign, the British maritime flag. Maybe the owner of the vessel was a Brit. If so, he or she certainly wasn't short of cash. As we passed close by the stern of the yacht, a little breath of wind opened the flag and I glimpsed something green on the red background of the flag apart from the Union Jack. I didn't have time to study it, but maybe this meant that the yacht didn't belong to a Brit after all.

As I had hoped, the views along the way were delightful. The coastline here was very rocky and the hills around the bay were covered in trees, interspersed with mature villas, some of them outstandingly beautiful. I was mildly surprised at how green it all was. No doubt the local authorities had imposed stringent construction regulations and the result was a remarkably unspoilt scene. We stopped halfway to Portofino in the little town of Santa Margherita Ligure where a handful of people got off, although the vast majority of the passengers were clearly headed for Portofino as we were. After barely two minutes, the ferry pulled away again and continued towards our destination.

The other surprise in store for me was how small Portofino was. I don't know what I had been expecting – maybe something like Monte Carlo with high-rise blocks and wall-to-wall housing, or at least an urban sprawl similar to the built-up slopes behind Rapallo, but such was not the case. As we rounded another rocky headland, the port opened up to us and I saw that Portofino really was tiny, situated in a little bay – and it had no doubt started life as a simple fishing port – with predominantly pink and cream buildings lining the shore around the harbour and an imposing castle on the hill above. The steeply sloping hillside behind these houses was covered in trees with occasional large villas peeking out between the branches. Altogether, it was probably smaller than my adopted home town of Montevolpone near Florence, and, considering Portofino's reputation as a playboy paradise, it wasn't what I'd been expecting. No flashy hotels, no historic casino and certainly no garish advertising. I glanced across at Anna.

'Nice-looking little place, isn't it?'

She smiled back. 'It's absolutely gorgeous, even if I was expecting something bigger.'

'Me too.'

The ferry pulled into a short jetty and virtually all the passengers got off, apart from a handful who were staying on to the boat's final destination around the corner to the north. Oscar, for whom this had been his first boat trip, appeared unmoved by the experience and merely cocked his leg against a stone bollard as a statement to other dogs that he was now claiming Portofino as his own.

We immediately made a couple of discoveries. First, the whole port area was pedestrians only and it was most pleasant not to have the background roar of traffic. The other – not altogether unexpected – find was that we certainly weren't the first people to visit the little port today. The place was absolutely heaving. Anna and I stood and just took it all in for a few minutes while, at my feet, Oscar did exactly the same, nostrils flared as he checked out the new environment. From the faces and the accents, it looked as though this place was every bit as cosmopolitan as Florence in the summer. There were quite a few Italian voices but for every Italian, there were probably three or four other nationalities ranging from French to Chinese, Scandinavian to Australian, alongside a considerable number of Americans.

We spent a very pleasant, if claustrophobic, hour walking around the little town, noticing luxury shops like Alexander McQueen and Gucci – needless to say without venturing inside – and a number of smart restaurants. Many had their menus on display outside and I checked out the prices to discover that they were probably in general twice or three times those of my local trattoria. A number of the menus were translated – or in some cases mistranslated – not only into English, but also frequently into Russian as well. These clearly played host to a broad mix of nationalities – especially the ones with deep pockets.

On our way back to the harbour, we stopped to buy ourselves a couple of cheesy focaccia sandwiches, which we ate perched on a stone bench in the shade, under the reproachful gaze of my dog, who clearly felt left out. As we consumed our snack, my eyes were drawn to three large motor yachts moored stern-on and I noticed that two of the three were flying the same Red Ensign with what looked like a green shield on it. After finishing our sandwiches, I led Anna over to get a closer look.

Standing by one of the yachts was a little group of uniformed officers. As we got closer, I could see that this consisted principally of an older officer dressed in an immaculate, white uniform, hung with gold braid. Along with him were a couple of younger officers, one male and one female, whose more practical white polo shirts had the words *GUARDIA COSTIERA* written on their backs. Evidently, these were members of the Coastguard.

I remembered my friend Virgilio back in Florence explaining to me that the Coastguard in Italy not only carries out the same functions as the equivalent force in the UK, ensuring maritime safety, but they are also a part of the Italian police force with an enforcement role as well. In effect, they are to the Italian coast and territorial waters what the *Polizia* or *Carabinieri* are on shore and they have the power to caution, arrest and investigate crimes committed on the water. He had once tried to explain the different roles of all the multiple Italian law enforcement agencies but by the time he had reached eight different entities, my eyes had glazed over. It has always struck me as a cumbersome system but it seems to work, although I do wonder just how well the competing forces manage to cooperate and collaborate.

This little group of officers had obviously just been speaking to one of the crew members from one of the big yachts and as the conversation ended and he turned away, I caught his eye, keen to satisfy my curiosity.

He had a badge on his left breast indicating that his name was Vincent, so I addressed him in English and it was clear that he understood. 'I wonder if you could just satisfy my curiosity for me. What flag is that?' I pointed at the Red Ensign with the green shield.

'BVI, the British Virgin Islands.' His accent sounded Australian to me.

'So does that mean you've sailed all the way over from the Caribbean?'

He shook his head. 'This boat's never been further than the Straits of Gibraltar but you'll find a lot of yachts are registered in BVI.' He gave me a little wink. 'For tax purposes.'

I thanked him, and Anna and I carried on with our leisurely stroll. Above us, the castle beckoned, but the narrow lane leading up towards it was so crowded, the people on it were almost stationary in places, and we decided to give it a miss for now. When we reached the end of the harbour directly beneath the castle, I was pleased to see half a dozen old-fashioned wooden fishing boats moored up and nets hanging in the sun to dry. Clearly, Portofino hadn't completely forgotten its roots. As the place was so crowded, we decided to find a café where we could sit and have a cool drink and Oscar could slurp up a bowl of water before we caught the ferry back to Rapallo. We would then return on the first boat next morning when hopefully, there wouldn't be so many people milling about.

By the time we made our return journey, the superyacht we had seen approaching had already dropped anchor just outside the breakwater at Rapallo and our route took us close enough to the stern of the three-decked luxury vessel to read the name: *Regal Princess*. I was just wondering whether it might belong to a member of one of the world's remaining royal families when I recognised one of the people on board and she wasn't royalty – TV royalty maybe, not real royalty. It was none other than Susie Upton, her flowing blonde hair partly hidden underneath a straw hat the size of a sombrero as she sat by the pool and read a book. I glanced across at Anna.

'Guess who? I presume the noisy group from the restaurant last night are staying on board that yacht.' The thought that leapt unbidden into my mind was whether the two men I had overheard in Lucca might now be aboard the *Regal Princess*, and whether the object of their wrath was still alive. Wisely, I didn't mention this to Anna. We were on holiday, after all.

Anna nodded. 'I presume they were moored up somewhere nearer to Lucca and they've cruised up the coast today. A rather nice way to spend a holiday, don't you think?'

'But you need a whole heap of money to rent one of those.'

'Or to own one…'

5

SUNDAY MORNING

After an excellent meal in Rapallo on Saturday night, we were up early to catch the nine o'clock ferry back to Portofino. It was another gorgeous day and even at this time, the temperature was already well into the twenties. This early on a Sunday morning, the ferry was only about half full and I hoped this would bode well for Portofino itself being a lot less claustrophobic than the previous day. When we left the harbour, I saw that the luxury yacht on which I had spied Susie Upton and her friends was no longer anchored just beyond the breakwater and I wondered where they had gone.

I didn't have to wait long to find out. As we approached Portofino, we passed close alongside the yacht, close enough to read the name on the stern. The vessel was now moored barely a couple of hundred metres from the entrance to the bay and I wondered if they had spent the night in Rapallo or had sailed over here yesterday evening. There was nobody visible on deck and I presumed they were still sleeping off the excesses of the previous night – assuming they had been indulging in food and drink to the same extent as they had done in Lucca.

My hopes were well founded and we were delighted to find that Portofino was far less crowded at this time of the morning. In consequence, we were able to walk up the path to the castle without hindrance. Close up, the castle was even more impressive with its massive defensive walls many metres thick, built of block after block of hard, grey stone. The upper part of the building had been transformed into living accommodation, but it still retained its unmistakable defensive feel and I could well imagine it being an impressive fortress in its day. The castle itself bore the very un-Italian name of Castello Brown. When we paid our five-euro entrance fee, we were handed a sheet that explained that the castle in its dominating position above the little harbour had originally been called Castello San Giorgio. It had fallen into disrepair in the seventeenth century but in the nineteenth century had been purchased by a gentleman with the impressive name of Montague Yeats-Brown, the local British Consul. He had restored it and transformed it back into residential accommodation. It had subsequently been sold on again, but now it was the property of the town authorities.

Photos on the walls revealed the numerous famous faces who had visited here over the years, including Winston Churchill, Walt Disney and famous actors like Humphrey Bogart and Lauren Bacall, and it was easy to see why they had chosen to come here. The views from the windows and terraces over the bay with its flotilla of yachts and lovely cream and pink buildings were delightful, although the steep drops on all sides didn't do a lot my for my fear of heights. The wooded slopes of the unspoilt hills surrounding Portofino added a charming backdrop to the scene and, vertigo or no vertigo, it was a beautiful and historic spot.

Looking down the almost vertical cliff from the main terrace to the sea far below, the water was so clear, it was possible to see right to the bottom, and I was sure if I had brought my binoculars I would have been able to spot fish swimming about. As it was, I could see an orange, rigid, inflatable boat belonging to the Coastguard and several divers in the water, presumably carrying out a drill in a little rocky inlet towards the end of the peninsula. It was a charming place and it more than justified our decision to get up early to avoid the crowds.

We had already decided not to linger too long as we felt sure that on a Sunday, the town would fill up very quickly, so after a walk for Oscar and a couple of very good – if pricey – ice creams, we took the ferry back to Rapallo around mid-morning. As we chugged past the *Regal Princess,* I could see half a dozen people sitting around a table on the top deck under an awning. I recognised a couple of the faces from Lucca, although there was no sign of Susie Upton's comedic companion, Martin Grey, or the big man with the eyepatch. Maybe they were still snoozing.

Back at Rapallo, after a stroll along the promenade, Anna and I walked up to the cable-car station for an even more panoramic view of the area. Remarkably, we were the only two passengers on the cable car – presumably on a hot day like this, everybody else was heading for the beach – and the conductor turned out to be very chatty. Not having much of a head for heights, I was happy to talk to take my mind off the fact that we were now hanging a hundred feet above the hillside. When I told him that I was a private investigator, his face lit up.

'Are you investigating the death of the *contessa*?'

'What *contessa*?'

'Back in 2001, the Contessa Francesca Vacca Agusta – from the Agusta helicopter company – fell down the cliff from her villa and it was three weeks later before her body was found, having been washed all the way across to France by the currents.'

I glanced at Anna and could see that this wasn't news to her but it certainly was to me. 'How very unfortunate. But why do you think a private investigator might be interested?'

'There were all kinds of conspiracy theories at the time. Her husband had been one of Italy's foremost industrialists. He died a few years before her, after which she took up with some unsavoury and unsuitable men and there were all kinds of family disputes about her husband's will.'

'I see. So people thought she might have been murdered?'

He shrugged. 'People thought all kinds of things. You know what it's like when a celebrity dies in suspicious circumstances.'

'Well, I'm pleased to report that I'm not here to investigate that death or any death. We're just on holiday for a few days.'

When we reached the top and looked back, it was clear that we had climbed a considerable distance. Our friendly conductor told us that we were now over six hundred metres above sea level and the views of Rapallo and out over the bay to Portofino and beyond were spectacular. Anna and I left him there and climbed several steep flights of stone steps before making our way up through the trees towards the sanctuary. This little church dated back to the late Renaissance period and so was of interest to the Renaissance specialist alongside me. While Anna went inside to check out the interior, I waited in the shade of the trees outside with Oscar, pulled out my phone and looked up the story the cable-car conductor had told us.

The story contained many of the elements I had come across so often during my career with the Metropolitan Police: a wealthy man and a beautiful young wife, political intrigue, lust, jealousy, family squabbles and greed but in this case, more unusually, superstition. The villa where she had died had originally belonged to Lord Carnarvon, the man who had financed the expedition that had discovered the tomb of Tutankhamen. As numerous people involved with the dig had subsequently died under mysterious circumstances, the rumour had circulated that any who had been involved with violating the tomb of Tutankhamen were cursed and so, by extension, was this villa. Not surprisingly, the investigation that followed the death of the *contessa* had not dwelt upon this hypothesis, but it sounded as if the police had investigated all the other possible elements in considerable depth before concluding that the most probable cause of death had been suicide or an unfortunate accident. I slipped my phone back into my pocket and glanced down at Oscar, who had returned to lie panting at my feet after a fruitless chase of a squirrel.

'Portofino: it's a beautiful place to die, don't you think?'

He shook his head in response, but that might just have been his attempt to rid himself of the attentions of a very insistent fly trying to land on his nose.

When Anna emerged from the sanctuary, the two of us decided against trekking up the tortuous and very steep path to the very top of the Monte Rosa and went back down through the trees until we reached the little café alongside the cable-car station. One cable car had just left so, as it was almost noon and I was on holiday, I had no scruples about ordering myself a cold beer while Anna opted for mineral water, and the friendly woman at the counter very kindly produced a big bowl of water for Oscar. We sat in the shade and enjoyed our drinks, the only sound the hum of the powerful electric winch engine in the background. We chatted about the death of Contessa Vacca Agusta and Anna told me that it had hit the headlines for many months but without the police ever being able to make any kind of headway. I could imagine the frustration of the officers involved. Nobody likes an unsolved case.

Five minutes later, the cable car arrived, carrying a handful of people and the same conductor. When he spotted us, he came over to our table, and there was an animated smile on his face.

'Have you heard the news? There's been another murder in Portofino.'

I looked up with interest. 'Really? When did that happen?'

'My colleagues down at the bottom station have just told me. It's on local radio and all over social media. The Coastguard found the body in the water this morning. At first, they thought it might have been accidental, but apparently there was something about the body that indicated it had been murder. They're not saying what it was, but I bet there was a dagger sticking out of the middle of the back.'

This sounded a little bit too theatrical but, plainly, there must have been some indication of foul play. I immediately thought back to the scene I had witnessed from the terrace of Castello Brown earlier this morning. Presumably, the Coastguard boat and the divers had not been on a training run after all but had been recovering the body or searching for clues. Needless to say, me being me, the memory of the conversation I had overheard in Lucca on Friday night instantly sprang to mind and I pressed our friend for more detail. 'The body? Was it a man or a woman?'

'A man, apparently, and would you believe he only had one eye?'

All kinds of warning bells started ringing in my head. 'One eye? Are you sure?'

'That's what they're saying on the Internet. I've just been checking it out as we came up here now. The police have put out a call for information as they're trying to establish the identity of the guy.' He grinned at me. 'There can't be too many one-eyed men around, and surely if one of them has gone missing, somebody would notice.'

Somebody certainly had noticed and that was me. The

conductor told us the cable car would be leaving again in five minutes and while he went off for a coffee, I turned towards Anna, but she got in first. 'I can almost hear your brain churning, Dan. You think it's the man from Lucca, don't you?'

I nodded slowly. 'I really don't know, but you have to admit that it's quite a coincidence, considering that the yacht belonging to the people from Lucca is moored only a couple of hundred metres from where the body was discovered.'

I saw her nod in return. 'So what are you going to do about it?'

'If the police have put out an appeal for information, I suppose I should head to the nearest police station and report what I heard. If necessary, I should be able to identify the guy even though I don't know his name.'

She gave me a long-suffering look. 'So in the space of a few minutes, Dan the holidaymaker has suddenly become Dan the detective again.' She gave me a little smile but I could see that it was an effort for her. 'Now, why doesn't that come as a surprise?'

6

SUNDAY LUNCHTIME

The police station in Rapallo was a twenty-minute walk from the cable-car station and although we hugged the shady side of the streets, we were hot by the time we got there. I left Anna and Oscar at a nearby café and went in to tell my tale. I was greeted at the door by a young constable who asked me my business, and when I told him I thought I might have information about the Portofino murder victim, he led me to a nearby interview room where I was asked to sit and wait. It took ten minutes before a grumpy-looking uniformed officer with sergeant's stripes on his epaulettes arrived.

'I understand you have information about a body.' He was probably in his late fifties – about my age – and he definitely looked disgruntled. I glanced at my watch and saw that it was almost one o'clock. The penny dropped. I had interrupted his Sunday lunch. I tried to be as cordial as possible.

'I'm sorry to take up your time. I've been told that a body's been found at Portofino. That's right, isn't it?'

He nodded. 'I believe so. Now, I need to have your name and address, please.'

He produced a notebook and laboriously made a record of my details before dropping the pen and prompting me. 'What information do you have about the body?'

'I understand that the body is that of a man with only one eye. Is that correct?'

He hesitated for a few moments before replying uncertainly, 'I believe that may be correct, yes.'

Considering the case was already all over the Internet and local media, I was surprised to find him sounding so vague. Nevertheless, I pressed on. 'I think I might know who he is.'

He picked up his pen again and gave me an expectant look. 'Right, let's have the name.'

I shook my head. 'I'm afraid I don't know the man's name, but I think I know how you can locate him.'

He dropped his pen onto his notebook again and gave a little snort. 'You don't know his name...' There was a pause while he collected himself before continuing. 'If you don't know his name, what makes you think this is the same person?'

Seeing him looking sceptical, I tried again. 'He's part of a group of British tourists. I saw them in Lucca on Friday night and I've seen some of the group on a yacht moored off Portofino this morning – and I do know the name of the yacht. Like I say, I don't know the man's name, but I'm sure I could recognise him again. Alternatively, it should be a simple matter for you to send somebody out to the yacht to check whether they're missing a one-eyed man or not.'

He gave a heartfelt sigh – not dissimilar to the sort of noise Oscar makes when he knows he's got to wait until I've finished eating before he gets his food. 'All right, thank you. Please let me have the name of the vessel and I'll get somebody to look into it.'

I gave him the name, *Regal Princess*, and saw him duly write it down. To my surprise, he then closed his notebook with a snap and stood up. 'Thank you, Signor *Armestronga*, I'll get somebody to look into it.'

I was genuinely amazed. 'You don't want to take a statement from me?'

'No, we have your contact details. If we need to speak to you again, we know how to reach you. Besides, this is a matter for the Coastguard or *Carabinieri*. I'll pass the information on to them.'

Two minutes later, I was standing outside on the pavement under the blue and white *Polizia* sign feeling bewildered and vaguely annoyed. I thought back on the sergeant's final words to me and slowly began to realise what the problem might be. Presumably, his branch of the Italian law-enforcement service didn't have primary jurisdiction in this case. I remembered what my friend Virgilio had told me. As the body had been found at sea, the investigation would have been initiated by the Coastguard and, from what the sergeant had said, it sounded as though they were working in collaboration with the *Carabinieri*, rather than the *Polizia*. The *Carabinieri* carry out a very similar investigative and enforcement role to the police although they are in fact originally a part of the Italian military. Talk about complicated...

As I crossed the road and walked back to where Anna and Oscar were waiting, I found myself seriously doubting whether this information would even be passed on. The sergeant certainly hadn't looked particularly interested and if, as I had always suspected, there was a certain amount of competition between the different forces, it was quite possible that he just wouldn't bother. When I got back to the table where Anna was sitting, she must have worked out from my expression that all wasn't well.

'Trouble?'

I recounted the less than warm reception I had received from the sergeant and Anna gave me a little smile. 'What did you expect at lunchtime on a Sunday? I'm surprised the police station was even open.' She pointed to a glass of beer on the table in front of her. 'Sit down and have a drink. I got you that. It's alcohol-free beer in case you're thinking of driving anywhere this afternoon.'

I took a very welcome mouthful and reflected on my next move. In fact, it didn't take long. I wiped the froth off my lip and looked across at her. 'I think I need to go back over to Portofino to speak to the Coastguard.' Seeing a look of thinly veiled exasperation on her face, I did my best to explain. 'It won't take long, but I need to pass on this information to the people directly involved with the investigation. You get that, don't you?'

She gave me a resigned smile. 'I get it, Dan. The detective inside you won't let you rest until somebody takes you seriously. So does this mean you're going straight down to the ferry now?'

I noticed her use of the singular pronoun 'you', rather than 'we', and I took the hint. 'I won't be away long. Why don't you have a walk around town with Oscar or go on the beach or maybe just go back to the hotel and have a lie-down?'

She glanced down at Oscar, who was sprawled under the table with his tongue hanging out. 'I think I'll have a sandwich here and then he and I can go back to the hotel. I'll give him his lunch and then we'll both have a lie-down. The room should be nice and cool and, if not, I can always put on the air con. You go off and do what you feel you have to do.'

I drained my glass and stood up. Oscar didn't even bother moving, obviously far too weary – or maybe he'd heard Anna say 'lunch'. I gave Anna a quick peck on the cheek. 'I won't be long, I promise, but you know how it is. I feel I've just got to speak to somebody about this.'

A long-suffering expression appeared on her face. 'I know how it is, Dan, believe me, I know.'

* * *

I only just managed to find a seat on the ferry, which was packed, and I had no doubt that Portofino would be heaving with people. When we got there, I was relieved to see the *Regal Princess* still moored at the mouth of the bay, but the crowds on the quayside were every bit as bad as I had feared. The good news, however, was that I recognised a figure in a blue and white uniform at the far end of the quay by the fishing boats, so I filed off the boat and struggled through the mass of humanity along the dockside towards the young *Guardia Costiera* officer I had seen before. He was looking stressed and I didn't blame him.

'Good afternoon, Officer, could you spare me a minute or two?'

'Just a few seconds, I'm afraid, as we're in the middle of a murder investigation.' Unlike the police sergeant in Rapallo, he was at least doing his best to be polite.

'It's about that. Have you been able to identify the body yet? If not, I think I might know who he was.'

It was clear that I had immediately got his attention. 'That would be very helpful indeed, Signor...?'

I gave him one of my cards and I saw him study it before looking up at me. 'You're a private investigator? Can I ask what your interest in this affair is?'

I shook my head. 'None whatsoever. I'm here on holiday with my girlfriend, but I just happened to overhear a conversation when we were in Lucca on Friday night that might have a bearing on this case.' Seeing his obvious interest, I gave him a quick summary of what I'd heard on Friday night and my fear that the body in the water might turn out to be the big man I had seen in the restaurant with Susie Upton. He listened intently without interrupting until I reached the end of my tale and at that point, he nodded a couple of times.

'That's very interesting indeed, Signor Armstrong, but you have no idea of the identity of the two men you overheard?'

'Unfortunately, no, but I'm reasonably sure that they came from the noisy group in the private dining room.'

'Do you think you would recognise their voices again?'

I'd been wondering that myself. 'I'm not sure. Neither of the voices were very distinctive but, you never know, it might be possible. Of course, I might be completely wrong and the one-eyed man I saw might be having his breakfast on the yacht out there at this very moment, but I thought it was worth letting you know. What are you thinking of doing? Presumably you have to speak to your boss now.'

'Ideally, yes, but he went off to Milan yesterday evening and he's on the early morning plane to South Africa for a conference as we speak. We still haven't been able to contact him. Even if he decides to come straight back, the earliest we can expect him is late tomorrow or even the next day.'

'Is there a risk that the yacht will leave before then?'

'That's not a problem. I can get a message to the captain not to weigh anchor until he gets authorisation from us.'

I decided to plead ignorance. 'Are you working with the police on this?'

He shook his head. 'There isn't a police station here in Portofino, but we have a good working relationship with the local *Carabinieri*.' I saw him make a decision. 'In fact, if you could spare me another few minutes of your time, I wonder if you'd be kind enough to come with me to the *Carabinieri* barracks to speak to the lieutenant.'

'The lieutenant?'

'Lieutenant Bertoletti. He's the main investigating officer

here.' He held out his hand towards me. 'Thank you for bringing this to our attention, Signor Armstrong. My name's Solaro, by the way, Paolo Solaro.'

It took us an age to walk the three or four hundred metres to the *Carabinieri* HQ. The crowds of sauntering tourists were, if anything, even worse than I'd feared and I was thankful that Anna and I had decided to take the early boat for our visit this morning. The *Carabinieri* post occupied the ground floor of an apartment block in a narrow road and there was an older officer in uniform standing outside. I'm not too clued up on ranks in the *Carabinieri* but from the look of the stripes on his epaulettes, I had a vague feeling he was a *maresciallo* or marshal, roughly equivalent to a sergeant. He was smoking a cigarette, no doubt at the end of his Sunday lunch, and thinking of food made me realise with a start that I was hungry. Oscar would never have forgotten something as important as that but, for now, I had business to attend to. The *maresciallo* gave Paolo Solaro a nod as we walked up to him and the young man offered a few words of explanation.

'*Ciao*, Romeo, this gentleman has some interesting information about the identity of our dead body.'

The *maresciallo* immediately dropped his cigarette on the floor and stubbed it out with his foot. 'We'd better go and see the lieutenant.'

He led us inside, past a reception desk, to a door marked *Privato*. He punched in a code and we followed him into a corridor, at the end of which was a frosted-glass door. The *maresciallo* knocked and waited. Seconds later, a voice replied.

'*Avanti.*'

Inside the office, I found a *Carabinieri* officer in shirtsleeves sitting behind a desk cluttered with paperwork. It was stuffy in here and the only ventilation appeared to be a freestanding fan on top of a filing cabinet. Officer Solaro handed him my card and gave him a brief outline of what I'd told him. The lieutenant stood up and held out his hand in greeting to me.

'Thank you for bringing this to our attention. Please take a seat.' I saw him study my card for a few seconds but he made no comment about my occupation. 'Signor Armstrong, would you mind just running me through it in your own words, please?' He was an intelligent-looking man, probably in his mid-forties, with short, dark hair. He was clean-shaven and he looked fit.

I sat down opposite him while the other two officers stood behind me and listened in as I went through my story again. As I had suspected, the police sergeant over in Rapallo hadn't bothered to pass on my message yet. The lieutenant listened intently, throwing out a question every now and then until I reached the end of my account. He had been taking notes as I went along and now he looked up from his desk over my shoulder towards the *maresciallo* and issued orders.

'Veronese, contact the *Regal Princess*. See if you can find out if there's a man on board with an eyepatch. If there's never been one or there still is one on there, then I think we can probably eliminate them from our inquiries. If there was such a person on board and he's no longer there for whatever reason, tell them everybody has to stay on the yacht and it doesn't move until I come out to question them.'

The *maresciallo* gave a brief, 'Yes, sir,' and went back out again, after which the lieutenant looked across at me.

'As you said yourself, Signor Armstrong, this may be a completely different one-eyed man. Would you be able to wait for five minutes until Veronese has been able to speak to the vessel? Could I offer you a coffee? What about you, Paolo? A little espresso maybe?' Clearly his relationship with the Coastguard officer was a lot less formal.

The lieutenant spoke into his phone as Paolo Solaro pulled up a chair, and barely three minutes later, another officer appeared carrying a tray with three espresso coffees on it. While we sipped these, the lieutenant asked me about my work and I gave him a quick summary of my life to date.

'I worked in the murder squad at Scotland Yard in London for thirty years and a couple of years ago I retired and moved here to Tuscany. A good friend of mine in the Florence murder squad suggested I set up my own investigation agency and I've been doing that for the last year.'

'Thirty years in the murder squad? Were you a senior officer?'

'Not terribly senior, I was a detective chief inspector, a DCI.'

He was obviously familiar with the rank and he smiled. 'That's roughly equivalent to major in the *Carabinieri* or *commissario* in the Italian police, isn't it? You must have seen some things in your time.'

'Yes, but never a one-eyed man floating in the sea. Can I ask if you're sure it was murder and not suicide or maybe just an unfortunate accident?'

'Definitely murder.' I saw him hesitate before making a decision. 'This is restricted information, so please keep it to yourself, but the man suffered six stab wounds to the back, sides and neck. And as for suicide, you try stabbing yourself in the back.' His tone was dry.

'He was stabbed *six* times?' Without knowing it, the cable-car conductor had been pretty close to the mark. 'That certainly doesn't sound like the work of a professional hitman.'

'No, the pathologist said it looked like a frenzied attack with a fairly slim-bladed knife only about ten centimetres long.'

'Tell me, do you have photos of the victim? I should be able to recognise him if he is the one I saw.'

'I'm just waiting to get the photos back from the lab.' He gave me a rueful shrug of the shoulders. 'We're only a very small contingent here and some of the technology takes a bit of time.'

Beside me, the Coastguard officer coughed apologetically. 'It was my first experience of a murder victim, I'm afraid, and I didn't think to take my own photos. I just left it to the force photographer.'

There was a peremptory knock on the door and the *maresciallo* returned. 'Sounds like this might be our man, sir. I've spoken to the captain, a woman called Monica Devesi, and she confirms there was a man with an eyepatch on board the *Regal Princess* until just before eleven last night, name of Jerome Van der Groot, British national. She says that she'd heard that for some reason after dinner, he left the saloon in a huff. Ten minutes later, they heard the outboard motor on one of their little rubber dinghies being started up and a crewmember saw it heading for the shore. It never came back and neither did he, so when this was reported to the captain first thing this morning, she sent out a search party in another boat. They found the dinghy wedged against the rocks just along the coast from here, but they've seen no sign of him and nobody's heard from him since last night. We found the body washed up only a hundred metres further on.'

'When you say "wedged", was the dinghy moored up?'

The *maresciallo* shook his head. 'I asked them that and they said no, no attempt had been made to secure it. It's a miracle it got stuck in the rocks, or it and the body would have been washed way out to sea by the currents and goodness only knows when it would have been found again.' He glanced across at me for a moment. 'You maybe know the story of the unfortunate Countess Vacca Agusta twenty years ago. Her body wasn't found for over three weeks until it washed up on the shore in France.'

'Yes, I just heard about it this morning. So on that basis,

there's no proof that Van der Groot was actually still in the boat when it reached the shore.'

'That's quite correct.'

The lieutenant nodded approvingly and caught my eye. 'Looks like you were right, Signor Armstrong.' He returned his attention to the *maresciallo*. 'What time did you say the man, Van der Groot, left the *Regal Princess*?'

'The captain said it was around eleven.'

'Where was the boat moored?'

'About a kilometre off the coast, between here and Santa Margherita. She says they arrived there from Rapallo at eight yesterday evening and spent the night there before moving to their current position closer to Portofino at seven-thirty this morning. They haven't moved since.'

'Has anybody come ashore or are they all still on the boat?'

'The two crewmembers who came looking for the dinghy at six-thirty this morning didn't set foot on dry land and returned with it as soon as they found it. As far as the guests on board are concerned, the captain says none of them have left the yacht so far today.' He gave a little smile. 'By the sound of it, they've been hitting the booze pretty hard and, as a result, they're not too active in the mornings.'

I saw the lieutenant digest the information for a few seconds before turning to me. 'Signor Armstrong, I know you said you're on holiday, but I wonder if you might be able to give us one more hour of your time. You said you think you *might* be able to recognise the voices you heard in Lucca, so would it be possible for you to come with me to the yacht now? I won't do formal interviews at this stage because I'm sure your time is precious, but I would just like to have a quick chat to everybody on board with you listening in, in the hope of pinpointing the men you heard.' I was impressed to hear him then switch to pretty good English with a distinct but comprehensible Italian accent. 'As you can imagine, I have to use English quite a lot so I'm reasonably fluent and I don't really need the services of an interpreter, but the people on the yacht don't need to know that. I won't introduce you and if anybody asks, we'll just say you're helping with the language.' He switched back to Italian again. 'Would you be able to do that for us? I'd be very grateful.'

I checked the time. It was almost two o'clock now and if Anna had gone for a snooze after her lunchtime sandwich she probably wouldn't be surfacing before three so I reckoned I was safe enough. 'Yes, of course. I wish I could give you more of my time, but I'm here with my girlfriend and she's expecting me to spend our holiday weekend with her.' I caught his eye for a moment. 'I'm afraid my job's been causing a bit of friction between us.'

The lieutenant gave me a rueful smile in return. 'That sounds all too familiar. Thank you very much for your help.' He turned to the young Coastguard officer. 'Paolo, I wonder if in return for Signor Armstrong's assistance, you or one of your colleagues would be kind enough to run him back to Rapallo after we've finished talking to the people on the yacht?'

'Of course.' Officer Solaro gave me a little grin. 'I promise I'll get you back a lot faster than the ferry.'

7

SUNDAY AFTERNOON

The *Regal Princess* was even more impressive close up. I'd been on a luxury yacht once before during a big drug investigation over in the UK, but that had been less than half the size of this monster. As the bright-orange Coastguard rigid inflatable nudged up against the open platform at the stern, the vessel towered above us. A crewman in shorts and a light-blue polo shirt with the name of the yacht on his back and his name, Christopher, on his left breast, took our mooring rope and made it fast. We climbed aboard and followed him up a flight of steps onto the open deck, where the swimming pool looked very inviting. I had no doubt that had Oscar been with me, he would have made a beeline for it. Like most Labradors, he loves the water.

I was mildly surprised to see nobody by the pool, but when we climbed the next flight of steps to the deck above, I realised why. Here we found everybody in a huge open-plan living/dining room that Christopher – who spoke with an Irish accent – referred to as the saloon. There was a huge dining table at one end and a series of smart, white leather armchairs at the other. As far as I could see, the only concession to this being a yacht, rather than a room in a luxury hotel, was the fact that the armchairs appeared to be bolted to the floor.

I counted eleven people sitting around a massive dining table laden with plates, cutlery, and the remains of a meal as well as about a dozen wine bottles, by the look of them mostly empty. This appeared to indicate that the alcoholic indulgence of the group wasn't restricted to the evenings. There was an aroma of freshly made coffee in the air and it was clear that the guests were just finishing their lunch. I looked around with interest and immediately spotted Susie Upton sitting next to her fellow comedian, Martin Grey. Around them were five other men and four women. I recognised several of the faces from various TV shows back in the UK and from the restaurant in Lucca but was unable to name any of them. Needless to say, there was no sign of Jerome Van der Groot, the man with the eyepatch.

I intercepted a few curious looks but nobody commented and the lieutenant said nothing as we followed Christopher up another level to the bridge. This was a state-of-the-art environment packed with electronic equipment and computer screens. There were panoramic windows all around, giving a terrific view of Portofino and the bay of Rapallo. A slim, fit-looking woman, probably in her early fifties, stepped forward and held out her hand to the lieutenant.

'Welcome aboard. I'm the captain. My name's Devesi, Monica Devesi. How can we help you?' She was speaking in Italian and I felt pretty sure I could hear a northern Italian accent, but I've only been living over here for two years and I'm not too good at pinning down precise locations yet.

'Good afternoon, Captain.' The lieutenant was sounding respectful. 'My name is Lieutenant Bertoletti from the investigative branch of the *Carabinieri*, based in Portofino.'

The lieutenant shook hands with her and, as agreed, made no

attempt to introduce me or either of the two officers with us. 'Thank you for sparing me your time. I'm afraid I have to inform you that it's possible that the passenger who left last night may have been murdered.' He checked his notebook, 'Mr Van der Groot, Jerome Van der Groot.'

The captain looked genuinely shocked. 'Murdered? But how...?'

The lieutenant didn't go into any detail and quickly qualified his statement. 'A body was found in a rocky inlet below Castello Brown this morning. At the moment, we aren't sure if the body found in the sea is that of your former guest or not. We'd like to have a few words with the other passengers and see if we can confirm his identity. I just have one or two questions for you first, if you don't mind. Firstly, how many guests are you carrying?'

'Twelve, including Mr Van der Groot. They're all involved with a British TV company.'

'And how many crewmembers do you have on board?'

'Sixteen – plus myself.' I listened in awe as she listed them. There were more crewmembers than passengers on board the *Regal Princess*. One thing was for sure: a cruising holiday on something like this was only for the mega rich.

'And are all of the crew well known to you?'

She nodded. 'Most of them. The second officer, purser and engineer have been with me for two years now, ever since I took over as Captain. Luigi and Carlo, the chefs, have been working with me since January, along with all the hospitality staff, and the only relatively new crewmembers are Rick and Penny. They started in May.'

'Any problems with any of them? Any violence, drug taking, anything like that?'

She shook her head decisively. 'At the first sign of anything like that, they would have been out. They all know that I don't tolerate that sort of thing. No, if Signor Van der Groot really has been murdered, I'm confident it wasn't done by one of my people.'

'Excellent, thank you. Next question: how long has this group been with you and where have you come from?'

'Just over a week. We picked them up from Naples last Saturday and we're making our way around to St Tropez in France by the end of this week. En route from Naples, we've spent a couple of days visiting Sardinia, followed by the island of Elba.'

'Please can you tell me where you spent Friday night?'

'We were at the Marina di Pisa. The group were picked up by coach and taken to Lucca for a Bob Dylan concert.' I nodded to myself. That explained how they had ended up in the restaurant.

'Thank you, Captain.' The lieutenant lowered his voice slightly. 'Please could you tell me – off the record, I promise – how you've got on with this group?'

She shrugged. 'As far as I've been concerned, they've been no trouble. When we've visited places, they've always come back in good time and nobody's done anything stupid on board. As far as the company that owns the boat is concerned, I have a feeling they're going to get a shock when they see how much alcohol this lot have consumed, but, like I say, that's not my problem.'

'And would you say they've been a happy group? Have you been aware of any internal disagreements or strife?'

She hesitated for a few moments before replying. 'I don't mix with them that much, but nothing drastic has happened, and there have been few occasions when voices have been raised apart, supposedly, from an argument last night involving Mr Van der Groot. I didn't witness it myself, but the hospitality staff mentioned it this morning. Otherwise nobody's punched anybody and as far as I know, nobody's started throwing glasses and plates around.' She gave the lieutenant a smile. 'You'd be surprised how often that happens on board.' She lowered her voice. 'I would say that this lot are a fairly typical bunch of spoilt, rich people – but a whole lot more civilised than the group of footballers and their wives and girlfriends we had last month.'

The fact that the one-eyed man had been involved in an argument added to the likelihood of him having been on the receiving end of the threats of two men in the gents' toilet in Lucca. Had I overheard a murder being planned?

The lieutenant thanked her and we went back down to the saloon again. The guests were all still sitting around the remains of their lunch and Lieutenant Bertoletti walked over to the head of the table to address the group in English.

'Good afternoon, ladies and gentlemen. My apologies for interrupting your lunch. My name is Guido Bertoletti and I'm a lieutenant in the *Carabinieri*. I'm here because I'm investigating a murder.'

I stood behind him and studied the faces around the table closely. I distinctly read surprise and disbelief when they heard the word 'murder', but at least for now, I couldn't see any obvious signs of guilt as the lieutenant continued.

'We're still trying to establish the identity of the murder victim and I'm afraid there's a possibility it could be that it's your former companion, Mr Jerome Van der Groot.'

This time, the expressions of shock intensified but, interestingly, I didn't immediately see any signs of sorrow. After the way she'd been manhandled by the big man back in Lucca, I particularly studied Susie Upton's face, but saw only horror and disbelief, but little or no sadness. It would appear that Jerome Van der Groot had not been universally liked.

The lieutenant stepped closer to the table and looked around.

'In order to facilitate identification of the body, I wonder whether any of you might have a photo of Mr Van der Groot.'

There was a flurry of hands and a few moments later, several people were holding out phones towards the lieutenant. He took two of them, looked at the photos and then passed them across to me and the two officers. As soon as I saw the first photo, I recognised the man with the eyepatch I had seen with Susie Upton in Lucca and it instantly became clear that the two officers – who had seen the body – had also identified him. All three of us looked up and nodded. Just in case there could be any doubt, the *maresciallo* added, 'That's him, sir. That's the victim all right.'

He was speaking Italian but I saw several of the guests blanch. Clearly, they had understood. The lieutenant thanked the owners of the phones and handed them back. 'I'm very sorry, ladies and gentlemen, but there appears to be no doubt about it. The murder victim is indeed your former companion, Mr Van der Groot.'

'Listen here, lieutenant, but are you quite sure he was murdered?' The voice belonged unmistakably to Martin Grey. His thick Liverpudlian accent was immediately recognisable from the TV. I took a closer look at him. He looked as if he was in his early forties, but these days people in the public eye almost invariably manage to appear younger than they really are. He looked remarkably fit, he was stylishly dressed, and his lush brown hair was impeccably styled. I had a feeling he was one of those people who could climb through a bush and still emerge looking perfect when they came out of the other side.

The lieutenant nodded. 'I'm afraid so. There's no doubt at all.' He didn't go into any detail and I definitely approved. There was no point in broadcasting gory details that would only inflame media stories when the news reached the press. The lieutenant turned his attention back to everybody in the room. 'I'd like to go around the table asking you to tell me your names, when you last saw the victim, and if you think you know anything that might be of interest to my investigation – anything, however minor, you might have heard or seen last night between ten and midnight.'

He walked around the table and spoke to each of them one by one, and I walked just behind him, listening closely as the guests answered in turn, wishing I could pull out my notebook and list their names but deciding it was best not to look too closely involved. By the time we returned to the head of the table, we had learned little that advanced the investigation, but I felt reasonably confident that I might have identified one of the voices I had heard in the restaurant at Lucca.

The owner of this voice was a man probably around my age and he told the lieutenant his name was Edgar Beaumont. He was stockily built, with short, dark hair and horn-rimmed glasses. His voice had the exact same undertones hinting at possible Welsh origins that I had heard and I felt pretty sure he was one of the two men I had overheard at the restaurant. And if he was one of the pair, this meant that the other was quite probably sitting around this table now.

Beaumont was wearing a garish red and orange Hawaiian shirt that didn't suit him at all. Somehow, he gave the impression that he would be far more comfortable in a collar and tie. I couldn't see if he was wearing shorts, but it wouldn't have surprised me if he'd turned out to be wearing pinstriped trousers and polished leather shoes. He was that kind of formal-looking guy.

The red-haired woman beside him – sporting a wedding ring along with a sparkling engagement ring – was stunningly beautiful and I was mildly surprised that I hadn't noticed her in the crowd at the restaurant in Lucca but, of course, my attention had mainly been taken by Susie Upton and the man with the eyepatch. This woman was probably at least twenty years younger than Beaumont, and it was hard to tell whether she was with him or with the man on the other side of her who looked closer to her age – or whether indeed she was with neither. That man was probably in his early forties and he had a serious face that made me mentally earmark him as a lawyer or even a judge.

As for the identity of the second man I had overheard in Lucca, I'd managed to whittle the possibles down to four. I'd done this by a simple process of elimination, immediately discounting Martin Grey and three other men – Grey because his voice and Liverpool accent were unmistakable, while one of the others had a distinct American accent, one the sort of Glasgow accent you could cut with a knife, and the other a strange, high-pitched voice that I vaguely remembered from a sitcom that my ex-wife used to like. That left me with the lawyer type, Neil Vaughan, sitting alongside the beautiful woman, whose name was Tamsin Taylor, two men sitting side by side at the far end of the table both wearing black T-shirts, and the man on the other side of Susie Upton.

The T-shirt duo corresponded far more closely to my notion of how comedians should look. One, whose name I now remembered as Billy Webster, had the sort of beer gut that takes regular consumption of gallons of the stuff to attain. I could imagine him working his way up through the working men's clubs to his present TV position, a microphone in one hand and a pint mug in the other. Although his normal accent here was southern English, I remembered him producing a very convincing northern accent in a sitcom set in the wilds of darkest Yorkshire, where he played the role of a publican doing his best to drink his profits. He was probably in his early sixties but he looked about ten years older. The slogan across the chest of his T-shirt read, *I told myself I should stop drinking but I'm not going to listen to a drunk who talks to himself.* I wondered to what extent this was ironic or accurate.

The man beside him, wearing a T-shirt bearing the words, *NOWLEGE IS POWRE*, was about half the age of his companion. He had a tough-guy face and a mass of dark hair gathered in a loose ponytail, revealing glittering gold rings hanging from his ears that gave him a piratical look. His name was Doug Kingsley, not a name I recognised, but I vaguely remembered his face from something I'd seen on the TV back in the UK. He, too, spoke with a southern English accent but there was a certain cockiness to his tone that didn't quite sound like the man I'd heard in Lucca – but of course, that man had been furious about something or somebody.

The man sitting to the right of Susie Upton was quite soberly dressed in comparison, but he made up for his less flamboyant clothing by what was beneath it. His plain-blue T-shirt clung to his body so tightly, it revealed every muscle of his torso – and there were a lot of them on display. He was probably in his late thirties and from his sculpted physique, it looked as though he spent a lot of his time in the gym. He also had a similar metropolitan accent, marking him as most likely from south-east England or even the capital.

Something else emerged as we went around the table and this was that the murder victim had been unaccompanied. There was no grieving widow present to lament his departure and, in fact, I didn't hear a single expression of regret at his passing. This immediately made me think back to the scene I had witnessed in Lucca and the almost proprietorial way the big man had treated Susie. Had they been close and, if so, why was she exhibiting so little emotion now? What, I wondered, had Jerome Van der Groot done to make himself so universally disliked and, if such was the case, why had he been invited along on this holiday in the first place? For now, these questions had to remain unanswered as the lieutenant, true to his word, glanced at his watch and led the three of us to the far end of the saloon, out of earshot of the table. He turned first to the *maresciallo*.

'Veronese, I want you to start interviewing all the crewmembers. Find out if they saw or heard anything suspicious last night and get a call through to Forensics to come and check the dinghy. I'm particularly interested to see if there are traces of blood on it. I'll make a start on preliminary interviews with all the guests while Paolo makes sure that Signor Armstrong gets back to Rapallo for his urgent appointment.' He transferred his attention to Officer Solaro. 'Paolo, after that, I want you to come straight back here to help Veronese and me with the interviews.' After these instructions, he glanced across at me. 'What about the voices you overheard, Signor Armstrong? Any luck at identifying them?'

I told him that I was now pretty sure of one of the voices and that I had whittled the others down to just four but that I would really need to listen to them for longer to know better. I hadn't been able to make a note of their names as the lieutenant had gone around the table and I described the ones I couldn't remember to him so he could tick them off the list in his notebook. He nodded a couple of times and then held out his hand. 'Thank you very much for your assistance, Signor Armstrong. I'll check with all five of these men to find out if they visited the toilets in the restaurant in Lucca, if they were making threats and, if so, against whom. I hope your girlfriend will forgive me for depriving her of your company this afternoon.'

I shook his hand. 'You have my contact details. If there's anything else I can do to help, please just give me a call.'

8

SUNDAY LATE AFTERNOON

The ride back to Rapallo in the powerful, rigid inflatable boat was exhilarating – and, as promised, a whole lot quicker than the ferry – and Officer Solaro dropped me off at the jetty with a cheery wave at just before three. After a short detour to buy myself a focaccia sandwich, I was back at the hotel by twenty past three and received a warm welcome from both of the occupants of the room. Anna was propped up on a couple of pillows against the headboard with a book on Byzantine architecture in her hands and Oscar was stretched out on the cool, tiled floor and clearly too tired to give me any more than a lazy wag of the tail. Anna didn't wag her tail but she gave me a big smile.

'Well, how did it go? Has the ex-Scotland Yard man solved the murder and the perpetrator is safely locked up in jail?'

I sat down on the edge of the bed and smiled back at her. 'Not exactly, but at least the *Carabinieri* now know that the victim was indeed that guy from Lucca.'

Her expression became more serious. 'Wow, fancy that! What about the men you overheard in the restaurant? Have you managed to identify them?'

I told her all about my visit to the yacht with the lieutenant and she listened intently before looking up at me with a serious expression on her face. 'Well, you've certainly done your bit, Dan. The *Carabinieri* lieutenant sounds as if he's clued up and on the case, so please can we see if we can enjoy a few hours together now without you dashing off again like Sherlock Holmes?'

'Accompanied by the Hound of the Baskervilles?' I pointed at my canine companion, who was still flat out on the floor beside the bed.

Anna produced a little smile but there was no missing the edge in her voice when she picked up again. 'Seriously, Dan, how about switching it off for a few hours? After all, we are supposed to be on holiday.'

I leant over and kissed her. 'I'm sorry, sweetheart, but I felt I had to pass on that information. Anyway, now I'm all yours. What would you like to do? I know what I'd like to do...'

I slipped off my shoes and snuggled up against her but she shook her head and pointed towards Oscar, who had suddenly decided to get to his feet and was now standing by the bed, staring intently at us. 'You know the rule, Dan. No hanky-panky while Oscar is watching and taking notes. No, I feel like a swim and then maybe a little stroll along the promenade, followed by a Campari spritz and a romantic dinner under the palm trees. How does that sound?'

It wasn't quite what I had had in mind, but it did sound rather nice so, obediently, I put my shoes back on and we dug out our swimming things and a couple of towels. The helpful receptionist indicated on a map where the nearest dog-friendly beach was and we headed straight down there.

Italian seaside resorts, generally speaking, are far more regimented than French or, indeed, British beaches. This has always struck me as strange considering how individualist the Italians are in so many other ways, but *bagni*, as the highly well-ordered rows of sun loungers and parasols are called, are a fact of life over here and people pay thirty or forty euros a day for the privilege of renting a pair of sunbeds. In fairness, you normally get changing rooms and showers, as well as a bar for the essential caffeine fix and some of them even offer meals. Very few of these, however, cater for dogs and this afternoon, we headed for an unregulated piece of beach. This was predictably crowded but we managed to find a space between an elderly couple who had brought their own deck chairs and a young couple who spent the afternoon stretched out in each other's arms doing what I had rather hoped to do back in the hotel room.

We had a very pleasant afternoon splashing around in the water with a happy Labrador and an assortment of canine pals. From time to time, the ferry to and from Portofino came past, still packed with people and, inevitably, I found myself thinking about the murdered man. There was so much I didn't know about the case and – although I wouldn't have dreamt of mentioning it to Anna – so much I would have liked to know. As I floated around in the wonderfully refreshing water, occasionally having to repel attempts by my dog to climb on top of me and risk drowning me in the process, I couldn't help wondering just what had motivated somebody to murder the man.

All I knew about him was his name and that brief moment I had glimpsed him in Lucca, during which I had to confess, he hadn't immediately endeared himself to me. What had been strange, however, had been the meek submission of the glamorous TV comic/presenter to his rather rude approach. It had almost been as if he had had some kind of hold over her. His name had been Van der Groot and her name was Upton so presumably, they weren't related by marriage. Or were they? When I got back to the beach and Anna settled down on her front to dry out in the sun, I propped myself up on my elbows and pulled out my phone. I started by checking out Susie Upton.

I very quickly learned that this was her real name and that she was forty-four years old – although she looked younger. She had been married to a fellow actor called Roger Shore for a seven-year period, but that had ended in divorce ten years earlier. No children were listed and everything else in her CV sounded pretty standard. She had studied at RADA, the prestigious drama school in London, and had started off with bit parts in a number of TV series until she had found her comic niche in a sitcom about three penniless girls sharing a flat. From there, she had graduated to other comedy series and she regularly made appearances on quiz shows, game shows and so on, making her a familiar household name. She currently lived in Chelsea with a cat called Winston and her hobbies were listed as squash, swimming, cookery and foreign travel.

The Wikipedia entry didn't refer to other men in her life since her divorce so I checked her out on social media. Her Facebook page contained only photos of her in her various roles and promotional posts, and it didn't mention the name Jerome Van der Groot. I found numerous other references to her from media outlets. In particular, a four-page article about her in *Hello!* magazine made interesting reading.

This included a number of photos of her in her various TV roles and at sparkling showbiz events, and there were several of her in a series of skimpy bikinis on beaches, smiling alluringly at the camera. Apart from her comedic talents, with her long legs and mass of blonde hair, she was definitely a good-looking woman and she knew it. The article talked about her career and, predictably, it mentioned her partnership with Martin Grey in another sitcom a few years back, but all it said about her current relationship with him was that they were 'close friends'. It did mention a couple of other household names who had been romantically linked with her in the past, but she was quoted as declaring herself 'happily single' nowadays.

There was no mention in that article of anybody called Jerome Van der Groot, so I did an online search for him. It didn't take long. It turned out that he was Head of Programming at the TV company for whom Susie Upton and Martin Grey worked and, as such, no doubt a very powerful man. Thought of infamous Hollywood directors like Harvey Weinstein and their casting couches came to mind and I wondered if she and Van der Groot had had that sort of deal going on. If so, I felt sure she wouldn't have been very happy about it, and unhappiness can easily turn to something more lethal. Certainly, if I were leading the investigation, I would be taking a close look at Ms Upton.

But of course, I had to remind myself, I wasn't running the investigation and, indeed, I was no longer involved in the investigation, so I would be best advised to forget about the affair of the one-eyed man and let Lieutenant Bertoletti and his team get on with it. As Anna had said, he'd struck me as a good detective and I had no doubts about his ability to conduct a thorough investigation of the crime.

I glanced sideways at my girlfriend. My dedication to my job had been a prime factor in the deterioration of relations between me and my wife and that had ended in divorce. Now that I had been lucky enough to find Anna, it was very much in my interests to avoid anything like this happening again. She and I had recently moved in together and we were very happy. I had every intention of keeping it that way.

At the end of the afternoon, when we were all three dry again and I had managed to get Oscar to stop shaking himself and threatening to wet other the beach users, we went back up onto the promenade and strolled along past the old castle. My history expert told me that this had been built in the sixteenth century after an attack by Turkish pirates who had carried off twenty local girls into a life of slavery – or worse. The castle was a formidable-looking, grey, stone construction and I felt sure it would have acted as an excellent deterrent against any further pirate incursions – although that would have been of little comfort to the twenty unfortunate girls.

We turned inland after a short walk and found ourselves a little café in the pedestrian area. We sat down at a table in the shade of the buildings and I ordered a spritz for Anna and a cold beer for myself. The café described itself as dog friendly and there was a big bowl of fresh water for Oscar. When the waiter brought our drinks, he also brought a handful of treats that my ever-hungry Labrador accepted most willingly. This reminded me that I was hungry so I asked the man if he could recommend a restaurant around here and he nodded.

'If I were you, I'd steer clear of the restaurants on the seafront. Some of them are very good but some of them are sharks. There's a place only a couple of hundred metres from here called l'Aragosta. They do excellent seafood, if you like that kind of thing.'

We certainly did. As I had only had a sandwich for lunch, I was more than happy to head for the restaurant as soon as it opened at seven, and we were given a table outside in a narrow, pedestrian street opposite a park with a children's playground sheltered by umbrella pines. Here in the shade, with a light breeze blowing along the street, the temperature was most pleasant and Anna and I both relaxed, as did Oscar, who stretched out on the ground at our feet and was soon snoring happily.

Anna and I both chose grilled anchovies as a starter, after which she opted for grilled plaice while I went for my very favourite Italian dish – *fritto misto*. Since coming to live in Tuscany, I had developed a real taste for this simple but often exceptional mixture of fried prawns, squid, octopus, whitebait and other little fish. Unlike British fish and chips, there's no thick batter involved. Normally, the ingredients are just dusted in flour and then lightly fried. Tonight, my *fritto misto* was served on a platter with a sheet of absorbent paper beneath the fish to collect any excess oil. My rating of tonight's *fritto misto* was nine out of ten, which is just about as good as it gets. Accompanied by a mixed salad and some cold white wine, it was a delightful meal and a most pleasant evening in perfect company.

At the end of the meal, when I was trying to decide whether to have panna cotta or an ice cream, my phone started ringing. It turned out to be Diana Greensleeves, presumably now back in England. This came as a surprise. I hadn't been expecting to hear from her again. Had something happened?

'Hello, Mr Armstrong. I hope I'm not disturbing you.'

Of course she was, but what could I say? 'Hello, no problem. How can I help you?'

'I've just had a call from Heather.'

'That's excellent news. I'm sure your parents must be delighted.'

'I haven't told them yet.' I could hear concern in her voice. 'You see, she's got herself into a bit of trouble; well, to be honest, quite a lot of trouble, by the sound of it.'

'Where is she now?'

My ears pricked up when I heard the reply. 'She said she's in a place called Portofino. I've heard of it before but I'm not sure where it is. Isn't it on the Amalfi coast somewhere south of Rome?'

'No, it's actually quite a lot further north than that, still on the west coast but a lot closer to Genoa. Tell me about this trouble she's got herself into.'

'She didn't go into much detail because she didn't have time. Her phone's run out of battery – she never remembers to pack her charger – and she called me from a public phone, but it only took coins and she didn't have many. It sounds as though there's real trouble brewing between her and her boyfriend, but there's more to it than just a falling-out. She sounded really scared. I haven't heard her like that for years, not since she was a little girl. As soon as I heard that she was in trouble, I said I'd try and contact you and I'd ring her straight back. She's waiting by the phone right now.'

'As it happens, I'm not that far from Portofino myself now, so why don't I call her, and that way, she can explain everything direct to me and I can ask any questions? I'll call you back after we've spoken and let you know what's happening.'

'That would be wonderful, thank you so much. I'm so sorry to interrupt your holiday but she sounded really frightened.'

'No problem.' I glanced across at Anna, who was studiously concentrating on her fish. 'Let me have the number and I'll call her now.'

I've never liked coincidences. Could it be that the trouble in which Heather Greensleeves now found herself might have something to do with a dead Englishman found floating in the sea?

9

SUNDAY NIGHT

After giving Anna a very quick summary of what Diana had told me, I dialled the number of the public phone in Portofino. It was answered after just one ring.

'Hi, Di, did you manage to get through to the private investigator chap?' Her words came tumbling out in a rush and she definitely sounded flustered.

'Hello, this *is* the private investigator chap. My name's Dan Armstrong. Your sister tells me you're in a spot of bother.'

'Oh, thank God.' I could hear the relief in her voice. 'I'm scared stiff and I really don't know what to do.'

I tried to sound as comforting as possible because she definitely seemed to be really spooked. 'Why don't you start by telling me all about it?'

'It's Mario, the guy I'm with.'

'What about him?'

'That's the thing. I don't really know him that well. It was all a bit of a whirlwind romance. Don't get me wrong, over these last few days, he's been fine, but then everything changed last night when we met up with another boat.'

'Another boat? What happened?' Surely not the *Regal Princess*...

'We were moored up just off the coast not far from here – I'm in Portofino, I don't know if you know it – when the other boat came alongside. Mario had been tense all evening and when the other boat arrived, he became dead serious and he told me to lock myself in the cabin and stay there. At first I did but then I sneaked out and took a peek while they weren't looking and I saw them loading stuff from the other boat onto ours.'

'Was it a big boat?' Her answer reassured me – to some extent.

'Not really, about the same size as ours.'

'And what sort of stuff were they bringing aboard?'

'At least a dozen heavy boxes. It took two men to lift each of them. They stowed them down a hatch near the front of the yacht. The whole thing took less than twenty minutes or so and then the other boat disappeared off into the night.'

'And Mario?'

'Ever since then, he's been like a cat on a hot tin roof: irritable, nervous. I tried asking him who had been on board the other boat and he just told me to forget about it. I didn't mention that I'd seen anything, but I feel sure there's something dodgy going on.'

Two boats meeting in the dark and people transferring heavy boxes sounded very suspicious to me too. I had a feeling that young Ms Greensleeves had got in with some questionable company but, by the sound of it, there didn't appear to be a connection with Van der Groot's murder. 'Where are you now? Are you sure Mario isn't listening?'

'No, we landed here in Portofino a bit earlier this evening and had a meal down by the harbour. Now that he's met up with the other two guys, he said he needed to have a private word with them, so I told him I'd go for a little walk. I'm at a public phone and there's nobody close by, so I'm sure it's okay.'

'Who are these other two guys you've met up with?'

'I don't know. I think one's called Abdel or something like that, and I'm pretty sure they were speaking to each other in Arabic, but they're scary guys and I didn't like the way the bigger one was looking at me. The meeting was clearly pre-planned and Mario said they're going to be coming sailing with us for a few days, but I'm really frightened now and I don't know what to do. That's why I called Diana.' Although I knew her to be a grown woman of twenty-three, she sounded more like a scared child and I felt instant sympathy for her.

'Don't worry, I'll help you. Where's Mario planning on sailing off to?'

'That's the thing, he wouldn't say. He just said we were going to go south and not to worry, but I'm terrified at the thought of going off God knows where with these two scary guys, and I still don't know what's in those boxes.'

I felt sure that the first imperative was to get her away from these dubious characters as soon as possible. 'Right, Heather, I think we've got to get you out of there. As it happens, I'm only just across the bay from you in Rapallo and it's probably only a half-hour drive from here to Portofino. I think the best thing is for me to drive over and pick you up. Once I know you're safe, you can tell me the whole story and we'll see what our next step has to be.'

'That would be amazing, thank you so much.' I could hear the relief in her voice. 'But what about my stuff...?'

'Have you got your passport, your wallet?'

'Yes, they're here with me in my handbag.'

'That's all you need for now. Just leave everything else.'

I did a bit of quick thinking. Although the harbour area of

Portofino is pedestrians only, I had seen cars parked further up towards the *Carabinieri* barracks, so presumably I would be able to get access that far.

'Listen, it's going to take me about half an hour but I'll need another ten or fifteen minutes first to go back and get the van.' I looked at my watch. 'It's just gone nine now so, realistically, I would hope to be with you about nine forty-five. I want you to stay clear of Mario and his friends for the next forty-five minutes and I'll pick you up from the main piazza. It's just before you get to the *Carabinieri* station and you'll see lots of parked cars there.' I tried to think of a suitable landmark to help her. 'It's about a hundred metres further on uphill from the Alexander McQueen shop. Have you seen that?'

'I'm very close to it now. In fact, I've been looking in the windows.'

'Right, well, carry on up the hill to the square with all the parked cars and I'll meet you there around a quarter to ten. I'm driving a dark-blue VW minivan. Okay?'

'Thank you so very much. By the way, I've got long, blonde hair and I'm wearing a white top and a grey skirt.'

I stuck the phone back in my pocket and reached for my wallet, but before I could say anything, Anna leant across the table and tapped the back of my hand. 'Don't worry, you go and get that girl. I'll look after the bill and I'll take care of Oscar.'

'Are you sure? You didn't hear what she said, but it didn't sound good.'

'That's the impression I got from listening to your end of the conversation. Just go. I understand, really. Oscar and I'll meet you back at the hotel and I'll have a word with them to see if they can find somewhere for her to spend the night. If not, she can share with me and you'll have to make do on the floor with Oscar or on the couch downstairs.'

I got to my feet and leant across to kiss her. 'I love you to bits, Anna. You know that, don't you?'

'Just go, you idiot. Tell me all about it later.' She gave me a warm smile in return. 'And I love you too. Now go.'

* * *

I phoned Heather's sister in the UK while I hurried back to the hotel and told her what I'd learnt and what we were going to do. She sounded very relieved and grateful. I collected the van and set off, but it took me until ten to ten to get to Portofino. The little town is at the far end of a promontory sticking out westwards from the Ligurian coast and, although the narrow road that winds its way around the coast is only about ten or twelve kilometres long, I had to contend with a near constant stream of traffic coming the other way and even a huge truck that blocked the road for about five minutes. When I finally nosed my way into the square amid all the parked cars, I slowed to a crawl and looked around carefully, trying to spot Heather. In fact, she saw me first, because a figure in a short skirt emerged from the shadows and stepped towards the van as I inched my way down the hill. I opened the window and looked out. 'Heather? I'm Dan. Hop in.'

A broad, beaming smile spread across her face and she hurried around to the passenger side. She climbed into the van, slammed the door, and then surprised me by reaching across and giving me a hug and a kiss on the cheek. 'Am I pleased to see you! I've been skulking here in the shadows feeling absolutely terrified.'

'Well, you're safe now. What I suggest we do now is I'll see if I can find a parking space where we can sit, and you can tell me exactly what's been happening. The more I think about it, the more I think we may well end up calling in on the local *Cara-*

binieri. They're just up the road from here.' Seeing an expression of concern on her face, I did my best to reassure her. 'It's all right, they're good guys. I met several of them earlier today.'

'You've been talking to the *Carabinieri*? About me?'

'No, about a completely separate matter. I'll tell you all about it later. First things first, let's find somewhere to park and you can tell me the full story. Okay?'

I had to do two circuits of the car park until, just as I was beginning to think there was no hope, a very swish-looking Mercedes pulled out of a space and I made sure I drove straight in before anybody else could take it. I switched off the engine and turned towards Heather. She suddenly seemed very vulnerable and I did my best to sound reassuring.

'My girlfriend is checking with the hotel where we're staying to see if they can find a bed for you for tonight so, don't worry, you aren't going to be left out on the street. Now, go through the whole thing again, starting with how you met Mario until you phoned your sister.'

She repeated her story, and I learnt that she had first met Mario at a disco in Pisa only a couple of weeks earlier. I had a feeling her mother would probably have taken a very dim view of the fact that she had been prepared to go off alone with him on a yacht only five or six days after meeting him, but that was up to her. Maybe this most recent experience might give her the scare she needed to make her start behaving a bit more responsibly but, again, that was her affair, not mine.

Mario's boat sounded as if it was a reasonable-sized motor yacht, but nothing like on the scale of the one being used by the TV people. She and Mario had been sailing up and down the coast and had spent a couple of days at the Isola del Giglio before coming here. I recognised the name of that island from the catastrophic shipwreck of a huge cruise liner just off the island

ten years earlier. Mario had chosen to drop anchor almost a kilometre outside Portofino bay the previous night, telling her that all
of the closer moorings had been taken, but more probably it had
been a pre-arranged rendezvous point with the mysterious other
vessel.

They had stayed on their mooring throughout most of the day
today and it had only been late this afternoon that he had finally
brought his yacht into the harbour and moored up at the end of
the quay. The two of them had come ashore for an early dinner in
one of the quayside restaurants. Although it was clear that things
had been going reasonably well between the two of them until
the previous night, I got the impression that Heather had been
having increasingly serious doubts over the past twenty-four
hours about the longevity of their relationship, even before the
two scary Arabic speakers had put in an appearance.

The more I listened to her account of meeting up with the
unknown boat at eleven o'clock at night and the clandestine
loading of the suspicious boxes, the more I was convinced that
this would have to be a matter for the *Carabinieri*. The trouble was
that she clearly didn't want me to go to the authorities. I tried to
work out whether this was out of lingering affection for Mario or
whether she was worried for herself, but she stubbornly resisted
my attempts to get her to accompany me to Lieutenant Bertoletti
right now.

The other reason why I wanted to get the police involved was
because of the synchronicity of the timings. In spite of my original feeling that her problems weren't connected with the death
of Van der Groot, maybe I had been too hasty in dismissing any
connection.

The mystery boat had come up alongside them at around
eleven last night and, coincidentally, at that exact same time
Jerome Van der Groot had been travelling back from the *Regal*

Princess towards Portofino in a little rubber dinghy – and a huff. As far as I could gather, both Mario's yacht and the TV people's luxury yacht had been in the same sort of area just under a kilometre offshore. What if Van der Groot in his rubber dinghy had stumbled across what sounded very much like suspicious activity and had been stabbed as a result? This would explain why the dinghy in which he'd been travelling had never returned and, in fact, had been found not far from the body a hundred metres or so further down the coast from the harbour entrance. Could it be that these two stories were intertwined after all?

In the end, against my better judgement, I let myself be persuaded to accompany Heather down to Mario's yacht, which was moored at the far end of the quay, to make sure that she could collect her things and remove them without running into difficulties with him or his two companions. After that, she promised she would come with me to the *Carabinieri*.

I left the van where it was, deciding that at this time of night, there was unlikely to be a traffic warden on duty and having no desire to pay the outrageous tariff of five euros an hour for the privilege of parking there. As we walked down the narrow street towards the sea, there were still quite a lot of people milling around, but it was nothing like as crowded as it had been earlier.

When we got to the quayside, there were two surprises in store for us. The first was that the table outside the very expensive restaurant where Heather had left Mario and the other two men was now empty. The second surprise was considerably greater. Heather stopped dead and grabbed my arm with one hand, while pointing along the quay with the other. I followed her gaze towards the little remaining piece of fishing port at the far end and saw bright lights illuminating a motor yacht moored stern-on to the quay, with figures moving around on it and near it. The figures were mostly wearing Coastguard or *Carabinieri* uniforms and among them, I quickly recognised Officer Solaro standing on the quay, speaking into his phone.

We hurried along the quay towards him and as soon as he finished his conversation, I went up to him. He gave me a broad smile when he recognised me and an appreciative look at Heather with her very short skirt.

'Hello again. You can't keep away, can you, Signor Armstrong?'

'Something like that.' I indicated Heather. 'This young woman has a very interesting story to tell. Is the lieutenant about?'

He nodded. 'He's just gone back on board the yacht.' I glanced across and read the name of the boat on the stern – *La Fortunata*, registered in Livorno, not the British Virgin Islands. Maybe Mario didn't need the tax breaks.

'What about the owner of this yacht and his friends?' Heather spoke excellent Italian.

'They've been arrested and taken into custody. The lieutenant will be interviewing them later.' This confirmed my impression that something very dodgy had been going on, but I found myself wondering how the *Carabinieri* had managed to react so quickly. Had they had a tip-off?

Heather looked shocked when she heard about the arrests, but I nodded approvingly. 'Excellent, because, from what I've heard from Heather here, there might be some serious charges coming their way.' I caught his eye. 'Including a possible charge of murder.'

I saw his eyes open wide. Without hesitation, he pulled out his phone again and made a call to the lieutenant, who indicated he would come straight away.

When Lieutenant Bertoletti appeared, we shook hands and I introduced Heather. I then explained that she had until recently been a passenger on board the yacht that he and his officers were busy searching. His eyes lit up when I went on to outline what Heather had told me about the happenings of the previous night around eleven and the very real possibility that the murdered man from the *Regal Princess* might have inadvertently witnessed something underhand going on. By the end of my account, the lieutenant was looking very interested indeed.

'Thank you, Signor Armstrong. That's fascinating.' He looked across at Heather. 'I'm going to need to interview you, Signora, but that doesn't have to be right now. You look as if you could do with a good night's sleep. I'd be grateful if you would leave me your passport just to remind you to come back and see me again.' After she had handed over her passport, he transferred his attention to me. 'If I could leave her in your care for tonight, Signor Armstrong, could you possibly see that she comes back again tomorrow morning for interview? By that time, I will have had a chance to question the three men in custody and I may be able to tell you more about just exactly what happened last night. I have a feeling you'd like to be kept informed as this case develops.'

This sounded like an excellent plan and I immediately agreed. 'Definitely, thank you. What sort of time would you like us here?'

'I'm sure Officer Solaro would be only too happy to come and pick you up from Rapallo at, say, nine o'clock?'

'That would be excellent, thank you. Just one thing – would it be all right if my girlfriend and my dog come over to Portofino with me tomorrow? I'm afraid I'm going to be very unpopular with both of them otherwise.'

'No problem at all. Now, I need to get back on board the yacht. We've already located the suspicious boxes in the forward hold. We have yet to open them but we're pretty sure we know the contents.'

'Could I ask how it is that you've arrested the men and identified the yacht so quickly?' No sooner had I asked the question than I realised there was only one logical answer. 'Of course, you've had them under observation, haven't you?'

He smiled and gave me a little wink. 'I couldn't possibly comment...'

I smiled back. 'Understood. One thing: what's the situation with regard to the other yacht, the *Regal Princess*? The captain said they're heading for France. Might they be leaving some time soon?'

'No, they've been told to stay here until I give the authorisation for them to leave. From what you've just told me, I definitely need to speak to the captain and to a number of them again. As you say, they were moored quite close to this yacht and they may have witnessed the other vessel last night.'

'Did you get any further with what I overheard in the toilets?'

He gave a frustrated snort. 'I asked each of them if they'd been to the toilet in the restaurant and I discovered that no fewer than ten of the twelve had used the facilities. How much were these people drinking? Anyway, the bad news is that nobody admitted to saying the words you heard, although the one guy whose voice you thought you might have recognised did look decidedly shifty when I spoke to him.'

'Oh yes, Edgar Beaumont. By the way, I checked his name on Google and he's described as a senior TV executive. It looks like most, if not all, of the people on the yacht are from the world of TV.'

'Not just that, but they're all from the same TV company.' He flicked through the pages of his notebook. 'GreyratTV – that's one hell of a name – and guess who the CEO is... or rather was? That's right, the big boss was none other than our murder victim, Jerome Van der Groot.'

So as well as Head of Programming, Van der Groot had actually been the CEO. 'That might explain why nobody seemed to be particularly saddened by his death and why Susie Upton was so subservient to him. I'd love to be a fly on the wall when you interview her in more depth.'

He looked across and caught my eye. 'You can be more than that if you can spare the time. That way, you could listen to the men's voices one more time as well, in case you can pick out the other man you heard. We could do that tomorrow morning after I've spoken to this young lady. You're welcome to sit in and ask any questions of your own, but only if you can spare the time and if your girlfriend and your dog will allow it.'

'That sounds like a very good idea. I'll talk to Anna about it tonight and I look forward to seeing Officer Solaro and his speedboat tomorrow at nine. I'm sure Anna will understand that it's something I need to do.'

Even as I said it, I found myself wondering whether she would.

10

MONDAY MORNING

As it turned out, I didn't need to sleep on the floor after all, although when I broke the news to Anna that I felt I needed to go back in the morning to help with the investigation, I had a feeling she was thinking of turfing me out of, not only the bed and the room, but maybe also her life as well. Luckily, she was appreciative of the way I was helping the maiden in distress so she swallowed her exasperation and agreed to return to Portofino with me next day. I knew I was breaking my promise to try to concentrate on her and our holiday, but something deep down inside me wouldn't let me turn my back on a murder case – even if, as she was quick to point out, I wasn't being paid for my efforts.

Anna had been able to convince the receptionist to find a small single room for Heather, and the receptionist even very kindly managed to provide her with a comb and a little tube of toothpaste with a disposable toothbrush, although all her other stuff was still on board *La Fortunata* at Portofino. Heather thanked us most warmly, but her voice was weary and I told her she would feel better after a good night's sleep.

Anna was still asleep when I woke up early next morning, so I crept out of bed and took Oscar for a walk before breakfast. When I got back to the room, the atmosphere was a bit strained but Anna appeared to have accepted the fait accompli and she no longer tried to object to my 'playing detectives'. Of course, in spite of her choice of vocabulary, she knows as well as I do that murder isn't a game.

When we met up with Heather in the breakfast room at eight, she was looking much brighter than the previous night. Over breakfast, I told her about the death of one of the group from the *Regal Princess* and she sounded interested when she heard who was on board the yacht.

'Susie Upton and Martin Grey: they did that sitcom about the magician and his assistant, didn't they? My mum used to love that one. As for their huge yacht, I saw it yesterday morning. It was anchored only a couple of hundred metres further out than us overnight and it came past around half past seven in the morning, heading for Portofino. I asked Mario why we weren't going ashore as well, because I was getting fed up with just bobbing up and down with the shore half a mile away, but he said he wanted to wait. Like I told you last night, he changed completely the previous night when that other boat appeared and he was in a foul mood all day yesterday. He really snapped at me. My phone wasn't working and I had nothing to read, so I had a really boring day. It was late afternoon before he finally decided it was time to go into the harbour and that was a tremendous relief.'

This confirmed what I had thought. The rendezvous with the unknown boat had been pre-arranged and presumably Mario had wanted to keep whatever was in those boxes safely out of the way of prying eyes until the last minute. Knowing that he was scheduled to meet and pick up the two Arabs that evening, he had just hung around out at sea and wasted time. Little wonder

Heather had been bored and getting more and more disenchanted with him.

I found Officer Solaro waiting for us when we got down to the jetty and he gave us another exhilarating trip across the bay. Oscar clearly loved it and he stood on the foredeck, firmly braced with his legs splayed, his nose pointing into the wind and his tail wagging, while I kept hold of the end of his lead in case he might decide to jump over the side. Fortunately, Anna also found the trip exciting and she was looking and sounding more cheerful when we got to Portofino. After dropping us off on the quayside, Officer Solaro stayed on board the boat, telling me he was going off to do his 'rounds'. I presumed this to mean checking up on the multitude of different boats moored up in the bay and beyond. Anna and I had already agreed that she and Oscar would go for a walking tour of the town while Heather and I went up to the *Carabinieri* station. The good news was that there were far fewer people around first thing on a Monday morning and it didn't take us long to get there.

When we got to the barracks I found Maresciallo Veronese standing outside once more, this time without a cigarette in his hand, and he gave me a smart salute.

'*Buongiorno, Commissario.*' Word of my former rank must have spread.

I smiled back at him. 'Good morning, *Maresciallo*, but it's ex-*commissario* these days. How did it go with the three men you have in custody?'

'The two Arabs claim they only speak a few words of Italian, no English, not even French. We couldn't get a word out of them although they'd been sitting with Mario Fortunato when we picked them up, so how did they talk to each other – hand signals?' He gave a dismissive snort. 'The lieutenant's trying to get an interpreter, but whether that will start them talking is another matter. As for Fortunato, he's barely said a word except for bleating that he wants to see his lawyer. That's the way it is for these pros: say nothing, get an expensive lawyer and try to wriggle out of all charges.'

'You say he's a pro – what sort of pro? A pro smuggler?'

'He's an arms dealer, a middleman between factories in places like Slovakia, the Czech Republic and Austria on the one hand and a variety of clients all around the globe, some of them decidedly suspicious, on the other. The lieutenant will tell you more, but we've had our eye on this bunch for months now.'

'I see.' This confirmed my feeling that the speed with which the *Carabinieri* had impounded the yacht and arrested its occupants had to mean that the authorities had already had them in their sights. 'Well, I hope you manage to break down their wall of silence.'

He shrugged his shoulders. 'I'm not holding my breath.' He checked his watch. 'I expect the lieutenant's back in his office now. He spent the night here at the barracks and the last I heard of him, he was having a quick coffee. Come on, let me show you through to his office. If he hasn't come back yet, you can wait for him.'

In fact, Lieutenant Bertoletti was already at his desk when we were ushered into his office. He stood up to shake my hand and looked across at the *maresciallo*. 'Veronese, I'd like you to take this young lady to an interview room, please. I'll be with her shortly.'

I gave Heather a little wave and mouthed to her not to worry. In response to the lieutenant's gesture, I sat down opposite him and gave him a sympathetic grin. 'Tired?'

'Exhausted. I didn't get to bed until 4 a.m. and I was up again at six-thirty. I've had so many cups of coffee this morning that I feel light-headed, but at least I'm awake.'

'I gather from the *maresciallo* that your other guests aren't talking.'

He shook his head helplessly. 'Hopefully, in the next hour or so, the Arabic interpreter should be here, although we're perfectly sure that these two already speak Italian, if not English, so that means I'm not expecting any instant confessions. As for Mario Fortunato, he refuses to say anything until his lawyer gets here from Pisa, and that won't be until mid-morning at the earliest.'

'The *maresciallo* told me that they were involved with arms smuggling. Did you manage to get any clues off those boxes that were transferred from the other boat? Don't worry, I don't want to know what was in them.'

'The Forensic team are still studying them. What I can tell you is that our ballistics specialists say they should have no trouble identifying the origin of the highly sophisticated weapons in the boxes and, you never know, we might be able to get some prints off them and match them with some of the other suspects in this case. They were no doubt destined for some very unpleasant people – Veronese may have told you that this is a Europewide, if not worldwide, operation.'

'I gathered as much. I wish you luck.'

He smiled. 'Thanks, we need it.'

'Did you get any kind of reaction from any of the three when you mentioned Jerome Van der Groot? I presume if they weren't talking, you didn't get much.'

'The two Arabs looked completely blank but, as far as we're aware, they weren't on either boat the other night. As for Fortunato, he did at least say something when I put it to him. It wasn't much, but he just said, quite firmly, "I am not a murderer."'

I caught his eye for a moment. 'He would say that, wouldn't he?'

He smiled grimly. 'Indeed, although I have to confess that I almost felt inclined to believe him. Tell me, how long are you staying in Rapallo?'

'We're heading home tomorrow. Anna has a meeting at the university in the afternoon.'

'But you're here all day today? Would it be too much of an imposition on you if we were to put off our visit to the *Regal Princess* until this afternoon? That'll give me time to talk to Heather Greensleeves, our two Arabic speakers, and hopefully before lunch, Mario Fortunato's lawyer will have arrived and the guy might finally start talking.' He looked up and gave me a weary smile. 'To sweeten the pill, could I at least offer you and your girlfriend dinner tonight? A close friend of mine has a restaurant here with a good reputation, and it's the least I can do after you've given your time so freely. You do like fish, don't you?'

'That's remarkably kind of you and, yes, we both love fish, but wouldn't you prefer to go home and get yourself a good night's sleep?'

He laughed. 'A good meal and a couple of glasses of wine and I'll be fine. And, by the way, I haven't forgotten your dog. I'll make sure they give us a table outside on the terrace. The restaurant's less than a hundred metres from here and it's called La Conchiglia. Just turn left outside the door and walk up the road.'

'Wonderful, thanks. What are you planning on doing with Heather Greensleeves? From what she's told me, I'm convinced she had nothing to do with what happened the other night.'

'I'm sure you're right. I just want to get as much background as I can on Fortunato and every single detail she can remember about the other boat and the people on it. The Coastguard have been tracking several boats that might have rendezvoused with them, but if we can get a positive ID, that would be excellent. I imagine when we've finished with her, she'll want to go back home to Lucca, rather than hang around waiting to be reunited with Signor Fortunato.' He ran a weary hand over his stubbly cheeks. 'I think I'd better go and have a shave. Why don't you go and tell her what's happening and check that she'll be able to make her own way home. And you can give her a bit of good news: I got my people to pack up her stuff, and her bag's in the corner of my office, so she doesn't need to worry about trying to get it back from the yacht. Thanks for all your help and I'll see you this afternoon.'

I got up and the two of us went out into the corridor. He opened a door partway along and I saw Heather in there sitting at a table, looking nervous. The lieutenant left me with her and went off to have his shave. I explained what was happening and gave her the good news about her belongings, stressing that she wasn't a suspect but that the lieutenant was hoping she might be able to provide a few extra snippets of information that could help their inquiry, and she looked reassured. I said she would probably be out in the next hour or so and asked if she was happy making her own way back to Lucca. She assured me that it would be no problem at all for her to get the ferry and the train, and then jumped to her feet to come over and give me another hug.

'Thank you, Dan, and please give my thanks to Anna. You've both been super kind to me. Any time you're in Lucca, please give me a call and come and have something to eat. I'm quite a good cook, honest.'

I thanked her and told her I would be sure to call. After that, I went out looking for Anna and Oscar, deciding to walk down to the seafront and, if I didn't see her, to text her. In fact, I almost bumped into her halfway down the road as she was staring at a handbag in a shop window. I went over and was about to suggest I buy it for her as a peace offering for leaving her to her own devices when I saw the price and decided to leave that one for the oligarchs. Oblivious to my fleeting moment of almost generosity, she turned around when Oscar spotted me and dragged her in my direction.

'That was quick, Dan.' Her face lit up, but only until I broke the news to her that I would be going out to the yacht full of TV people this afternoon rather than this morning. She muttered a typical Italian expression of annoyance, which translates literally as, 'Pig misery!' Don't ask me why. I hastened to apologise and was seriously considering revisiting the idea of the handbag, even though it would probably have involved taking out a mortgage, when I was saved by the bell. Anna's phone started ringing. She answered and it was immediately clear that she'd been expecting the call.

'*Ciao*, Tamsin, that would be great. And you're sure you don't mind if I bring the dog?' She glanced across at me. 'Although I can happily leave my boyfriend behind – just say the word. Well, if that's okay, I'd love to. Hang on and I'll see what Dan says.' She looked down at me as I was scratching Oscar's ears. 'I bumped into an old friend a few minutes ago and she's invited us for lunch with her. She was just checking to see if it's okay. Are you going to be tied up with your *Carabinieri* friends or might you be able to spare me an hour or two of your precious time?'

I hastily assured her that I would be only too delighted and I heard her relay the information to her friend. Her last words were intriguing.

'You'll come and collect us? Twelve-thirty. Perfect. We'll be waiting at the jetty.'

She dropped the phone back into her bag and turned towards me.

'That was a woman called Tamsin Taylor. She used to work for a company making historical TV documentaries and she and I worked together four years ago when she was making a programme about the Palio in Siena. I was advising on the historical side of things and acting as interpreter. It was quite fun, certainly a lot more fun than my time on the movie last year where I met you. No murders in her programmes, I'm pleased to say. She's now working for a new TV company and she's here with a bunch of other TV people holidaying on a yacht and that's where we've been invited for lunch.'

'Tamsin Taylor...?' I recognised that name and I must have looked completely gormless because she actually burst out laughing.

'That's right, Sherlock, we've just been invited for lunch on board the *Regal Princess*.'

My head was spinning. On the one hand, this would be an excellent way of mingling with the people on the boat in an informal manner, but the complication was that they had already seen me in the company of the *Carabinieri*. At the very least, people were going to be suspicious of me, maybe hostile. I did my best to explain the problem to Anna but, ever pragmatic, she just shrugged her shoulders.

'So what? Did you do any interrogating or questioning or whatever you call it when you were on the boat yesterday? In fact, did you say anything to anybody?' Seeing me shake my head, she continued. 'You're English and you speak Italian. We'll just tell them you were helping out with translating. That doesn't mean you're connected with the police. It'll be fine, you'll see.'

I hoped she was right. Certainly, the idea of going back aboard the *Regal Princess* appealed to my investigative instincts, but whether it would further the murder investigation remained to be seen.

11

MONDAY LUNCHTIME

At half past twelve, we were waiting on the jetty as instructed when a sleek, highly polished wooden launch purred up to collect us. It was driven by Christopher, the deckhand from the *Regal Princess*, and alongside him was Anna's friend, Tamsin, whose face I immediately recognised from the previous day. She was the very good-looking woman who had been sitting between Edgar Beaumont, my number one suspect with the vague Welsh accent, and the serious lawyer type, Neil Vaughan.

She didn't immediately recognise me but when she did, Anna gave her the interpreter story and she appeared to buy it. We stepped down into the launch and took seats on comfortable, red, velvet cushions. Oscar looked longingly at the cushions but had to settle for the floor, from where he was soon happily sniffing the breeze as we set off. While Anna and Tamsin carried on catching up, I reflected on what I might now be able to find out. I had phoned the lieutenant to tell him about the chance lunch invitation and he'd agreed that it was a very good opportunity to talk to the four suspects who might or might not have been the voices I'd heard in Lucca. At the same time, it would give me the opportunity to get a bit of inside information on the people on board.

Although the crew of the mystery boat and/or Heather's boyfriend – or more correctly, her *former* boyfriend now – were still the most likely candidates for Jerome Van der Groot's murder, there still remained a question over whether he might in fact have been killed by somebody on the *Regal Princess*. In particular, I wanted to do my best to identify the voices I'd overheard in Lucca, but I was also interested to know the dynamics of the group. Why were they all here? Had this been intended as a very swish business meeting or had Van der Groot simply been trying to say thank you to some loyal colleagues by taking them on an all-expenses-paid cruise? Had there been any arguments? Had there maybe even been a bit of bed-hopping going on that could have aroused jealousy?

It promised to be an interesting couple of hours.

We boarded the yacht by the rear platform as before and it was clear that this was the watersports centre as well as being the main access to the vessel. A grey rubber dinghy with a little outboard motor was moored to one side and I wondered if this was similar to the one that had conveyed the murder victim on his ill-fated last voyage. As far as I knew, that one was still being investigated by Forensics. A kayak and a couple of jet skis were lying on the low-level deck that protruded from the hull barely a few feet above the waterline. Alongside the jet skis, I spotted the man with the American accent I'd heard while I'd been listening in to the lieutenant's questions around the lunch table yesterday. He was wearing a wetsuit and looked as if he'd just been out on the water. With him was one of the female guests, whose face I recognised but I couldn't remember her name. She was also wearing a wetsuit and was in the process of being helped out of scuba-diving gear by a female deckhand. Clearly, the *Regal Princess* offered more than limitless alcohol.

Anna and I followed Tamsin up to the deck above and I kept a good grip on Oscar's lead when he clapped eyes on the swimming pool. Given half a chance, he would have belly-flopped in and splashed the three people sitting on the edge of the pool with their feet in the water. This little group consisted of two men and a woman. The woman sitting between the two men, wearing a light-blue swimming costume, was Susie Upton, and her companions were the same two who had been flanking her at the lunch table the previous day: Martin Grey, the Liverpudlian comic, and the muscleman whose name I knew to be Adam Phillips but whom I had already mentally christened Mr Muscle. Interestingly, Martin Grey's hand was resting on Susie Upton's thigh. When she set eyes on Oscar, she jumped to her feet very nimbly and came around to give him an effusive greeting. His tail started wagging immediately; he likes it when women make a fuss of him – and who can blame him?

Tamsin introduced Anna and me and repeated my interpreter cover story, which, again, appeared to be accepted at face value. We chatted idly about the weather, Labradors and the beauty of Portofino, but Susie made no reference to the murder investigation. However, a few moments later, we were joined by the guy with the muscles and his first question after being introduced to me was, 'Have the police caught Jerome's murderer yet?'

I shrugged. 'I've no idea. The lieutenant told me they've managed to get a police interpreter to help out now. I was just an emergency fill-in yesterday.'

He seemed to accept the fact that I no longer had any involvement with the investigation, but it was clear from what he said next that the murder had been the main topic of conversation here on the yacht ever since the previous day. 'What I can't understand is why the police think it was murder. Isn't it much more likely that Jerome just fell over the side of the little dinghy and drowned? He'd had a real skinful by that time of night, so it doesn't surprise me in the slightest that he might have fallen in. You should have seen the state he was in – not just drunk, but absolutely furious. He wasn't behaving rationally. Anybody could see that.'

I'd been listening carefully to him and had to admit that his southern English accent might indeed have been the voice I'd heard plotting – or at least letting off steam – at the restaurant in Lucca. I still couldn't be sure, but mentally I put a little tick alongside his name. From what he'd just said, it was clear that the news that Van der Groot had been stabbed before drowning hadn't percolated through, and I certainly wasn't going to tell them, so I continued to plead ignorance. 'I don't know the details but, from what the lieutenant said, there could be no doubt that it was murder. What was Jerome Van der Groot so angry about?'

Before Mr Muscle could answer, a familiar voice cut in, this time sounding decidedly prickly.

'Just internal company stuff. It wouldn't mean anything to you.' Martin Grey had also come across to join us. He stopped short of telling me to mind my own business, but the implication was clear. I had to admit that he looked good in his swimming trunks – and he knew it. His muscle tone was perfect – although his muscles bulged far less than the man alongside him – and his all-over tan was flawless. He made no attempt to approach Oscar, who glanced at him and then ignored him. He has a canine sixth sense about which humans are dog friendly and which aren't.

I took the hint and just shrugged my shoulders. 'Who knows? Certainly too much alcohol and a ride in a little dinghy in the middle of the night doesn't strike me as a very good mix.'

Leaving them there, Anna and I followed Tamsin up the next

flight of stairs to the saloon, where we found half a dozen people standing around with glasses in their hands. After making the introductions and relaying my cover story, Tamsin led us across to a well-stocked bar where a female member of staff was standing. She was wearing the regulation *Regal Princess* polo shirt and her name tag indicated that she was called Vanessa. She gave us a friendly smile and asked what we'd like to drink. As usual, Anna opted for a Campari spritz and, for once, I asked for the same. I'm normally a beer drinker at this kind of event, but somehow on a multimillion-dollar yacht in the bay of Portofino, it seemed only right and proper to be drinking something a bit more sophisticated. I smiled to myself. At least I hadn't gone the whole hog and asked for a vodka Martini, shaken not stirred.

While Anna and Tamsin chatted about historical matters, I wandered about and looked around, Oscar sniffing everything he came to. Fortunately, he soon broke the ice with the other people, and I found myself drawn into conversation with them. As before, they asked about the investigation and I gave them the same story – saying that it was nothing to do with me. When they realised that I couldn't shed any light on police business, their topic of conversation very quickly gravitated back to company affairs, and I listened closely while at the same time trying to appear only casually interested.

It quickly emerged that roughly half of the people on this cruise were performers, mainly comedy actors, while the other half came from the production or administrative side of the company. I don't know what I'd been expecting from a bunch of comedians – maybe non-stop jokes and banter – but the mood was sombre. Mind you, it was hardly surprising that under the circumstances, nobody felt much like laughing.

The good news was that both of the men who'd been sitting at the far end of yesterday's lunch table were here now and I concentrated as much on how they were speaking as on what they were saying. It very quickly became clear that Billy Webster, today wearing a different – but equally voluminous – T-shirt, this time advertising his own UK Tour 2019, had either been indulging liberally in the open bar this morning or he was still drunk from the night before. He didn't say very much, but what he did say was liberally laced with fruity expletives that would have scandalised a sailor. In essence, he was asking all and sundry, as well as the heavens, to explain why he'd managed to find himself on a boat with a murderer. I could understand his concern, although I would probably have expressed it a bit less colourfully.

Alongside him was Doug Kingsley, his stubbly chin indicating that he had probably just rolled out of bed. Today's T-shirt bore the slogan: *EDUCATION IS IMPORTANT BUT COMEDY IS IMPORTANTER*. I listened carefully to his voice and Webster's but, annoyingly, I was unable to make a positive voice ID for either of them. In the end, all I could do was leave them on the list of possibles alongside Adam Phillips, AKA Mr Muscle.

The previous day, I had mentally pigeonholed Mr Muscle as being in his thirties but, close up, he might even have been a few years older. When I queried his position in the company, it came as something of a surprise to be told that he was in Accounts. Somehow, I had imagined him as being a daredevil TV presenter abseiling down cliff faces and white water rafting in the Rocky Mountains. Interestingly, although he was bulging with impressive muscles, he wasn't very tall and, compared to Kingsley, I wondered just how tough he might prove to be in a fight. Still, I told myself, I had no desire to get involved in a fight and I assumed the same would apply to most of the people here. Apart, of course, from the person who had murdered Jerome Van der Groot.

Ten minutes later, we were joined by Susie Upton, now changed out of her costume into a tight top and an even shorter skirt than Heather had been wearing. Without make-up, she was looking a little more like her real age, but there was no question that she was a very good-looking woman who wasn't afraid to put herself on display. I thought it might be interesting to study her relationship with the equally beautiful and considerably younger Tamsin Taylor and I noticed that they almost ignored each other. Tamsin was still chatting happily to Anna about the Medici so, after a few moments hovering near them, Susie went over to the bar and ordered herself a gin and tonic. Either Vanessa at the bar was naturally generous with her employer's supply of alcohol or she knew Susie of old, because I was amazed to see her half fill a tall glass with gin before adding ice and a slice of lemon and passing it across the counter, accompanied by a little bottle of tonic. Susie tipped barely half the tonic into the glass and turned towards me, treating me – or more probably Oscar – to a beaming smile.

'So, you live here in Italy, do you, Dan? How wonderful. If I didn't have to be in London for my job, I'd love to settle over here, probably to Tuscany.'

I smiled back while Oscar went over and rested his head against her knee. 'That's where I live, just outside Florence, and I love it.'

'What is it you do, Dan?'

Over coffee in a harbourside café this morning, Anna and I had been discussing what my answer to this question should be and we had come to the conclusion that it was probably best to avoid mentioning my work as a private investigator – at least at first. Instead, I told Susie about my literary ambitions. 'I'm a writer. I write detective stories set in Italy.' This was in fact quite true as my first book, *Death Amid the Vines*, had come out this spring and was selling well. My second book had already been delivered to the publisher and would be coming out in the late autumn.

Her smile grew even broader. 'How exciting! Do tell me about it, won't you?'

I gave her a brief synopsis of the first book and she looked absolutely fascinated, producing a series of oohs and aahs. Of course, I told myself, to showbiz people, hyperbole was everything, so I probably shouldn't count on her going out and buying herself a copy as soon as she got back to the UK. Still, I had to admit that she was easy to talk to.

A few minutes later, the atmosphere abruptly changed. I felt a tap on my shoulder and found myself confronted by Martin Grey, now also changed out of his swimming kit into a smart designer polo shirt and shorts. He was looking far less friendly than Susie Upton, and Oscar must have sensed it as well because he ostentatiously turned away and padded across to the other side of me, staying well out of the comedian's way.

'Chief Inspector Armstrong, pray tell me why we've suddenly managed to find ourselves with a private investigator in our midst?' The Liverpool accent easily lends itself to a threatening tone and, from his belligerent expression, it was clear he was playing to the gallery. The chatter around us died away as I suddenly became the centre of attention. Grey must have noted an expression of surprise on my face because he held up his phone and shook it gently in front of me. 'Mr Google had quite a lot to say about you, Chief Inspector, but it didn't say why you're here, so do tell. We'd love to know what you're investigating.'

Fortunately, I'd come across any number of difficult characters in my time and I knew that the best way to handle them was to stand up to them. I gave him an innocent smile in response. 'That's easy, Mr Grey, the answer's nothing. I'm no longer in the police force and I'm not here in an official capacity. I'm just having a few days' holiday with my girlfriend.'

'That sounds like a load of bull to me.' He looked out around the faces of the rest of the group. 'Are you convinced?'

If he'd been expecting a rousing show of support, he was to be disappointed. Nobody said anything, although I could tell they were at the very least curious to know why I was here. Encouraged by this, I turned the question back on Grey. 'Like I say, I'm just having a few days off and I'm only here because Anna knows Tamsin. The last thing I want is to intrude on your holiday so if you'd prefer me to leave, that's fine by me, but before I go, please, do tell me, *is* there something I should be investigating here?'

He was good. He almost showed no reaction, but there was just a fleeting millisecond when I felt sure I saw something on his face – maybe guilt or at least disquiet – before he collected himself and shook his head.

'Apart from Billy's liver and Susie's knickers, there's nothing around her that needs going into.'

Before I could reply, I felt a hand on my arm as Susie Upton mounted a show of support. 'Martin, for the love of God, can't you just behave for once? Dan's here with Anna and she's here because Tamsin asked her to be here. It doesn't matter whether he's a private investigator or a lion tamer. His job has nothing to do with you. Just because Jerome's gone doesn't mean that you call the shots. Behave yourself and let everybody else have a good time, even if you want to be an old grouch.'

'Susie, Susie, Susie, calm down, calm down.' His tone and his manner were dismissive and I could feel the tension rising in Susie through her hand on my arm. Unperturbed, he carried on. 'There's no need to be so frickin' defensive. I was just asking the gentleman if he was currently involved in an investigation. What's the harm in that?'

'Martin, you're an ass.' I was mildly surprised at her mild choice of language, but the insult must have hit home all the same. For a moment or two, his assumed air of bonhomie slipped and there was a real edge to his voice when he responded.

'And you're a slut.'

This time, I actually heard a couple of sharp intakes of breath among the others but Susie just gave my arm a squeeze and looked up at me. 'I think it's time for lunch, don't you, Dan? Let's go and make sure we get a seat a long way away from him. Being near him would make me lose my appetite.'

There was no need for her to specify to whom she was referring. Clearly, there was no love lost between the two actors, but I had been surprised by the venom attached to his accusation. Whether her insult or his far stronger response had any basis in fact was something I would have dearly loved to find out.

12

MONDAY LUNCHTIME

Lunch was excellent, but I'd been expecting no less – after all, the *Regal Princess* boasted a chef *and* a sous-chef. It started with a choice of cold lobster salad or cheese soufflés – or both – and was followed by steamed turbot in a blue cheese sauce or, for the meat eaters, wonderful, tender fillet steak. The food was accompanied by ice-cold white Burgundy and a powerful but highly aromatic Rioja – although I noticed that Billy Webster stuck with pint mugs of beer. I opted for the steak as my main course and I couldn't help noticing that the wooden-handled steak knives looked remarkably similar to the description I had received of the murder weapon. Might there be one missing? I wondered.

The meal was immaculately served by two Filipino stewards and the mood around the table – at least at our end – soon lightened up. Susie had placed herself to my right and Anna was on my left with Tamsin beyond her. Susie was good company and in chatty mood – no doubt the large gin and tonic had helped in that respect. If she had been hurt by Grey's insult, it didn't show. I couldn't help remembering the way his hand had been resting on her thigh down at the pool and I wondered exactly what her relationship with him was. Surely if they were intimate, then calling her a slut would appear to show that all was not rosy between them.

As we ate, I gradually discovered more about my lunch companions and their all-expenses-paid cruise. As I had surmised, the trip had been sponsored by GreyratTV, as the brainchild of the CEO, Jerome Van der Groot, with the intention of combining business with pleasure. I learned that several hours each day had been devoted to plenary sessions discussing programming for the next twenty-four months. Tamsin told us that the company, while specialising in entertainment programmes, was further subdivided into different categories such as quiz, game, stand-up and so on. The representatives of each of these different disciplines had had to pitch ideas to the general assembly for discussion in the course of the cruise and then decisions had been taken on whether to go ahead or not. In all cases, the ultimate arbiter had been Van der Groot himself and I could easily see how internal rivalries could have developed and how he could have made himself popular with some, but deeply unpopular with others.

But deeply enough for somebody to commit murder?

On a more personal level, I learned that partners had not been invited and so there had effectively been twelve unaccompanied individuals here, eleven since the death of Jerome Van der Groot. Tamsin told us that she'd been married for only six months and was regretting being separated from her husband for two whole weeks but, like the others, she had accepted that it was just part of the job. Her job, I discovered, was that of producer/director of the best known of the quiz shows. This must have made quite a change from historical documentaries but presumably it had seen her career follow an upward trajectory. Anna was excellent at digging out bits of scandal from those around us – like the fact that Martin Grey had been slapped across the face by Louise from Payroll after he'd tried to grope her by the pool.

Susie surreptitiously pointed Louise out to me on the opposite side of the table to Edgar Beaumont, where she was engaged in earnest conversation with the man with the Glaswegian accent who was apparently the head of PR. Louise Challenger was the serious-looking woman I had spotted earlier on the watersports deck. With her tightly pulled-back hair and glasses, she certainly didn't look as if she fell into the 'slut' category. I could well imagine her outrage at being assaulted by the foul-mouthed Liverpudlian.

It all sounded par for the course with this sort of work/leisure environment, but I was unable to unearth any deep and lasting grudges, the sort that can lead to murder. The sad fact of the matter was that by the time we reached the excellent *crème brûlée*, I was no nearer to knowing who might have wanted to murder Jerome Van der Groot than I had been before sitting down to eat.

Things got a bit more interesting at coffee time. This was served along with the offer of a very good Cognac, but I thanked the steward and accepted the coffee and declined the hard stuff. In fact, I'd been going easy on alcohol all meal as I was trying to keep my mental faculties reasonably sharp. A glance at my watch told me that it was almost half past two by this time, and I'd told the lieutenant I would give him a call before three, so I was just wondering about thanking Tamsin and asking for a lift back to the harbour when a furious row broke out at the far end of the table. Predictably, this involved Martin Grey. There was the sound of a fist banging on the table hard enough to rouse Oscar from no doubt sweet dreams of squirrels and food and he looked up with an indignant expression on his face. The thump was followed by an expletive-filled outburst from the comedian. This translated into printable English as:

'Who do you think you're talking to, you little worm? Now that Jerome's gone, I'm the most senior person here so if I say that's what we do, then that's what we do.' I was impressed that he managed to include the F-word no fewer than five times in these two short sentences. No mean feat.

The 'little worm' in question was Doug Kingsley, the young comic, and he looked equally furious as he jumped to his feet and picked up his half-full glass of red wine. He fixed Grey with a malevolent stare and, when he spoke, his voice was filled with venom.

'For feck's sake, Martin, who do you think you are? Just because you treat that poor wife of yours like dirt, doesn't mean you can do it to me. You're going to apologise to me right now, I mean it, this very minute, or I won't be responsible for my actions.'

A more uncertain look crossed Martin Grey's face as his eyes focused on the red wine while his hand reached up in a protective gesture towards the little crocodile on his immaculate sky-blue polo shirt. There was a tense standoff for about fifteen or twenty seconds before he replied in a more reasonable voice.

'There's no need for violence, Douggie. I was simply saying that you have no authority over me.'

The glass of red wine drew a couple of inches closer to Grey's face. 'That doesn't sound like an apology to me, Martin. I'll count to three and then first it's the wine, then it'll be the glass, and then it'll be my fist. One... two...'

'All right, all right, I'm sorry. I shouldn't have used that language. Abject apologies and all that sort of thing.'

The insincerity and the sarcasm in his voice was clear to everybody and for a moment, I had a feeling he was going to get a face full of red wine anyway but, finally, Doug Kingsley set the glass down, turned dismissively and headed off down the stairs towards the sun deck. I glanced sideways at Susie, who was looking quite unmoved by the scene, and lowered my voice. 'Is that sort of thing a common occurrence?'

She threw me a little smile and nodded. 'With Martin, yes. I had to empty a plate of vindaloo into his lap a few months back. He can be an unbearable little oik and of course, now that Jerome's died, he thinks he's God Almighty.'

So what had the 'unbearable little oik' been doing with his hand on her thigh? Deciding not to pursue that line of enquiry for now, I concentrated on company matters. 'Is it true that he's the most senior person here? Is he going to take Van der Groot's place?'

She shook her head vehemently. 'Of course he's not. He's just an employee like the rest of us, even if he has been with the company a bit longer than most. There are two or three people here who've been in the company longer than him and occupy more responsible positions, like Edgar for instance. He's the head of Accounts but he's also Company Secretary and generally acknowledged as Jerome's number two. Let's face it, Martin's just a comedian. He's like me and what do we do?' A more cynical note entered her voice. 'We say silly things and we try to make people laugh. It's not exactly rocket science. Martin's not a director or a producer and he's certainly not a manager. *He* might think he's God's gift, but he's the only one who does. There's no way he could get himself into a senior managerial position even if it was offered to him; first, he couldn't organise a piss-up in a brewery and, second, he's even more detested by most people than Jerome was.'

I had already pretty much worked that out for myself but I queried it with her anyway. 'Van der Groot wasn't popular, then?'

This time, a far more serious expression appeared on her face. 'Popular? You must be joking! Jerome was a slimy toad. You couldn't believe a single thing he said. He treated everybody – from the cleaners to the producers – appallingly and, to make matters worse, he had final say on all major decision-making and he made mistake after mistake, so the result is that the company's now in deep financial trouble.'

I sat there for a few moments and digested that information. Why on earth, if the company risked insolvency, had Van der Groot taken the decision to spend probably as much as a hundred thousand pounds on a two-week luxury cruise for everybody? It made little sense. I had no doubt that the people around me were well paid and stood to lose a lot if the company collapsed so, if Van der Groot had been running the company into the ground, had somebody maybe decided to get rid of him permanently in order to save GreyratTV and their livelihoods? Murder was certainly a far more radical solution than a vote of no confidence at a board meeting, but after this little scene, it was clear that tempers were running high among the GreyratTV staff.

This fracas seemed to be the sign for everybody to get up from the table and start leaving the room. I shook hands with a few people and thanked Susie for her company – she dropped to her knees and gave Oscar a warm send-off before he and I followed Tamsin and Anna back down to the launch. When we reached the watersports deck, there was nobody around, and Tamsin stopped to apologise for the scene we'd just witnessed and to pass on a bit more useful information.

'I'm sorry about Martin. He's been getting worse and worse recently. Just because he's the public face of the company – along with Susie and the others, of course – he thinks that gives him the right to throw his weight around. On Saturday night, he was getting quite impossible and Jerome called him out right in front of everybody and gave him a real stripping-down. I've never seen Jerome so furious and I've never seen Martin so angry in his turn.

I really thought they were going to start physically attacking each other at one point.'

This certainly was significant. Could it be that Martin Grey had decided to take his revenge on his boss in such a radical way? But, from what I'd just seen and heard, Martin Grey wasn't the only person with a short fuse. Doug Kingsley had sounded quite vicious in his altercation with Grey and I had a feeling that if he and Jerome Van der Groot had crossed swords, the comic with the earrings might have resorted to violence. Seeing as Tamsin was in talkative mood, I glanced around to check that we weren't being overheard and then asked her a question that had been preying on my mind.

'Could I ask why Martin Grey called Susie a slut? Was that just a random insult or is he basing that on something linked to her behaviour perhaps?'

I noticed that Tamsin also took a surreptitious look around before answering. 'No, of course not, although she's no saint. As far as Martin's concerned, it all stems from his narcissism. For ages now, he's been peddling a rumour – quite unfounded, I'm sure – that the only reason Susie has done so well in the company is because she's been sleeping with the boss.' I saw her exchange glances with Anna. 'You never met Jerome, did you? But, believe me, he wasn't the sort of man that any woman with an ounce of self-respect would consider as a bedfellow.' I saw her actually shudder. 'Like I say, Martin always has to be top dog, and it's pretty clear to me, and I'm sure it was clear to everybody including Jerome, that Susie can run rings around Martin in terms of professionalism, public popularity and just plain intelligence. And, deep down, I'm sure Martin knows it's true, but this just makes him more and more sour towards her. Hence the insults.'

Anna was looking surprised. 'And yet the two of them can

appear side by side on TV and you'd think they were the very best of friends.'

Tamsin gave her a wry smile. 'What happens in front of the camera and what happens away from it are two very different things.'

This reminded me that half the people on this boat were actors. I'd met quite a few talented actors in my time – not in a comedic but in a criminal sense – and I knew that an innocent smile often concealed hidden guilt. Yes, Martin Grey and Doug Kingsley might appear to be rude and argumentative, but could it be that other less aggressive members of the GreyratTV staff were skilfully concealing hidden depths? If there was a murderer here on board the *Regal Princess*, his or her identity was far from clear.

13

MONDAY AFTERNOON

As soon as we reached the jetty and I'd waved farewell to Christopher in the launch, I pulled out my phone and called Lieutenant Bertoletti. He answered immediately and told me that he was in his office if I wanted to drop in. I explained to Anna that I would only be a few minutes and then I promised that would be the end of my involvement with this case. I left her looking a lot happier than she had been this morning, sitting on a bench in the shade with Oscar at her side. I struggled through the crowds to the *Carabinieri* station and found Maresciallo Veronese standing outside as usual. As before, he gave me a salute when he saw me and addressed me as *Commissario*. I decided there was no point in trying to correct him as this would probably be the last time I would see him anyway.

'Good afternoon, *Maresciallo*. I'm just going in to see the lieutenant. What sort of morning have you had?'

'Frustrating. The lieutenant will tell you all about it. The two Libyans claim that they're old friends of Mario Fortunato and they just happened to bump into him by sheer chance here in

Portofino.' He shot me a sceptical look. 'And I'm Father Christmas, right?'

'And what about Fortunato himself? Did his lawyer appear?'

'Yes, but I don't think the lieutenant got much out of him either. Come on, he can tell you himself.'

He led me through to the lieutenant's office and left me there. The lieutenant was looking a bit less tired but, just like the *maresciallo*, I could tell he was frustrated. I could well understand and I gave him a sympathetic smile.

'I gather that your three suspects haven't provided you with any kind of breakthrough.'

'My three suspects have hardly said anything. The Libyans claim they know nothing and want to speak to their embassy in Rome, accusing me of harassment. Fortunato continues to deny everything, including a mystery vessel arriving in the night, as well as any knowledge of the boxes in his hold, even though I've told him his girlfriend witnessed their transfer from the other vessel. He says she must be mistaken and hinted darkly that she'd been smoking pot. We did find a stash of marijuana in the main cabin but whether that was for her use or his, I have no idea.'

'What about her? When you spoke to her, did she manage to give you a decent description of the other boat?'

He shook his head sadly. 'Not really: similar size yacht to the one she was on, but because it was dark, she barely glimpsed the name and can't remember what that was. She has little or no experience of boats, and she didn't even notice if it had a mast or not. So, no, not a lot of help. We've taken a statement from her and we have her contact details, but we sent her away just after ten. She's probably back in Lucca by now. The trouble is that, without her evidence, we still can't get a positive ID on that other boat – assuming there really was one and it wasn't just the product of a drug-induced dream. What about you? How did it go on board the *Regal Princess*?'

I gave him a rundown of what I'd learned, starting with the bad news that I'd been unable to identify the other voice I'd heard in Lucca. I saw him nod gloomily and I went on to give him the other bits of information I had gleaned, finishing off with a brief summary.

'So what does that give us? The victim was generally disliked by all and particularly hated by Martin Grey. Douglas Kingsley, the younger comedian, looks like a tough character, although I'm not sure I could see him committing murder, and I'm not aware of him having had any particular arguments with the victim. There's the question of the company maybe facing insolvency, but I fail to see how that might have provided grounds for killing the boss. To be honest, without sitting down and giving each of them a full in-depth interview and checking their records, I'm struggling. What about the crew? Did Maresciallo Veronese get any joy when he interviewed them?'

'Nothing of any value. The deckhand who was on anchor watch that night claims that he saw nothing and heard nothing apart from the outboard motor on the dinghy starting up when Van der Groot set off for the shore. Veronese said the man wasn't particularly cooperative.' He consulted his notebook. 'Name of Heinrich Schiller, German national, goes by the name Rick on board the yacht, and Veronese wondered if he might even have a criminal record as he was very negative, almost insolent. I haven't checked him out yet. I've been waiting to see if you'd come across anything interesting, but I'll get onto the German authorities now. According to Schiller, all he says he could see when he heard the sound of the dinghy engine was the shape of a single person sitting in the boat as it disappeared into the dark, heading for shore, but there was no way he could identify who that was.

Apart from that one sighting, he claims no other boats came or left or even passed near them between sunset and dawn.'

'Van der Groot stormed off at the end of a major argument that night. I'm not sure, but it was probably with Martin Grey.'

'I'll check that out. Veronese and I are on our way back to the yacht this afternoon.'

'And when you spoke to the people on the yacht yesterday, did they tell you what they did after Van der Groot stormed off? Did they get up and leave as well or just stay in the saloon?'

'We didn't have long with each of them so I'll ask for more detail this afternoon, but, from what people told me, after the meal had finished, some started heading back to their cabins, one or two went for a late-night swim in the pool, a couple opened yet another bottle of wine and stayed in the saloon but, otherwise, nothing much happened. Very few of them have solid alibis so I suppose almost any of them could have followed Van der Groot and killed him. We asked each of the guests if they'd seen anything of Van der Groot after he stormed off and they all said no, but I find it hard to believe that he just disappeared into thin air. To make matters worse, although the yacht has a CCTV system, it's been out of action for the last two or three days and I gather they're calling into Genoa later in the week to get a replacement part fitted. It's infuriating.'

I knew how he felt. 'That's a great pity. There's a part of me that still thinks there's something not quite right on the *Regal Princess*, but I suppose I'm coming around to having to accept that it might not have been one of them after all. Maybe Van der Groot just happened to be in the wrong place at the wrong time, and he was murdered by Mario Fortunato or the crew of the boat that brought the cases of weapons to stop him revealing what he'd seen.'

Bertoletti nodded slowly. 'But of course we have no conclusive proof that there was a second vessel there, so that leaves us with the possibility that as Van der Groot was passing Fortunato's boat, he spotted him doing something compromising – whatever that might have been – and Fortunato decided to kill him to shut him up, but I'm just clutching at straws.' He gave a frustrated snort. 'Who knows? Maybe Van der Groot was killed for some completely different reason. It might even have happened after he landed here in Portofino. He arrives at the harbour and somebody's lying in wait for him. They jump into the dinghy, knife him, then tip the body into the water and push the dinghy out into the current and that's that. But why? And more to the point, how did they know he was coming? I haven't done checks on all the phones on board the *Regal Princess* yet, but I suppose it's just possible somebody on board phoned here to tip the killer off, but why?'

'Why indeed? Could it just have been an opportunistic robbery?'

'Anything's possible. When the body was found, there was no phone, wallet or passport on him but the murderer might have taken them just to give the impression of a robbery or just to slow the investigation.' He shrugged helplessly. 'Like I say, anything's possible.'

'By the way, have your Forensics people checked the dinghy used by the victim yet?'

'Yes, I got the results a couple of hours ago. Definite traces of blood and in fact some faint bloodstains still visible on the floor of the dinghy. The lab has analysed the blood and confirms that it matches the victim's. He was either knifed in the dinghy or it was used when disposing of the body.'

'Yes, but if somebody came with him in the dinghy from the *Regal Princess* and murdered him en route to the shore, or if somebody knifed him on the yacht and then took the body away in the dinghy to dispose of it, how did they get back to the yacht? The German on watch says no other boats came near that night and the yacht was several hundred metres from the shore.'

'More like eight hundred metres: a good long way.'

I let my mind roam for a few seconds. None of these scenarios seemed very likely but, without evidence, there was little we could do apart from come up with hypotheses and try to shoot them down. My thoughts were interrupted by the lieutenant's voice.

'What about Susie Upton, the comedian? What was that you said about her maybe having had a relationship with the victim? Might that have gone sour?'

'Your guess is as good as mine, but my gut feeling – and that's all it is – is that I think it's unlikely she was involved with the victim, but anything's possible, I suppose. When she spoke to me about him, she made it clear that she found him repulsive. Yes, she might have been lying, but I tended to believe her. I didn't see her as that venal. To be honest, I rather liked her, but I've been wrong before.' I glanced across the desk at him. 'What's your next move?'

'I can't keep the *Regal Princess* here much longer without charging somebody, so I'll have one more go at questioning everyone on board, including Susie Upton, and if nothing new emerges then I'll have to give the captain permission to carry on with the cruise.'

I remembered something that had occurred to me earlier. 'I had a very nice fillet steak for lunch on board the yacht today and I noticed that the steak knives correspond pretty closely to the description you gave me of the murder weapon. I don't know whether you think it might be worth getting them to check if they're missing one?'

'It can't do any harm – but I must make sure we tell the person doing the check to say nothing to any of the guests. The less gory detail gets out to the media, the better. Mind you, even if one's gone, it doesn't really get us any closer to knowing who might have stolen it and used it.'

I glanced at my watch and stood up. 'I'm sorry I haven't been able to give you a positive ID on the voices I overheard, but maybe that was a red herring anyway. It could be the people I heard were from a completely different group – there were loads of English speakers in Lucca that night for the concert – and even if they were from the *Regal Princess*, maybe they were just letting off steam. From what I've seen and heard today, there's been a pretty tense atmosphere on board all week – and a lot of alcohol being consumed. Anyway, I've promised my girlfriend and my dog a decent walk so I'd better go. Sorry I haven't been able to help more.'

'You've been a lot of help. I look forward to saying thank you properly at dinner tonight. See you at seven. Tell your girlfriend that my wife will be there so she won't be left to her own devices if you and I start talking shop. La Conchiglia, okay?'

'If we start talking shop, I'm afraid you might find me in the sea with a steak knife sticking in *my* back.'

* * *

Anna and I spent the rest of the afternoon together and I worked hard to get back into her good books. My original idea had been to climb up the steep hillside above Portofino and walk for two hours to the Abbey of San Fruttuoso and then return to Portofino by ferry, but a helpful notice at the bottom of the hill indicated that it was a 'moderate to hard' climb. The temperature was in the low thirties and I knew Anna wasn't very keen on hiking, so I wisely chose an alternative route. This was the *Passeggiata dei Baci*

– the Path of Kisses – that led from Portofino around the rocky coastline to Santa Margherita. It was almost pan flat and the views across the bay to the south towards the distant Cinque Terre were delightful. There weren't too many people using the path and we even managed to stop in one or two secluded places for a few *baci* of our own.

I had brought Oscar's bowl, a small bag of dog food and a big bottle of water in my backpack and the highlight of his walk was without question when I gave him his lunch, now delayed by several hours. He has an impeccable internal body clock and it had been telling him that he was hungry for some time now – and he had been telling me with insistent prods of his nose. Needless to say, he hoovered it up in a matter of seconds and then finished off his meal with a bellyful of water – not quite as nice as lobster and fillet steak, but he's always been more interested in quantity than quality.

When we got to Santa Margherita, we walked along the harbourside until we found seats at a table under the trees directly overlooking the marina. Like Rapallo, it was packed with pleasure craft ranging in size from rowing boats to what I would formerly have described as 'gin palaces' – although I now knew they were small fry in comparison to where I had recently been wined and dined on something three or four times their size. The buildings ringing the harbour were the same mix of ochre colours as Portofino but it lacked the beautiful little bay and the old castle on the hill. The busy road running parallel to the harbourside further detracted from the charm of the place, but it was very pleasant all the same and I sensed that Anna might be beginning to forgive me for allowing work to encroach on our precious free time together.

There was more of a general family holiday vibe here and there were kids at most tables with nervous parents constantly checking that they didn't run out into the road. As for Oscar, he happily sprawled on the cool stone beneath our feet as we ordered freshly pressed lemonade for ourselves.

We had only been there for five minutes or so when Anna's phone started ringing. I heard her say, 'Hi, Tamsin,' and then a few seconds later, she passed the phone across to me. 'It's Tamsin, she says one of the men on the yacht wants to speak to you.' She didn't look impressed.

I took the phone from her. 'Hi, Tamsin, thanks again for your hospitality today. We've just been trying to walk off all the wonderful food.'

'Hi, Dan, you're very welcome. Listen, I've got Neil beside me: Neil Vaughan from Accounts? I don't know if you remember him. He'd like a word, if you can spare him the time.'

'Yes, of course I remember him. I'd be happy to talk to him.'

Now what, I wondered, was this about? A couple of seconds later, I heard a man's voice. In spite of what I'd just said, I was still trying to place Neil Vaughan, but as soon as I heard the voice, I recognised it. It was the man who had originally been sitting alongside Tamsin, one of my possibles for the Lucca restaurant conversation, and the one I had notionally pigeonholed as a serious lawyer type. So he was an accountant rather than a lawyer – my first guess had been a good try, but no cigar.

'Hello, Mr Armstrong, this is Neil Vaughan. I'm one of the GreyratTV group on the *Regal Princess*. I wonder if I could have a word with you about a serious matter.'

'Hello, Mr Vaughan, how can I help?'

There was a momentary hesitation and when he spoke, it was in muffled tones. I had a mental image of him leaning out over the side of the boat so as not to be overheard. My curiosity increased as he murmured into Tamsin's phone. 'I believe you said you're a private investigator. That's correct, is it?'

'Yes, although, as I said, I'm a private investigator on holiday at the moment.' My eyes caught Anna's for a moment and I saw her nod in approval at mention of the word 'holiday'.

'Yes, I'm sorry to interrupt your break, but we have a situation here that needs to be looked into urgently.'

'What sort of situation?'

'I work in the accounts department and I've been getting increasingly worried over the past months about irregularities.'

'When you say irregularities, do you mean that money's been going missing?'

'That's exactly what I mean.' There was another long pause. 'And I'm afraid that Jerome's death might be connected with it.'

'In what way?'

'I have a horrible feeling he might have discovered that somebody's been fleecing the company and that person, whoever it was, decided to silence him.'

I took a few moments to digest what I'd just heard. This could potentially add a different dimension to the whole case, but I still tried to distance myself from the official investigation as far as anybody on the *Regal Princess* was concerned. 'I happened to bump into the *Carabinieri* lieutenant this afternoon and he told me he was coming out to the yacht to do some more interviews. Have you seen him and did you tell him this?'

'Yes, I've seen him, but no, I didn't tell him, because I thought it was just too awful to contemplate.'

'So why involve me now?'

'After he left, I needed to talk to somebody about this so I took Tamsin into my confidence, and she told me I really needed to speak up. I was wondering whether maybe you could be persuaded to come and investigate my suspicions before we get the UK police involved. In the meantime, I'd be grateful if you'd go to the lieutenant and tell him about my concerns in case this might influence his investigation. You can say that I'm happy – well, not happy, but you know what I mean – to tell him all about it but, as you can imagine, I'm just concerned that if my accusations turn out to be groundless, I may have endangered my career. You can probably imagine how you would feel if one of your colleagues accused you of embezzlement, let alone murder.'

'Yes, indeed. Do you have a particular person in mind as a suspect?'

There was a pregnant pause before he replied, his voice barely audible now. 'I wouldn't like to accuse anybody unjustly, but there are only very few people with access to the company's affairs who could have been able to take the money.'

'And are these people on the boat with you now?'

I swear I heard him gulp. He then cleared his throat before replying tersely, 'Yes.'

'All of them?'

'Yes.'

I did a bit of quick thinking. It was five-thirty now and I would be meeting the lieutenant at seven. The complication, of course, was that Anna would be with me and I had promised to devote myself solely to her from now on. The fact was, however, that this was a murder case. I knew that this was serious enough for me to have to override any sensitivities Anna might have. I told myself I could have a couple of minutes at the beginning of the evening passing on this information to the lieutenant and then he could decide what steps, if any, he wanted to take. 'Okay, Mr Vaughan, thanks for telling me this. I need to speak to my girlfriend to see whether I have time to get involved with the investigation, but I'll certainly get a message to the lieutenant. Don't worry, I'm sure he'll handle it sensitively and you don't need to be afraid. As far as my involvement is concerned, I'll get back to you if you give me your number.'

He sounded relieved, gave me his phone number and thanked me profusely. When the call ended, I relayed the gist of the conversation to Anna and she nodded a couple of times – not so much in agreement as in resignation. She made no direct comment but I thought I might just have caught a low murmur of, 'Here we go again.'

14

MONDAY EVENING

We took the ferry back from Santa Margherita to Portofino just before seven after I'd had a chance to try to convince Anna that I wasn't going to get involved, and that this was now all going to be handled by the *Carabinieri*. I told her that all I was going to do was to act as an intermediary, relaying the message from Vaughan to the lieutenant, and then I would wash my hands of the whole affair. In spite of my best efforts, she didn't look convinced, and equally worrying was the fact that Oscar didn't look convinced either. Dumb animal he may be, but that nose of his doesn't miss much.

La Conchiglia, the shell restaurant, was a two-minute walk from the *Carabinieri* barracks and when I gave the lieutenant's name, a friendly looking woman sitting at a table on the terrace jumped to her feet and held out her hand towards us.

'Good evening. You must be Guido's friends. I'm Marina, his wife. He's just called me to say he's been held up but he'll be here in five minutes.' She gave us a little smile. 'Knowing him, that may well turn out to be ten minutes or more, but he promises he's coming.'

We all shook hands and sat down. Oscar went over to make friends with Marina, and Anna was soon telling her about her work at the university in Florence. It turned out that Marina was a teacher of history at the *liceo* in Rapallo and they discovered that they had a lot in common – not just being unfortunate enough to be partnered with detectives.

In the end, it was almost twenty minutes before the lieutenant arrived, sounding most apologetic. 'I'm so sorry to be late, but a Greek sailor and a Turkish sailor from two different yachts decided to get very drunk and restage the Trojan war down at the harbour. I've just been dealing with them. Too much wine, I'm afraid.' He pulled out his chair but before sitting down, he glanced down at the table. 'Talking of wine, I can't see any on the table. Are you just drinking water? I need to sort that out straight away.'

He turned and headed through the door into the restaurant, so I got up and followed him. As Anna and Marina were still happily chatting, and Oscar was fully engaged in begging for breadsticks from the soft-hearted Marina, I thought this might be the perfect opportunity to talk shop without disturbing the two women. Inside, I found the lieutenant being embraced by the owner, a jovial man with a fine restaurateur's stomach. The lieutenant – 'Call me Guido' – introduced me and we discussed the choice of wine. The owner told us he'd just taken delivery of a few dozen bottles of white from a new producer near Bolgheri in southern Tuscany and he insisted on opening one and filling three glasses so we could taste it before making a decision. It was excellent and Guido asked him to put a bottle on the table for us. When the *padrone* went off to organise the wine, I took Guido to one side and related what Neil Vaughan had told me. He listened intently before responding.

'That could well be very interesting. We're getting absolutely

nowhere with Mario Fortunato and I've got the Libyan embassy –
and the public prosecutor – on my back to either charge or
release the two Libyan nationals. Fortunato has been steadfast in
denying he could possibly have participated in murder and,
without proof, I'm not sure there's much more I can do to link
him to the murder. Mind you, I won't be releasing him. There's
the little bag of weed found in the cabin, but that's hardly a criminal offence these days, but, of course, we can get him for possession of contraband arms. The thing is, I'd love to get him for
something bigger.'

'Did you get any joy out of the people on the *Regal Princess*
this afternoon?'

He shook his head. 'Not much. I interviewed Schiller, the
crewman who was on anchor watch the night of the murder, and
he stuck to his story of not having seen or heard anything apart
from the dinghy leaving but, just like Veronese said, I thought he
was acting a bit suspiciously. I'm at a loss to think of any reason
he might have had to murder one of the guests, but I'm certainly
not ruling him out for now. The woman, Susie Upton, struck me
as pretty straight but, given her profession as a television
performer, maybe it was just a good act. I tried pressing her on
whether the murder victim had made inappropriate advances
towards her in return for promotion and she denied it most forcefully, insisting that she would never have stooped to anything as
base as that. The other comedian, Martin Grey, came across as
very full of himself and decidedly slippery, but he still totally
denies having had anything to do with the murder, although it
sounds as though the big argument that night did involve him.
When I pressed him about his allegations of something going on
between Susie Upton and the victim, he started backtracking, so
maybe it was just a story he made up like Anna's friend on the
yacht said.'

'And the other men on the *Regal Princess*? Are they still not admitting to having been involved in the Lucca restaurant conversation I overheard?'

'Absolutely not. I couldn't even get a hint of anything suspicious from any of them except for Edgar Beaumont. You were pretty sure about him being one of the people you heard but he still denies it, but there's something about him that makes me think he's lying. The trouble is that I know, just like he knows, that there's nothing more I can do without finding the man he was talking to. Just to make matters worse, the Coastguard radar trackers have now informed us that there were actually as many as seven vessels in the area that night that might have passed close to Fortunato's boat. The problem we face is that we have no evidence against any of them so we can't stop and search all those boats – there would be one hell of an uproar.'

He drained the last of the wine from his glass and set it down on the bar before reaching over and clapping me on the shoulder. 'You have at least one small success to your name. I got the purser – in the strictest confidence – to check the steak knives, and he confirms that, instead of having the full two dozen, they now only have twenty-three. Not that this helps us a lot as it's without doubt lying somewhere at the bottom of the sea now, but it does increase the likelihood of the murderer being on the yacht. All we can do is keep trying, can't we? What about you? Are you going to take on the case of the missing money? If you want to start questioning people on board the yacht, I'm going to hold it until tomorrow late afternoon, but then I'll have to let them go.'

I found myself in a really difficult position. Every investigative bone in my body was telling me that I couldn't let a murderer get away scot-free. If it wasn't Fortunato or his friends, I was now ever more convinced that the killer was to be found on the *Regal*

Princess and yet here I was, about to walk away from the investigation. And that didn't sit well with me.

Of course, any intervention by me was complicated by the presence of my girlfriend sitting outside on the terrace talking history with Guido's wife. Anna had been feeling justifiably miffed that our relaxing long weekend away together had turned into more of a busman's holiday for me and, in consequence, a frustrating one for her. I owed it to her to turn the job down and stick by her side even though Neil Vaughan's telephone call had now handed me a golden opportunity to get back on board the yacht and start asking questions of my own. The problem was how Anna might react if I went down that road and, to make matters worse, she had an important meeting in Florence the following afternoon so I was up against it from a time point of view. Before I could give Guido an answer, I felt his hand, still on my shoulder, give me a reassuring squeeze before he released his hold.

'I've got a good idea of what's going through your head, Dan. You and I are both familiar with juggling the pressures of work and home life. Take your time; you don't have to make a decision now. Let's go and eat and then you can talk it through with Anna later. You have my phone number. If you decide you want to go back on board early tomorrow morning to start sniffing around to get to the bottom of the allegations of financial irregularities being made by Mr Vaughan, we can go out to the boat together. I'm going to have to go there anyway to follow up with him but, I'll be quite honest, I need all the help I can get at the moment.' A smile crossed his face. 'But think of it this way: if you take Mr Vaughan's contract, you will at least be being paid for your time and not just donating it generously like you have been doing so far.'

I gave him a sincere smile. 'Thanks, Guido, I appreciate that.

You're right, I need to talk it over with Anna, but I really would like to get to the bottom of what's happening. The trouble is that I need to get away tomorrow by noon at the latest as Anna has to be back in Florence by five. I'll give you a call later this evening or, more probably, first thing tomorrow morning when I go for a walk with Oscar on my own, say between seven and seven-thirty.'

'That's fine but remember this – I still want to catch this murderer, so don't think you'll be leaving things in limbo if you decide not to be involved any more. But, like I say, two heads are better than one. If you decide not to carry on any involvement, I will understand, and you can rest assured that I'll still be on the case. At least you being here has meant that I've been able to meet and make friends with a fellow professional from a different country and that's always good. Now let's get back outside to Anna and Marina and make sure we talk about anything at all, as long as it isn't murder.'

I swallowed my wine and followed him out to the terrace. The meal that followed was excellent even though, with everything we had eaten at lunchtime, Anna and I were unable to do it real justice. We all started by sharing a wonderful platter of mixed seafood antipasti loaded with everything from crab to squid, prawns to scallops. Guido tried to insist that we had a plate of pasta before the main course and I resisted manfully until we finally hit on a compromise. Anna and I would share a plate of the house speciality *spaghetti alla marinara*.

I've always quite liked pasta and since moving to Italy, I've inevitably consumed an increasing amount of it, whether *pasta fresca* or *pasta asciutta* – that's the hard, dry stuff you find in packets on the shelves. I've had tagliatelle, lasagne, ravioli and pappardelle – plus a load of other types whose names escape me – but this was the first time I'd ever been served a plate of spaghetti where there was more sauce than pasta. The plate was absolutely piled high with clams and mussels in their shells and, with just a hint of freshly made pesto – the Ligurian speciality – in the sauce, the resulting taste was exquisite.

In spite of Anna's protestations that she was still full from lunch, I noticed that even she very quickly shed her scruples and the two of us managed to clear the plate, much to the chagrin of my ever-hungry dog whose nose had told him exactly what we humans were eating. I bought him off with a couple more bread-sticks but I could tell he was feeling hard done by. The proprietor, who came out to check that everything was all right, must have intercepted a longing look from the Labrador because two minutes later, a waitress emerged with the remains of a T-bone steak that somebody hadn't been able to finish. Oscar's eyes lit up and the rest of the evening was punctuated by sinister crunching noises from beneath the table as he enjoyed his very own feast.

As we ate, we chatted, and I discovered that Guido and Marina had been married for five years and lived in an apartment in Rapallo. This, he told me, was partly for Marina's convenience for her teaching job, but also because property prices in Portofino were astronomical. He told me ruefully that even a general in the *Carabinieri* would find it hard to afford a two-bedroom flat here. I could well believe it. This tiny little place was clearly the domain of the super-rich, and I wondered who had been out to catch what we were eating tonight. Where did the fishermen live and how did they manage to survive in this playground of the wealthy?

The pasta course was followed by another massive platter, this time of grilled fish. I counted at least seven different species but could name only a couple of them. What they all had in common, however, was that they tasted great. With a simple mixed salad as accompaniment, it was outstanding.

I was just sitting back with a cup of coffee, after having

managed to summon the self-control to refuse a dessert, when a phone started ringing. For once, it wasn't mine. It was Guido's. As calls go, it wasn't the longest.

'Hello. What? Where? I'll be with you in two minutes.'

He reached for his coffee cup and drained the last of it before standing up. I could see him doing his best not to catch my eye, but I couldn't miss the expression of shock and exasperation on his face. His wife must have seen it as well because she reached out her hand, caught hold of his arm and looked up at him.

'What is it, Guido? What's happened?'

'There's been another murder.'

Her hand flew to her mouth in disbelief. 'Two in three days! Where's this one?'

This time, he definitely did make eye contact with me. 'It's on board the *Regal Princess*.'

I felt as stunned as he did and a sudden feeling of premonition settled on me. Surely it couldn't be Neil Vaughan so soon after voicing his suspicions but, significantly, without naming names. With a feeling of dread, I looked up at Guido and asked the all-important question.

'Who is it?'

The answer wasn't what I was expecting.

'Heinrich Schiller, the deckhand. His body's been found in a pool of blood.'

Although every investigative bone in my body was screaming at me to leap to my feet and accompany Guido to the yacht, he pre-empted any action from me by laying a calming hand on my shoulder, preventing me from having to make a difficult decision. 'I'm sorry but I have to go. Don't worry about trying to pay the bill; I've already spoken to the owner. Before you say anything, Dan, I'll go out to the boat with my people now. There's no need for you to get involved. We'll talk in the morning, all right?' He turned to his wife. 'I'm sorry, my love, but you know how it is. Will you give Dan and Anna a lift back to Rapallo?' He bent down to kiss her, shook hands with Anna and me and disappeared at the double.

I stayed in my seat as bidden, but it was a struggle.

15

TUESDAY EARLY MORNING

I couldn't get off to sleep that night. If I'm totally honest, it was probably in good part my own fault for having eaten far too much in the course of the day but, more specifically, it was because my brain had been churning. The two subjects preventing me from dropping off had been the murders at Portofino and my relationship with Anna. Of the two, I knew that Anna was the more important to me, but thirty years in the murder squad leave their mark. Yes, I loved Anna dearly, but at the same time, it was now crystal clear that there was a psychopath at large on the luxury yacht. I spent ages telling myself over and over again that Guido Bertoletti was a committed, competent detective and it was his job, not mine, to bring the killer to justice. A fat lot of good that did me. I still found myself lying there staring blankly at the ceiling until somewhere around two o'clock in the morning.

At that point, I was roused by a movement from the floor beside the bed and a couple of seconds later, a cold nose gave my shoulder a nudge. I rolled over to see a pair of big, brown eyes, now glowing green in the moonlight filtering through the shutters, staring at me intently. At first, I wondered if Oscar was telling me he wanted a comfort break, but he only gave me that one nudge, whereas I knew from experience that if he had wanted to go out, he would have kept on headbutting me. Evidently, his canine radar had picked up the fact that I was troubled and he was trying to offer support. I pulled one arm out from under the sheet and scratched his ears while I outlined my problem to him in a whisper. He gave no reaction until I reached the end of my exposé.

At that point, after a momentary pause for reflection, he farted.

As a cloud of near toxic gas wafted over me, I recoiled and bumped into Anna. She's normally a heavy sleeper but presumably tonight she had also been struggling to get to sleep as she sounded wide awake when she pulled the sheet over her head and addressed me from within it.

'I'm hoping that was the dog, Dan.'

I joined her under the sheet. 'Not guilty, your honour. It was definitely Oscar. That's the trouble when he gets hold of a bone. Sorry I woke you.'

'I wasn't really sleeping.' She rolled towards me and caught hold of my upper arm. 'I've eaten too much.'

'Me, too, but it was good, wasn't it?'

'Both meals were excellent, but food isn't the only reason you've been lying there talking to your dog, is it?'

'You heard that?'

'Only odd words, but enough to know that you're struggling to know what to do.'

'I know what I have to do, it's just that I'm finding it hard to turn my back on years of conditioning.' I reached across with my hand and let it rest against her cheek. 'My number-one priority is you. I know that, I hope you know that, and Oscar now knows that. I brought you away for a few days for a nice, relaxing holiday and what have you had? Me charging off all over the place, pretending I'm in the murder squad again while you've had to sit around and twiddle your thumbs. I'm really sorry and, however much my instincts are telling me to get involved with the people on that yacht, I know where my responsibilities lie. And that's with you.' To reinforce the point, I kissed her.

She kissed me in return and then gave my arm a squeeze. 'I know that, *carissimo*, but I also know what drives you. It's that Hercule Poirot brain of yours that just can't switch off.' She leant over and gave me another kiss. 'And I love you for your brain, so I have a suggestion. Tomorrow morning, sorry, this morning, I think you need to go back over to Portofino and go out to the yacht with Guido. Between the two of you, I know you'll be able to sort things out.' Before I could reply, she placed a finger on my lips. 'I can easily walk down to the station tomorrow and catch a train that'll get me to Florence by lunchtime. My meeting isn't till five and there are loads of things I have to do for work, so I'll just go back to my place and get on with that while you do your best to solve the mystery here. All right?'

Just in case I might be thinking of omitting to give credit to my four-legged friend for initiating this conversation, two heavy paws then landed on my bottom and the next thing I knew, I had fifty or sixty pounds of canine bone and muscle climbing all over me. By the time I had managed to persuade him to return to his place on the floor and had thanked him formally for his intervention, Anna had finally stopped laughing. I rolled back towards her and saw her face, no longer covered by the sheet, smiling at me.

'You're sure you don't mind?' I gave her a kiss for good measure.

'Of course I don't mind. I'll go back to the never-ending arguments between Pope Julius II and Michelangelo while you go and solve your murders. We all have our areas of expertise. Go and use yours.'

* * *

I woke up at six-thirty on Tuesday morning and took Oscar for a walk. The beauty of getting out so early was that the temperature was delightful, the air almost fresh, and the traffic on the streets around the hotel far lighter than I knew it would be later on in the day. We walked to a nearby park that I had found the previous day where Oscar had the chance to run around retrieving pine cones for me to throw for him. While the game continued, I pulled out my phone and texted Neil Vaughan, telling him I would be happy to investigate the missing money, and then I called the lieutenant. His phone was answered by *Maresciallo* Veronese.

'Lieutenant Bertoletti's phone.'

'Good morning, *Maresciallo*, it's Dan Armstrong. How did it go on the *Regal Princess* last night?'

'Good morning, *Commissario*, it certainly looks like the same perpetrator. The man was lying on the rear deck of the yacht with his throat cut and a steak knife still sticking into his heart. The pathologist said he must have died almost instantly, so whoever did it knew what they were doing.'

'And they cut his throat as well as stabbing him through the heart! They certainly wanted to make sure he was dead. Did the pathologist say which blow came first?'

'The throat, apparently – that accounts for all the blood.'

I digested what he'd said. The choice of murder weapon certainly seemed to indicate that this latest murder had been committed by the same person who had killed Van der Groot.

'Any chance of prints on the knife?'

'Forensics were there until two and they say there are at least some partials. We'll fingerprint everybody this morning and it would be great if we found some that matched, but we're not getting our hopes up yet. The pathologist's doing a post-mortem as we speak but he doesn't expect to find anything much apart from the stab wounds.'

'Any suspects?'

'Nothing for now. At that time of night, half of the people on the yacht were already in bed and most of the remainder looked as if they were too drunk to have been able to get down the stairs to the rear deck, let alone stab a fit thirty-year-old. The lieutenant stationed two officers on the boat overnight and he's confined everybody to the area. We're going back over again this morning to do formal interviews. Ah, here he is now. I'll pass you over to him.'

A couple of seconds later, I heard Guido's voice. 'Good morning, Dan. I hope you slept well.'

'Ultimately, yes, but Anna and I were doing a bit of talking first. The decision we've come to is that she's going back to Florence by train and I'm going to accept Mr Vaughan's proposition, so I'm up for a visit to the yacht as soon as you like.'

'Excellent. Do you want me to send a boat over to Rapallo to pick you up?'

'Thanks, but I have to leave the hotel today, and that includes moving the van. The place is completely booked tonight and for the rest of the week, so I thought I'd drive over because, if all else fails, that means I can sleep in the van. Somehow, I don't think I can afford Portofino prices.'

He laughed. 'I can help with that. I'll find you a bed here at the barracks if you need it and I can even offer you a free parking space. Just park in any of the yellow parking spaces at the top of

Piazza della Libertà and I'll get you a permit. What time can you be here?'

'It's almost seven now. Probably around eight-thirty if that's okay with you.'

'Perfect, see you then. I'll fill you in on what happened last night when you're here.'

After a quick breakfast, I kissed Anna goodbye and loaded Oscar into the van. Fortunately, at this time of the morning, the road to Portofino wasn't too busy and I managed to get to Piazza della Libertà at just before eight-thirty. As instructed, I parked in one of the restricted spaces right in front of a sign indicating graphically that transgressors would find their vehicles towed away. I hurried up to the *Carabinieri* station where I found Maresciallo Veronese in his usual spot outside. We shook hands and he ruffled Oscar's ears before leading me in to see the lieutenant, who greeted me with a smile.

'Come in, Dan, sit down. Veronese, will you see that a parking permit gets put on Dan's car? What's the make and registration number?'

After the *maresciallo* had gone off to make sure that my van didn't end up being towed away, Guido ran through the events of the previous night.

'I got out to the yacht at just before eleven. There were a lot of pretty drunk people sitting around looking stunned, but about half of the guests had already disappeared to their cabins. We took statements from the captain and from the crewmember who discovered the body, but otherwise I put everything on hold until this morning. The anchor-watch guy found the body curled up in a foetal position in a pool of blood and although he saw the horrific cut across the throat and knew the man was dead, it was only when we turned the body over that we found the knife in his heart.' He caught my eye. 'Another one of the steak knives, but I'm not broadcasting the fact.'

'An opportunistic weapon and the same killer by the sound of it, unless it was a copycat murder – although nobody's supposed to know that Van der Groot's murder was committed with one of the yacht's own knives. Strange that they left the knife there to be found. I'd have dumped it in the sea.' I caught his eye. 'Of course, this makes it almost certain that the killer is to be found on board the *Regal Princess*, and that means that our idea of the first victim being stabbed by Mario Fortunato and his mysterious henchmen is much less likely.' I was secretly pleased that this indicated that Heather Greensleeves hadn't hooked up with a killer after all. I had rather liked her.

'I agree. We need to focus on the people on board the *Regal Princess*. As for the murder weapon being left with the body, I know what you mean, but maybe in the heat of the moment, the killer panicked. What are your plans now? You're very welcome to sit in with me, or do you want to do your own thing?'

I'd been thinking about this on the way over. 'I think it might be better if I distance myself from your investigation – at least initially. Maybe that might encourage a few of the guests that I interview to open up to me about things that they wouldn't have wanted to discuss with the police. In fact, Neil Vaughan has just texted me to offer to send their launch to pick me up, so I think I might take him up on that. That way, you and I will arrive separately and that should further distance us in the eyes of those on board. I'll text you when I've finished and if you do the same for me then we can meet up back here and discuss our findings. How does that sound?'

Guido agreed and I sent off a text immediately to the yacht asking for a ride. While waiting for a reply, I floated an idea that had been running through my brain since hearing of the murder of the deckhand.

'One of the main problems we've had as far as the first murder's concerned is that the information we were originally given was that a lone figure had been seen leaving the yacht in a dinghy and that neither that person – assuming it was Van der Groot – nor the dinghy came back. This, of course, made it likely that Van der Groot had been murdered on his way to the shore after witnessing Fortunato and his cronies up to no good or maybe he got himself killed after arriving in Portofino. The finger of suspicion now definitely points at both murders having been committed by somebody on the *Regal Princess*, but the man who provided that information is now our second murder victim, so what does that mean as far as the first death's concerned? Did Van der Groot's murderer think that the deckhand might have been able to identify him? If so, was Schiller killed by Van der Groot's murderer to shut him up? Alternatively, was Schiller lying about what he saw? Was he maybe a willing accomplice or even the sole murderer? Did Schiller stab Van der Groot in the dinghy when it was still with the yacht and then tip the body into the water, untie the dinghy and then dream up the story of having seen it going off with Van der Groot in it?'

Guido had clearly been thinking along the same lines. 'I've spoken to the Coastguard and they say definitively that if the dinghy and the body had been dumped over the side of the yacht out there where they were moored on Saturday night, almost a kilometre from the coast, both would have drifted way out to sea, rather than ending up on the coast where they did. So the body and the dinghy must have been dumped much closer to the coast, but that doesn't make sense unless the killer was then returned to the *Regal Princess* by another boat and nobody noticed the sound of the engine, but if so, who on earth was driving that? There must have been an accomplice.' He glanced at me. 'Maybe the same two men you heard in Lucca.'

This had been worrying me, too. 'Point taken. Besides, even if Schiller did kill Jerome Van der Groot – and God knows why he would have done – then who killed him?'

Guido nodded slowly. 'Like you say, if Schiller murdered Van der Groot, who murdered *him* and why? Revenge – somebody knew Schiller had done it and wanted him to get a taste of his own medicine? I seriously doubt it. From what I've been told, I don't think there's a single person on board the yacht who liked Van der Groot enough to buy him a drink, let alone avenge his murder.'

I felt sure he was right about that. 'I agree, and that makes it even less likely that Schiller killed Van der Groot in the first place. But if Schiller was murdered because the killer was afraid of having been spotted, the problem is how did the killer know that he or she had been seen? Surely if the murderer had realised on Saturday night that they'd been recognised, they would have disposed of the witness immediately, not waited two days to do it. And as for Schiller, surely he would have told you as soon as he saw you on Sunday.'

'Not necessarily.' Guido leafed through some papers on his desk and produced a sheet. 'The German police have been very efficient and they sent us through their report on Schiller yesterday evening while you and I were having dinner. Veronese and I both thought he was a suspicious character and it turns out he did indeed have a criminal record in Germany: not for violent crime, but for extortion. He was jailed for eighteen months a few years back. It seems he specialised in getting compromising information about people and then blackmailing them in return for keeping quiet. Getting a job on a yacht like this full of wealthy and, in some cases, famous people must have provided him with all sorts of opportunities.'

This was really interesting – although it didn't reflect well on the thoroughness of the staff vetting procedures used by the owners of the *Regal Princess*. I looked across the desk and caught Guido's eye. 'Of course, that would explain why there was the delay before killing him. Schiller must have seen something the other night so he approached the murderer on Sunday or Monday, presumably asking for money, threatening to expose them if they didn't pay up. How's this for a scenario? Van der Groot's murderer arranged to meet Schiller last night on the rear deck of the yacht to hand over the cash, and while the German was distracted, maybe counting the money, our murderer cut his throat and stabbed him.'

'Exactly what I've been thinking – although there's still the conundrum of how Van der Groot's body ended up where it did. What this means is that we're now almost certainly looking for a double murderer, and it's 99 per cent certain that he or she is on the *Regal Princess*.'

I nodded in agreement. 'Or there were two murderers. Otherwise, how did Van der Groot's killer get back to the ship? It's looking highly unlikely that Mario Fortunato and the other arms smugglers killed Van der Groot so does this mean you'll have to release them now?'

'I'm still holding onto him and the Libyans until this afternoon, by which time I've been promised the results of fingerprint and DNA analysis from the boxes of arms found on Fortunato's boat as well as the knife sticking in Schiller's heart. But if they come back clean, then I don't really have much option but to release the Libyans and all I can charge Fortunato with is possession of contraband weapons. Yes, the public prosecutor says that will definitely see him go to trial, but with good lawyers – and his kind always have good lawyers – he's unlikely to get a lengthy sentence.' He gave an exasperated sigh. 'It's infuriating. We wanted to roll up the whole chain all the way back to Bratislava or wherever. Still, at least we can put him away for a bit and it might slow the provision of illegal arms for a while, but it's not the conclusive result we were hoping for.'

At that moment, my phone bleeped and I saw a text telling me that the launch was on its way to the jetty to pick me up. I stood up, gave Guido a wave, and Oscar and I headed down to the waterfront for our trip out to the *Regal Princess*. As I walked down the narrow street, I couldn't help reflecting that I was soon going to come face to face with one or even two murderers. I glanced down at Oscar beside me.

'Just like old times, eh, buddy?'

He glanced up at me, but I noticed that he didn't wag his tail.

16

TUESDAY MORNING

Neil Vaughan was on the launch when it arrived at the jetty and I saw him talking to the deckhand at the wheel. As a result, the boat moored up and Vaughan climbed out. We shook hands and he outlined what he wanted to do.

'The launch will wait for us. I'd like to find a quiet spot around here where you and I can sit down and talk first without being overheard. That damn yacht is far too claustrophobic. Everybody knows everybody else's business.'

As we headed for a waterside café, I deliberately didn't mention the recent murder, hoping to make it look as if I had had little or no contact with the *Carabinieri* and their investigation. It didn't take long before Vaughan broke the news of Schiller's death to me and I made sure I looked suitably shocked before asking if he had any details of what had happened or any suspicions as to who might have done it. He waited until we'd found a table at the far end of a café terrace with nobody around us before he answered.

'It happened last night after dinner and the police were all over the yacht until past midnight. The deckhand who found the body said the victim had his throat cut.'

'And you have no idea who might have done it?'

He shook his head. 'I just don't understand it. If my theory that Jerome might have been murdered because he was about to unmask the person who's been stealing from the company is correct, then what possible involvement might the deckhand have had?'

I decided that it wouldn't do any harm to voice the possible blackmail scenario Guido and I had been discussing. I ran through this quickly, pretending it had just struck me and ending up with the words, 'So if this latest victim had identified Van der Groot's killer on Saturday night and was trying to blackmail him or her, the murderer might have killed him instead of paying him off.'

Vaughan looked appalled. 'So this means that I'm living on a yacht with a serial killer!' His face paled. 'God knows who'll be next.'

I tried to offer some comfort. 'Try not to worry too much. I'm sure the *Carabinieri* are on the case and the lieutenant struck me as a good man. You never know, maybe my inquiries into the financial irregularities you mentioned will result in some information that might help him unmask the perpetrator.' I waited until a waitress had taken our order for two coffees before pressing Vaughan on the subject of the company's finances. His answer was fascinating.

'Everybody had it in for Jerome, and I'll admit that he wasn't the most pleasant of characters. The simple fact of the matter, though, is that the company's now in dire financial straits, but it certainly wasn't all down to poor decisions on Jerome's part.' He looked up and caught my eye. 'Like I told you on the phone, I'm

virtually certain that somebody's been stealing from the company
– and not just a few pounds here and there. I've been looking
back through the accounts for the past twelve months and I've
discovered a number of payments to an anonymous account in
the Cayman Islands totalling somewhere in excess of two million
pounds. There might be more. I would need to spend quite a few
days going through everything line by line, but you can't syphon
off two million pounds a year from a company our size without it
having a huge impact on our solvency.'

I gave a little whistle. 'Wow, that's serious embezzlement. And
you have no idea who might be behind this?'

Although we were hundreds of metres from the yacht,
which was still lying at anchor out at the mouth of the bay, and
there was nobody close enough to hear what we were saying,
he still looked around apprehensively before answering.
'Jerome was the CEO and he had overall control, and Company
Secretary and head of Accounts is Edgar, Edgar Beaumont.
Both would have had full access, but there are two other people
as well who could have done it.' He gave yet another cautious
look over his shoulder. 'And they're both on this cruise too.
They're Adam Phillips and Louise Challenger. Like me, Adam
works under Edgar in Accounts and Louise is the payroll
specialist. They both know all the passwords and have full
access.'

I was scribbling in my notebook as he produced these names
and I recognised Adam Phillips as Mr Muscle and Louise from
Payroll as the woman who had apparently slapped Martin Grey
after allegedly being groped by him at the pool. When I had
finished writing, I looked up. 'Might there be anybody else,
maybe somebody not on this cruise?'

'No, even producers like Tamsin don't have access to the
accounts. I'm afraid it has to be one of those three...' He hesitated

for a moment before giving me a nervous smile. 'And me, of course. That's four people.'

I smiled back at him. 'I think I can discount you for the very reason that you came to me about this in the first place. It makes no sense that the perpetrator of the fraud should bring in a private investigator to look into what he's done. But, assuming you're correct about the missing money, there are indeed *four* possible suspects, but you're not one of them.' I saw an expression of mystification on his face so I explained. 'Four people: Adam Phillips, Louise Challenger, Edgar Beaumont and, of course, Jerome Van der Groot.'

'But Jerome's dead...' The bafflement on his face increased.

'But that doesn't mean he might not have been involved with the fraud. Any of them might have been. Tell me something: why did you come to me instead of going to Edgar Beaumont with your suspicions? He's the head of Accounts after all, or are you suspicious of him?'

'No, no, of course not.' He hesitated. 'At least, not really...'

'But you knew that there was a chance he might have been involved, didn't you? What if he was in it together with Jerome Van der Groot? Suppose Edgar Beaumont decided to kill Van der Groot so as to get 100 per cent of the missing money, rather than half?'

I studied the expression on his face as he explored that suggestion, and I saw comprehension slowly dawn. 'So you're really saying that Jerome might have been one of the people stealing from the company?'

'It's a possibility. After all, it's not as if it's his company, is it? I presume he's on a salary like you are, maybe plus a bonus, but the excess profits go back into the business or to the shareholders. Is that right?'

He nodded. 'Yes, it's a public limited company. We're all on salaries plus some of us get a bonus – although the way things are looking, there won't be any bonuses this year. And you think Jerome might have been working together with either Adam, Louise or Edgar to defraud the company? Surely not!'

'Well, you know them better than I do, but money can do strange things to people. Of course, it's possible that Jerome Van der Groot did it all himself and one of the other three found out about it and was so enraged that they murdered him. What do you think of that hypothesis? I'm sure you find the idea of fraud repugnant, but do you think any of your colleagues could have felt strongly enough about a momentous discovery like that to murder the perpetrator?' He shook his head and I nodded. 'I agree with you that it's unlikely. Surely anybody finding out that the boss had been on the fiddle would have gone straight to the authorities.'

'Well, that's what *I* certainly would have done.' He looked up as the waitress returned with our coffees and waited until she'd left before continuing.

As I waited to hear what he might have to add, my eyes roamed over the beautiful scene before us. Wooded hills sloped down to the perfect ultramarine-blue sea whose colour was high-lighted by the multitude of mainly white boats floating around serenely in it. Here on shore, it was getting busier and happy tourists were milling about, phones in hand, taking thousands upon thousands of photos of this iconic spot. As a location for two gory murders, it seemed incongruous.

Vaughan's voice tore me away from admiring the scenery. 'Going to the authorities is exactly what I intend to do. Hopefully, with your help, I'll be able to identify the guilty party, and then I'll have no hesitation about going straight to the police back in the UK.'

'I'm glad to hear it, Mr Vaughan. Now, think hard: what's your feeling about our three potential suspects for the fraud and even the murders? Don't forget, we're talking a cold-blooded killer here. Which of them, if any, do you think might have been capable of killing?'

He answered immediately. 'None of them, surely. I can't believe it. Louise is too young, and she's a woman. There's no way she could have done something like that.' I decided not to mention any number of female murderers who had come my way over the years and I let him carry on considering the remaining two men. 'Edgar, he can be bad-tempered and pretty tough, but it's a big leap from shouting at somebody to killing them. As for Adam, he may look like Mr Universe, but he wouldn't hurt a fly. I'm sure of that.'

'So you're saying that you don't think any of them might have committed either murder. What about fraud? Do you think any of them might have stooped to stealing from the company?'

He had to stop and think for a few moments. 'Murder's murder, but stealing is something else. I still can't imagine any of the three stooping so low, but I suppose in the right circum-stances and if the right opportunity presented itself, one of them might have decided to take the money. Two million pounds is a life-changing amount.' He looked up again and caught my eye. 'But I honestly couldn't even begin to guess which of them it might have been.'

I took a sip of coffee before veering off the subject of fraud. 'Going back to Van der Groot's death, this fraud business is certainly a possible motive for murder, but what about other motives? In my experience, financial gain is a powerful motivator, but so is love or lust. Do you think there were any jealous husbands or spurned women here who might have wanted revenge on Van der Groot?'

He looked genuinely gobsmacked. 'You mean Jerome having

an affair? I think that's out of the question. After all, he wasn't the type.' Realising what he'd just said, he corrected himself. 'No, I don't mean he was... you know...' He looked acutely embarrassed. 'Not wishing to speak ill of the dead, but I honestly can't think of any women here or elsewhere who would have been interested in him in that way.'

'But what about women that *he* might have been interested in? Being propositioned by your boss can't be a lot of fun. Might something like that have been behind his death?' I was waiting for him to repeat Martin Grey's allegation that Susie Upton had been trading sexual favours for advancement in the company, but he just shook his head blankly. 'I can't, no, I really can't, but maybe if you speak to some of the women on board... Ask Susie, she knows everything about everybody.'

Over the next ten minutes, I got him to talk me through how he'd come to the conclusion that somebody had been stealing from the company and pressed him to name his first choice of culprit. He remained unable or unwilling to point the finger at anybody in particular so after we'd finished our coffees, I told him what I wanted to do next.

'Let's go back to the yacht now. I'd like you to tell Edgar Beaumont the two of us need to speak to him in private. Once we have him on his own, tell him about your suspicions and tell him that you want him to take the decision on behalf of the company to engage my services to investigate. Whether he's innocent or guilty, I'm sure he'll have to agree to my starting to ask questions, and if he's guilty, I might be able to get some clues from the expression on his face when you tell him about it. Okay with you?'

He agreed and we both stood up. He called the waitress and paid for the coffees, saving the ticket and putting it into his wallet. He then enquired about my rates and I produced one of my printed sheets for him, which he read line by line before folding it meticulously in half and then in half again and tucking it safely into his wallet as well. Anna always laughs at me for having a supply of these sheets in the van, but as I often tell her, it's best to be prepared. I wasn't in the Boy Scouts all those years ago for nothing.

On the journey over to the yacht in the launch, neither of us spoke, but I had my hands full making sure that Oscar didn't suddenly decide to go for a swim. Arriving on board a luxury yacht with a wet and smelly dog wouldn't be an auspicious start to my investigation. I checked to see if the Coastguard launch was already lying alongside the *Regal Princess* but it was clear that Guido and his *Carabinieri* team had decided to give me a bit of time and space before they began their own investigation. When we boarded the yacht, I noticed that both of the grey inflatable dinghies were now back on the watersports deck. Presumably, Forensics had finished with the one with the bloodstains and had returned it ready for the yacht's departure – whenever that was going to be now that Schiller had been murdered as well. One half of the low deck had been taped off by the *Carabinieri* and a bored-looking officer was sitting in the shade, keeping watch.

I checked the time as we walked up to the saloon and saw that it was almost nine o'clock. There was nobody using the pool or sitting around it, but this was probably as a result of the events of the night before. I could well understand that nobody was feeling in a cheery holiday mood after something like that. There were only four people sitting at the table having breakfast: Tamsin Taylor, looking aghast; a visibly plastered Billy Webster, who looked as though he had been there all night; Doug Kingsley, with his nose buried in a cup of coffee; and, fortunately, Edgar Beaumont. I greeted them all with a little wave of my hand but said nothing as Neil Vaughan went over to his boss and whispered in his ear. Beaumont looked puzzled, then shocked, and immediately stood up. Ignoring the curiosity on some of the faces of the others around him, he pointed towards the door leading to the guest accommodation.

'If you'd both like to follow me to my cabin, we can speak in private.'

17

TUESDAY MORNING

The cabin belonging to the Head of Accounts was much larger than I'd been expecting and it had an actual window, rather than a porthole, through which there was a beautiful view of the rocky cliffs below Castello Brown. In fact, from here to where Jerome Van der Groot's body had been washed up was probably only a hundred and fifty metres or so but, of course, I reminded myself, on the night of that murder, the yacht had been almost a kilometre further out from the shore. The cabin was luxuriously furnished, and a glance through the open door to the bathroom revealed that to be equally sumptuous. Apart from the double bed, there were also four small armchairs around a coffee table and it was here that Neil Vaughan and I were invited to sit down. Oscar was allowed to stretch out on a soft white rug alongside me and he gave me a disbelieving look as he did so. I found myself hoping that it would still be in pristine condition when he got up again. Black Labrador hair does tend to stand out against a white background.

Edgar Beaumont indicated a selection of bottles on a tray behind him. 'Can I offer either of you gentlemen a drink?'

Considering that it was still breakfast time, I decided to give the booze a miss and just thanked him. Neil Vaughan did the same and we watched as Beaumont poured himself a generous glass of neat Scotch. Might this signify that he had a drink problem or might it indicate a guilty conscience, meaning that he needed a bit of Dutch courage? When he'd taken a seat opposite us, I let Neil Vaughan do the talking, and he gave a slightly nervous, but clear and well-reasoned, summary of the situation he had discovered and ended by indicating that the inescapable conclusion he'd come to was that somebody must have been embezzling the company's money on a grand scale. As a result, he had thought it best to bring in a completely independent investigator to get to the truth of the matter and he hoped his boss would approve. He removed the sheet containing my terms and conditions from his wallet, carefully unfolded it and handed it across. The two of them then had a discussion with lowered voices and I studiously kept my attention on the view through the window and did a bit of thinking.

As Vaughan had revealed his suspicions to Beaumont, I had kept my eyes very carefully on the older man, trying to detect any signs of guilt. It had been a hard task because almost as soon as he'd begun to register all the facts, I'd seen a whole host of expressions cross his face. These had ranged from surprise and incredulity to disbelief and then anger. It was a convincing performance, but there was just something about his reaction that didn't quite ring true. Call it an old copper's hunch, but I got the feeling that maybe at least some of this news hadn't come as a complete surprise to him. As he and Vaughan continued to talk quietly between themselves, I sat back and wondered about Edgar Beaumont.

Was Beaumont the embezzler? Had Van der Groot found out and accosted him about it on Saturday night, only to end up dead as a result? Alternatively, had Beaumont murdered Van der Groot because he'd discovered that the person dipping his hands in the till had been none other than Van der Groot himself, and he'd taken radical steps to rid the company of the thief rather than risk a very public scandal? If he had been one half of the conversation I had overheard in Lucca – and I was increasingly convinced that he was – this would explain my feeling that maybe the news hadn't been totally new to him. Had he and the other man been discussing having discovered the identity of the embezzler? If that was the case, it could indicate that Beaumont might have had an accomplice in murdering their boss. Was this really credible? Would a couple of media executives really murder an embezzler rather than let the law take its course? I had serious doubts.

This begged the question of who his accomplice might have been. Presumably, it must have been the other man I had heard in Lucca. One thing was for sure: that couldn't have been Heinrich Schiller, as he had allegedly spoken with a noticeable German accent. So why kill Schiller? To silence a blackmailer who claimed to have seen something on Saturday night, or for a completely different reason? As for the identity of the accomplice, unless some other rabbits popped out of the hat, it seemed ever more likely that that person had to be Adam Phillips, AKA Mr Muscle, because I had definitely heard two *male* voices. And I intended to interview him next.

I tried hard for a moment to dismiss the conversation I'd overheard in Lucca. The fact was that I couldn't be absolutely sure that the two men had belonged to the *Regal Princess* group, so it was always possible that they had been two completely different men with no connection to this company. As soon as I did this, of course, it brought the only woman with access to the accounts into the frame as well, and this was Louise Challenger, the payroll specialist. Beneath her severe, bookkeeper exterior, could there be a murderer lurking there? Was she the person who'd been stealing the money and had she killed Van der Groot after being confronted by him? If so, had she been the target of a blackmail attempt by Schiller that had ultimately signed his death warrant as well? She didn't look the murdering type but, over the years, one thing I've learnt has been that there isn't one single, easily detectable type of murderer. Given the right circumstances and motivation, killing somebody isn't just the domain of the psychopath. I was looking forward to speaking to her.

Any further conjecture was interrupted by the sound of Edgar Beaumont's voice. This time, his attention was directed at me.

'Mr Armstrong, I don't need to remind you how delicate this information is and how damaging it could be in the wrong hands. Our company has a good name and our shareholders trust us. Something like this, if revealed to be true, could seriously damage confidence in us and potentially even ruin the company. If you are prepared to pursue this case for us – and I agree with Neil that you should – I need it to be absolutely understood between us that anything you discover stays out of the public domain.'

I nodded. 'You can rely on my integrity. I spent thirty years in the Metropolitan Police and if you like, I can let you have names of referees who can attest to my honesty and professionalism.'

He nodded a couple of times in return. 'Thank you, but that won't be necessary. Neil has just told me that he's already vetted you fully.'

I glanced sideways at Neil Vaughan and he produced a little smile. 'A quick search on the Internet gave me your background, and as a result, I asked my mother to call a friend of hers about you. I needed to be sure before I approached you, and you'll be pleased to hear that you received a sparkling bill of health.'

'A very sensible precaution, Mr Vaughan, but why your mother? May I ask the identity of her friend?'

'The former Metropolitan Police Commissioner. She and my mother are golfing partners.'

It's not often that I'm at a loss for words, but the fact that the former head of the force had remembered a humble DCI was a shock to the system. Finally regaining the power of speech, I thanked him and returned my attention to Edgar Beaumont.

'As I said, you can rely on my discretion, but I have to warn you that if I uncover evidence of lawbreaking, I'll have no choice but to refer it to the police.' I saw him nod, but was that just a little flicker of uncertainty I could see on his face? It disappeared as quickly as it had come and he replied in firm tones.

'Of course, Mr Armstrong, I wholeheartedly agree. We must make sure we do everything strictly by the book.'

I carried on. 'You also need to know that I'm not an expert in financial matters. In order to obtain a successful prosecution, you'll have to submit your accounts to scrutiny by specialists in the field, but that's some way down the road for now. Mr Vaughan tells me that, as far as he's concerned, there are only four people still alive who have access to the company's accounts and they're all here on this boat. Is that correct or is there anybody else? Maybe IT people, secretaries, former staff members?'

'Definitely not. Apart from the Inland Revenue, there's nobody else.'

'And these people are yourself, Mr Vaughan, Louise Challenger and Adam Phillips, is that correct?' He nodded and I carried on. 'In that case, I'd like to interview each of them individually. I've already had a long talk to Mr Vaughan so that's done. When would it be convenient for you and me to sit down together, just the two of us?'

Before Beaumont could answer, Neil Vaughan jumped to his

feet. 'Why don't I go and see if I can print out some of the irregularities I've identified? While I'm doing that, you two can have
your talk, if that's convenient for you both.'

Beaumont gave him an approving nod. 'A very good idea, Neil.
Go off and do that. Mr Armstrong and I can go through everything right now.' As Vaughan made his way to the door, his boss
called after him. 'And thank you most sincerely for bringing this
to my attention.'

I couldn't help wondering to what extent he meant it.

I waited until Neil Vaughan had left before launching into a
series of questions. Although I started by asking about very practical matters relating to the accounts, audits and the security of
the accounting system, I also did my best to introduce a few other
questions relating to Van der Groot's murder. In particular, I
asked Beaumont where he'd been on Saturday night after the
victim had got up from the table in the saloon and stormed off in
a huff.

He looked at me for a few moments before answering. 'I've
already given the police the answer to this. I can't see how my
whereabouts that night can be relevant to an investigation into
our accountancy problems.'

I felt that this was either very naïve or a deliberate attempt at
dissimulation, but I spelled it out to him all the same. 'Two
people have been murdered, Mr Beaumont. As far as I know, the
police are still searching for a motive. To my mind, the small
matter of a few missing millions might well prove to be sufficient
motive for at least one of the murders, don't you think? The loss
of the money and the murders may be linked, so an investigation
of one naturally leads to an investigation of the other.'

There was a pause while I saw him consider the implications
of what I'd just said. Finally, a resigned look appeared on his face
and he answered my question. 'I still find it hard to believe that

anybody here would have been prepared to commit murder – and *I* certainly didn't – but, if it helps your inquiry, I can tell you that I left the saloon that night shortly after Jerome stormed out, and I went back to my cabin. As far as I'm aware, most of the others did the same. It was almost eleven o'clock at night, after all.'

'Can anybody corroborate that?'

'If you mean did I have company in my room, the answer's no. I walked back from the saloon with Louise and she left me at my door. I'm afraid that's the best I can do for you in terms of an alibi, apart from just repeating that I don't go around killing people.'

I added a few stock phrases about having to ask difficult questions as a matter of routine and then drew him back to the accounts. 'Do you think it's possible that Jerome Van der Groot might have discovered the irregularities in the accounts before his death?'

'Are you saying you think he might have been murdered by the embezzler?'

'That's exactly what I'm saying. Anybody convicted of stealing millions of pounds would face a long period in prison. Trying to avoid that would definitely be a motive for murder.'

I waited as he formulated his answer and while I watched his face, I couldn't help thinking that none of this was coming as a major surprise to him. When he finally replied, his tone was cautious. 'I suppose it's possible but unlikely. Jerome was a very busy man and all this week, he'd been dealing with proposals and counter proposals for all our future programming, so I question whether he would have had the time to make an in-depth study of the accounts.'

'And of course there's another option: might Jerome Van der Groot have been the embezzler himself?'

'Jerome?' I saw him jerk upright in surprise. 'You think he might have been stealing from the company? No, definitely not.

It's unthinkable. Jerome has been CEO for ten years now and GreyratTV is... was very much his baby. There's no way he would ever try to steal from it. It would have been like stealing from himself.'

'You're sure of that?'

'Absolutely.' I had to admit that he looked pretty convinced about what he was saying so I moved on. 'And what about you, Mr Beaumont? How come it's taken one of your subordinates to discover something as massive as this? Surely you have overall control of the accounts and this should have been your responsibility?'

He answered almost immediately and the expression on his face looked like one of contrition. 'You're right, of course, I *am* responsible, but only in the same way that the captain of this yacht is responsible for everything that happens on board. If the engineer drops his coffee into an electric engine and it blows up, that can hardly be blamed on the captain.'

He was right, of course, but I prodded him a little more all the same. 'But we're not really talking about a cup of coffee, though, are we? We're talking about a large sum of money going missing. I don't know much about accountancy and I haven't had a look at your books, but it occurs to me that whoever did this must have made a very good job of covering his or her tracks. This wasn't done by an intern playing around on the computer, was it? This brings us back to the four of you. If we assume for the moment that you and Mr Vaughan are in the clear, that only leaves us with two other possibilities: Louise Challenger or Adam Phillips. I know you may find this distasteful and I promise I won't quote you, but could you tell me in your opinion which of the two would be more likely to have done it?'

I saw his eyes studying the now empty whisky glass in his hand and I rather got the impression that he would have liked another. The thought crossed my mind again that maybe he had a drink problem. If so, this could have been responsible for him neglecting his duties and allowing the embezzler to get away with theft on a massive scale. Of course, somebody who's very drunk can also make terrible decisions and do awful things – even commit murder.

I had to wait at least half a minute before he replied to my question about the other two suspects.

'I honestly don't know. Yes, both of them are good at their jobs and good with figures. Both know the passwords and have access to all areas of the accounts. The fact is, however, that Adam has worked for the company for five or six years now and Louise for three. We've never had any trouble with either, so I find it hard to believe that they might have suddenly developed into embezzlers.'

'And are you aware of any money problems either of them might have had? Maybe a gambling problem? Some other forms of debt?' He just shook his head so I decided enough was enough for now. 'Thank you very much, Mr Beaumont. I'd like to speak to Adam Phillips now. Would it be possible to assign me a cabin where I can talk to him in private?'

He stood up immediately. 'I'll get onto it right away. But first, I think I need to make a general announcement to everybody, explaining why you're here.' He caught my eye for a moment. 'Would you agree with that course of action?'

I'd been thinking about this already and I decided that there was little to be gained by trying to keep things secret. After all, there were supposedly only two people here apart from him and Vaughan who could possibly have had access to the accounts, and I was about to see the first of them almost immediately. I nodded in agreement.

18

TUESDAY MORNING

I interviewed Adam Phillips in a smaller cabin on the lower deck, and, from the objects lying around, it looked as though it belonged to the ship's engineer. This was less luxurious than the guest cabins above, but it still gave me ample space to sit down facing my interviewees. Adam Phillips came in wearing a sweat-stained T-shirt advertising the Mr Olympia competition 2021. It looked as though it had had a lot of wear since then. He apologised, saying that he'd been in the gym working out. The fact that this yacht boasted a gym didn't really come as a surprise. Given that it also had its own pool, it wouldn't have surprised me to learn that it had a casino and a disco on board as well. He sat down opposite me, his arm and shoulder muscles threatening to burst through his clothing but, to my surprise, I saw him visibly trembling. Was this in reaction to the news he'd just been given by the head of Accounts or maybe just a natural reaction of the body after violent exercise?

Alternatively, was it guilt?

I started with the easy stuff. 'Your name is Adam Phillips?'

'Yes.' He had to stop and clear his throat. 'That's correct.'

'And I believe you've worked for the company for five or six years.'

'It'll be six years in September.' He was leaning towards me with his elbows on his knees and I could see his fingers twisting and twining nervously.

'Have you always worked in the accounts department?'

'Yes, I'm a qualified accountant.'

'Do you enjoy your job?'

'Very much...' I saw him take a deep breath. 'Is it true what Edgar just said? Have you been hired to investigate missing money?' He looked worried but somehow not altogether surprised and my suspicions deepened so I didn't pull my punches.

'It appears that over two million pounds have been stolen.'

The expression of shock remained on his face but whether this was at the amount of missing money or at the prospect of being uncovered remained to be seen.

I kept going. 'I want you to be completely honest with me: do you know anything about this? I'm not accusing you of anything, I'm just asking if at any time you've had suspicions that something underhand was going on. I imagine you spend a lot of time looking at the company's accounts so you'd be well placed to pick up any irregularities.'

For a moment, it looked as though he was going to say something, but then he stopped and I could see him think twice. I didn't press him; I just gave him time until he finally made his decision. When he spoke, his voice was little more than a whisper.

'Can you promise me that what I say will be treated with the utmost confidentiality?'

'Of course.' This was sounding promising.

'The answer to your question is yes.' There was another long pause. 'Several months back, around Easter time, I became suspicious about large sums of money being transferred to what looked like an anonymous account. I did a bit of checking and managed to trace it to a bank in the Cayman Islands – I'm sure you're aware that's a tax haven – and the more I thought about it, the less I liked it.'

I tried to sound as encouraging as possible. 'So did you do anything about it? Presumably your first port of call would have been your direct superior, and that's Edgar Beaumont, isn't it?'

He nodded and another long pause followed before he finally came to the point. 'Please, for the love of God, don't tell Edgar that I told you this, but I found myself wondering whether he might have had something to do with it.' I saw him run the back of his hand across his forehead to wipe the sweat away, and this time, I felt sure it had nothing to do with his workout. 'You see, Edgar's been involved in a very messy divorce. It's common knowledge in the company. On a couple of occasions, he's let slip that his wife is trying to bleed him dry – those are the exact words he used. When I got suspicious about money going missing, I couldn't help thinking that he might have had something to do with it.'

'Does that mean you just kept quiet or did you speak to somebody else about your suspicions?'

'I couldn't stay quiet about something as serious as that. After all, if money was going missing, I could even find myself being under suspicion so, after a number of sleepless nights, I went to Jerome Van der Groot.'

'And you told the CEO everything?'

I saw him nod.

'And how did he react?'

'He was obviously very shocked and he thanked me for having had the courage to come forward. Reluctantly, I told him of my doubts about Edgar and he confided in me that he'd also been suspicious about him for some time.'

'And what happened then? Did Jerome Van der Groot go to the police or did he approach Edgar Beaumont directly?'

'Jerome told me he wanted to do everything he could to avoid a scandal and he said that until we had concrete proof that it really was Edgar, he wanted me just to keep an eye on things and report direct to him if I noticed any other suspicious transactions.'

'So you have no idea if he spoke to Edgar? What about suspicious transactions? Did you come across any others after that?'

He shook his head. 'Absolutely none. If it was Edgar, he must have got wind of my suspicions and stopped. I presume Jerome must have confronted him about it, and maybe Edgar confessed and paid the money back – but if he did, I haven't seen any big sums being paid in – or maybe it wasn't Edgar at all. I really don't know. I'm afraid that's all I can tell you. Jerome never spoke to me about it again but, seeing as no further money was going missing, I just assumed Jerome had sorted it somehow.'

'Thank you. Please could you tell me where you were and what you did on Saturday night when Jerome Van der Groot stormed off from the dinner table?'

'I sat there with the others for a minute or two before going back to my cabin. We were really quite shocked. Everybody knew that Jerome had a short fuse, but I'd never seen him so furious before.'

'And could you tell me who he was furious with and what it was all about?'

'Mainly with Martin – you know, Martin Grey, the game-show host.' He caught my eye for a moment. 'Nothing unusual there. Martin picks fights with everybody.'

'Fights?'

'Not real fights, arguments. He has a habit of rubbing people up the wrong way.'

'But this argument wasn't about this missing money?'

'God, no, I would have remembered that. No, it might have been a programming thing but, whatever it was, it really angered Jerome and he was absolutely fuming.'

'Thank you, and don't worry, I'll be very circumspect with all the information you've given me. Now I need to interview Louise Challenger. Could you ask her to come and see me, please?'

He stood up and left the room, still looking very nervous, and I reflected on what he'd said and the overall impression he'd given. It was interesting that the big argument on Saturday night hadn't been about the money after all. Maybe my next interviewee might be able to shed more light on that. In spite of my initial doubts, I tended to believe what Adam Phillips had told me, but the fact of the matter was that although he claimed to have reported his suspicions to the CEO, Jerome Van der Groot was no longer around to confirm or deny. Mr Muscle might never have reported anything because *he* had been the thief. It could be this had been a hastily prepared cover story following the murder of his boss. The next question, needless to say, was exactly what involvement he might have had in that. Had I just been talking to a very credible-sounding actor intent on avoiding a conviction for murder – maybe double murder?

Louise Challenger looked equally nervous when she came into the room. Today, her hair was hanging loose and she was wearing quite a pretty, flowery blouse and a fairly short – but not Susie Upton short – skirt. Certainly, she didn't look as school-marmish as the first time I'd seen her. Oscar, always delighted to have a female visitor, got to his feet and wandered over to rest his head on her knee. This appeared to give her some encouragement and she even managed to summon a little smile.

'What a lovely dog. What's his name?'

'It's Oscar, and am I right in thinking that your name is Louise Challenger?' She nodded and I continued. 'As you've probably heard from Mr Beaumont, I've been asked to investigate some irregularities with the company's accounts. Could I start by asking if this comes as a surprise to you?'

'It certainly does. Edgar didn't go into any detail. What's been happening? Has money been taken? A big sum?'

'In excess of two million pounds, I believe.'

I saw her sit back with a shocked expression on her face – although she might just have been a good actor.

'Two million pounds? But how? Who?' She sounded genuinely stunned.

'That's what I've been engaged to find out. From what the others have told me, it would seem that only Jerome Van der Groot, Edgar Beaumont, Neil Vaughan, Adam Phillips and you had access to the accounts. Is that correct or have I left anybody out?'

'No, that's everybody. But surely you don't think...?' She was still doing a very good job of looking horrified.

I ignored her question. 'You're absolutely sure about there's nobody else? No secretaries, trainees, interns?'

'Absolutely not. We're the only people with access, but...?'

This time, I did reply to her unposed question. 'Now that Mr Van der Groot has been murdered, we're left with just four possible perpetrators. I'm trying to identify which of you this might be.'

The expression on her face was one of horror, but she pulled herself together and looked me square in the eye. 'Well, I can tell you right now that I had nothing to do with it.'

'That's good to hear but, tell me, if you *had* wanted to make payments to an outside bank account, could you have done so?'

She answered immediately. 'Yes, of course I could. That's the main part of my job. I pay people, but everything I do is vetted by Neil and Edgar and, of course, by Jerome.'

That sounded pretty conclusive. 'I now have a more difficult question for you: assuming that you're telling the truth, and seeing as Jerome Van der Groot is dead, that only leaves three possible perpetrators. Have you ever had any suspicions about any of them?'

She immediately shook her head but I sensed a lack of conviction. I waited some time for her to actually put her thoughts into words. 'It's unthinkable that any of my colleagues would have done anything so awful. I certainly can't believe it of Adam or Neil.'

I immediately picked up on her omission. 'What about Edgar Beaumont?'

I had to wait before she answered and she was clearly choosing her words carefully. 'Edgar's been having problems, money problems. He's in the middle of an acrimonious divorce and every now and then, he moans to me about it, but I genuinely can't imagine him resorting to theft, particularly on such a grand scale.'

'And what about Jerome Van der Groot?'

She looked up sharply and caught my eye again. 'Jerome? But he's dead...'

'Indeed, but he might have been squirrelling money away, mightn't he?'

I had to wait even longer while she explored what appeared to be a completely new concept. Finally, she replied, but I noticed that she didn't look me in the eye this time. 'No, that doesn't sound right, besides, he's dead...'

There seemed to be little more I could get out of her about the accounts so I queried the big argument on Saturday night and her answer to this was more informative.

'It was between Jerome and Martin.' She shot me a quick glance. 'You were here yesterday, weren't you? You heard Martin – he can be a real pain. He and Jerome had a massive argument.'

'About what?'

'I don't know all the ins and outs of it, but I'm pretty sure it was something to do with industrial espionage.'

Now it was my turn to look surprised. 'You're going to have to explain that to me.'

'Like I say, I don't know much about it, but I think the cause of all the trouble was that Martin's been in talks with one of the other TV channels.'

'With a view to leaving your company?'

'I honestly don't know. Maybe he was just feeding them ideas, but, whatever it was, it really got to Jerome. Any company that can dream up a fresh game-show or comedy-show format could potentially make many millions. In consequence, any ideas have to be kept strictly confidential.' She paused for a moment before a thought must have occurred to her. 'The best person to ask is Susie. She was sitting next to Jerome as usual and she knows everything there is to know about what goes on here at GreyratTV.'

I made a mental note of the fact that Susie Upton's usual spot had been alongside the big boss and continued with my questions. 'This has nothing to do with the inquiry into the accounts irregularities, so you're under no obligation to answer, but just to satisfy my curiosity, what's the relationship between Susie Upton and Martin Grey? One minute, I hear them insulting each other and the next, I see Grey with his hand on her thigh. What's that all about?'

'Martin puts his hand on everybody's thigh – including mine!

I wouldn't read too much into that. As an outsider, I think Martin's secretly jealous of Susie because anybody can see that she's more popular than he is. He's got such a massive ego, this really gets to him and he's always sniping at her as a result. But at the same time, he absolutely drools over her. Anybody can see that.'

'But she doesn't return his affection?'

'Definitely not.'

'Do you think anybody else here is attracted to Susie?'

If she was puzzled to see the possible connection between these questions and the missing money, she didn't show it. I saw her pause for thought for a few seconds before replying. 'I don't think so. Of course, there was always Jerome.'

'What makes you so sure about that?'

'Just the way he behaved alongside her.' She raised her eyes from Oscar for a moment or two and looked at me. 'He was always very... I don't know the word really, maybe "possessive". He was very touchy feely with her, he insisted on her sitting with him and I've seen him put his hand on her bottom.' Her expression soured. 'I certainly wouldn't have let him do something like that to me.'

'And do you think anything ever happened between them?'

She shrugged. 'I really don't know, but I doubt it. Susie's a flirt. Everybody knows that, but I don't think she would stoop that low.'

'Thank you. I now only have a couple more questions for you. First, what did you do on Saturday night after Jerome Van der Groot stormed off?'

'A number of us got up and exchanged looks, but nobody said much. Then I just went back to my cabin and went to bed.'

'Can anybody confirm that?'

She had to think for a few moments. 'I walked back with

Edgar. We stood outside his door for a couple of minutes and chatted – just about Italy and this cruise – and then I went to my cabin. I was on my own all night if you're looking for an alibi, but I'm not the sort of person who goes around murdering people.'

'Thank you and, finally, can you think of any connection there may have been between the murdered deckhand, Heinrich or Rick Schiller, and anybody in your group?'

She shook her head but then added, 'You could ask Susie. She knows pretty much everything that goes on around here.'

I thanked her for her cooperation and asked her if she would mind asking Susie Upton to come and talk to me. Clearly, the glamorous presenter was the fount of all knowledge here on the *Regal Princess*.

After the door had closed behind Louise, I reflected on what I'd heard from her and the others. Of the five people with access to the accounts, I was increasingly feeling that the suspects had now reduced to just two men: Edgar Beaumont and the late Jerome Van der Groot. As far as the other three were concerned, I had tended to believe them, although I still had the feeling that Adam Phillips had not been completely open with me. The next problem was going to be pinning something on either of the two – the dead man or the one who was still alive. Back in the days when I was at Scotland Yard, I would have sent the company accounts to the team of forensic accounting specialists who are specially trained to go through item by item, line by line, double-checking source and destination of every payment and correlating this against who might have authorised it. It's a long and painstaking job, but I had a feeling this would now be the only way of getting to the bottom of GreyratTV's missing millions.

The other interesting piece of information was the fact that Jerome Van der Groot had clearly had the hots for Susie Upton – even though she had been adamant in denying any relationship with him of that ilk, and my brief glimpse of the two of them together in Lucca hadn't struck me as overly affectionate. But what if Martin Grey had been right? Maybe her denials were just an act? Had she been cynically prostituting herself to her boss so as to get ahead? If so, might this have led to a situation where she couldn't take it any longer and had decided to resort to drastic action? Was the murderer a woman rather than a man?

19

TUESDAY MORNING

Susie Upton arrived looking flustered. Although Oscar managed to bring a smile to her face, I could hear more than a hint of irritation in her voice when she sat down to talk to me.

'The *Carabinieri* are back again. They've been asking everybody about this latest murder victim. Surely his killer has to be somebody in the crew, doesn't it? We barely knew the guy.'

I shook my head. 'Not necessarily. You have to admit that it's quite a coincidence that there have been two murders in three days. I suppose the police have to consider that the two might be linked in some way.' I decided to test her powers of deduction. 'I've been trying to think of any way they might be linked – can you?'

She paused for thought for a few seconds and I studied her while she was thinking. Today, she was wearing a different bikini with a very loose, white, cotton shawl thing wrapped around her. I'm sure there's a technical term for it, but women's fashion has never been my strong point. As before, she was looking alluring, but today there was also clear concern or annoyance on her face as she ventured a guess.

'Could it be that this deckhand and whoever it was who killed Jerome were working together? What if they had a falling-out and one killed the other? No honour among thieves and so on.'

'You might be right, but the question that still needs answering is why Jerome Van der Groot was killed in the first place.' I saw her nod in agreement and I continued. 'As I'm sure you've heard, the reason I'm here asking questions is because Edgar Beaumont has asked me to investigate what looks like serious embezzlement. Several million pounds, I believe.'

I saw her eyes widen. 'Millions of pounds gone missing? Wow! Edgar said money had disappeared, but I hadn't realised it was that much.' There was a pause while this registered with her. 'But I don't think I'll be able to help you. I'm very much at the sharp end, in front of the camera. I don't have access to the accounts and, even if I did, I probably wouldn't be able to make sense of them. I have an accountant who does all my tax returns and things like that. Who do you suspect?'

'I was going to ask *you* that. I'm not suggesting that you're involved, but I wonder if you've heard anything that might help me? Maybe somebody with a gambling habit or big debts, or maybe somebody who has a grudge against the company?'

Again, there was a pause while she thought it through. Finally, she produced her answer. 'I really can't imagine anybody here doing something like that. Certainly it would have to have been somebody with access to the accounts, so that limits it to just a few people. Any of us involved with actually making the programmes wouldn't have had the opportunity. Of those with access, I do know that Edgar's in big trouble with his wife's divorce lawyer trying to take him for everything he's got but, if he called you in, it can't be him. Of course, there's always Martin. He has absolutely no moral compass at all, but I can't see how he could have got access to the accounts.'

'Talking of Martin Grey, I gather Saturday night's big argument was between him and Jerome Van der Groot. I heard it might have been something to do with industrial espionage. You're sure it had nothing to do with the accounts?' I already knew the answer to this last question but, as I was ostensibly here to investigate the fraud, I did my best to link my question to it.

She answered immediately. 'It wasn't about the accounts. Call it what you like, but the fact of the matter is that Martin's been selling us out to the competition. I've noticed quite a few times over the last couple of years that just as we're coming up with, say, a new quiz show for teenagers, one of the other channels gets there first. To start off with, I thought it was just coincidence, but more recently, I've been having serious doubts. When I heard that Martin was responsible, it came as no surprise, but I thought it was shameful, even for somebody like him.'

'What's going to happen to him? Will he lose his job?'

'Almost certainly. On Saturday night, Jerome told him in no uncertain terms that he wouldn't forgive such a breach of trust, and that he wanted him out. He said he was going to give the host role for *Comics on the Run*, our headline show, to me and you can probably imagine that that went down like a lead balloon with Martin. He was spitting blood. Obviously, that decision will now have to be ratified by Jerome's replacement as CEO. Short term, I imagine that will be Edgar, and there's no love lost between him and Martin, so I'm pretty sure he'll rubber-stamp it.'

This was very interesting. Suddenly, we had another possible motive for murder. Might Martin Grey have killed Van der Groot as revenge for firing him – particularly as this meant that his job was going to the woman of whom he was secretly jealous? Of course, as Susie had just said, the decision would be up to Van der Groot's successor, who might or might not decide to treat him more kindly, but it certainly did open a completely new possible avenue of investigation. I wondered if Guido Bertoletti had been made aware of this. If not, I fully intended to tell him.

'Thanks for that. I've almost finished with the questions now. Can you think of anybody in your group who might have known the crewman who was murdered – Rick Schiller?'

She shook her head. 'No idea, I'm afraid. If he was the one I think he was – tall with blond hair – he was a good-looking guy. He wasn't really my type, but maybe he was carrying on with one of the female crewmembers and it all turned nasty? Some internal jealousy perhaps?'

'Who knows? Anyway, thanks. The last question relates to Jerome Van der Groot. I imagine you knew him fairly well. In your opinion, do you think *he* might have been the person responsible for stealing the millions?'

She had to stop and think. 'I really don't know. I suppose anybody can fall into temptation, but I can't see him as a thief. He was a funny guy; not funny ha-ha, often rude and more than a bit creepy, but that doesn't make him an embezzler.'

'But I gather that you were always by his side. Was there anything going on between the two of you?'

Her expression changed to one of clear annoyance. 'The lieutenant was asking the same question. It's all because Martin's always slagging me off, spreading malicious rumours, isn't it?' She looked me straight in the eye. 'The idea of having sex with Jerome makes me feel physically sick. I couldn't care less whether you and the lieutenant believe me or not, but that's the truth. As for Martin, if I had to list the number of times I've been groped, mauled and propositioned by him, we'd still be here talking tomorrow.'

There was a real edge to her voice now and I felt convinced that she was telling the truth. Interestingly, although she'd told me she found the idea of sleeping with her boss abhorrent, she hadn't actually denied it. Now that he was dead, of course, this would no longer be a problem for her. Could it be she had taken direct action to remove him from her life? I tried changing tack.

'As far as the dead crewman's concerned, can you think of any connection between him and any of your group? Has he ever been seen sneaking around the guest cabins?'

She shook her head. 'Not that I'm aware of. I don't think he was involved with any of our group. I normally keep my ear pretty close to the ground but I haven't heard anything like that.' She looked up at me. 'I can ask around if you like, although I'm not sure what connection there might be to the missing money.'

'Thanks for the offer. Please do. I've no idea what the connection might be either, but I'm trying to investigate all possible leads.'

She produced a smile, but that might just have been because Oscar had stretched out with his head on her foot. 'Leave it to me. I'll see what I can dig up. I'm sorry I haven't been more helpful.'

'But you have been, thank you very much.'

Much to Oscar's chagrin, she stood up. 'Good luck finding out who's been stealing the money.'

'Thanks, I have a feeling I'm going to need it.'

After she'd left, I pulled out my phone and checked out the man whose name kept cropping up. A search for Martin Grey on the Internet revealed numerous pages of items about him, and his social-media feeds were full of glossy photos of him doing charity skydives and triathlons, and a load of showbiz hype, indicating that he had no scruples about gratuitous self-promotion. In every photo, he was looking at his very best and I had a sneaky suspicion that Photoshop might have been involved in a number of these. There were a few photos of him at sporting events and on the beach and I had to agree that he had clearly been looking after his body. Mind you, most people involved with the media do that these days.

I couldn't see any mention of him touting for jobs with other companies, but there were several articles from the tabloids underlining what I'd already learned here on the yacht. Martin Grey had wandering hands and a number of women had accused him of getting far too up close and personal, although there was no mention of prosecutions. I was particularly struck by a photo of him with his wife at some evening gala and – although maybe I was just already predisposed to feeling suspicious – I had a feeling that the smile on his wife's face was decidedly forced. All in all, nothing new and certainly not a great character reference for the man.

I was still scrolling through various articles when there was a tap at the door and Guido Bertoletti peered into the cabin. I beckoned to him to come in and sit down and he closed the door carefully behind him first. Oscar jumped to his feet, delighted to see his new friend, and positioned himself alongside Guido as soon as he had sat down.

'*Ciao*, Dan, how's it going?' He scratched Oscar's head as he spoke to me.

'I've picked up a few more bits of information, but not an enormous amount. As far as the stolen money's concerned, my gut feeling is that it has to have been either Edgar Beaumont or the first victim.'

'Jerome Van der Groot embezzled his own money?'

'Except that it wasn't his. He was just the CEO and he would have been on a salary like the others. I'm not saying it was definitely him, but I reckon it was one of the two unless there's some other person that had access to the accounts. What about you? Any progress on the death of Heinrich Schiller?'

'Not very much, I'm afraid. It was his night off and he'd been into Portofino for a few drinks with one of the other crewmembers.' He consulted his notebook. 'Jeanne Toulousain, French national. They took one of the rubber dinghies and came back around eleven-thirty. The Frenchwoman claims she then went off to bed on her own and he went off in the other direction. She looked quite upset about his death but that doesn't prove anything. As far as I can gather from the other crewmembers, Schiller had a bit of a reputation with the ladies and the captain had already spoken to him twice about not getting involved with women on the yacht.'

I gave that a bit of thought. 'I suppose one of the female guests or crew might have had a little fling with him and that might have led to one of the others killing him out of jealousy, but it's flimsy at best. One bit of information I did pick up is that the big argument immediately before Jerome Van der Groot's death was indeed with Martin Grey, but it wasn't so much an argument as almost certainly the end of Grey's career in the company. Apparently, he'd been passing on company secrets to some of their competitors and, by the sound of it, Van der Groot was livid and sacked him. That might provide a motive for murder. A bit excessive, I agree, but everybody says that the two men were very drunk and very angry.'

'That could well be significant. I'd better have a serious talk to Mr Grey.'

At that moment, my phone started ringing and I was mildly surprised to see that it was Heather Greensleeves.

'Hi, Heather. All well?'

'Hi, Dan. Yes, everything's fine, thanks. I wonder if you could get a message to the *Carabinieri* lieutenant for me.'

'I can do better than that. He's sitting right opposite me now. I'll pass you over.'

It wasn't a long conversation but I could tell from what I heard and from the expression on Guido's face that it was the news he'd been hoping to hear. When the call ended, he handed the phone back to me with a broad smile on his face.

'Heather Greensleeves sends you her love but, more important than that, she's just remembered the name of the other boat she saw on Saturday night. She was watching a programme on ancient Greek mythology and it suddenly came to her: *Poseidon*.'

I produced a satisfied smile. 'The god of the seas – with a bellyful of contraband arms. That's excellent news. The next question is where it is now. It's been, what, two and a half days since it came up alongside Mario Fortunato's boat, so I suppose it might be anywhere by now.'

As I spoke, Guido was calling his office with the news. I was amazed to find that they were able to call back barely five minutes later having already traced the vessel. He listened intently before ordering his people to come and collect him. At the end of the call, he told me what he'd just heard.

'At last, a stroke of luck. Under normal circumstances, we would've been struggling to locate a vessel that size. Apparently, it's something called a Beneteau Swift, a fifteen-metre motor yacht, and only vessels over thirty metres in length need to have marine trackers on board by law. As it happens, a quick search has revealed that it's currently at a boatyard in Lavagna, only half an hour along the coast from here, waiting for a replacement rudder after running onto rocks while sailing too close to the cliffs in the dark. Ironically, it was one of our own Coastguard vessels from Lavagna that towed it into port. I'm going over there now. What are your plans?'

'I need to do a bit of thinking and then I suppose I'd better report back to the Head of Accounts, although I'm going to have to be very careful what I say. At the moment, Edgar Beaumont is just about my number-one suspect for the stolen millions.'

'Could I ask a favour of you?' I nodded and Guido continued. 'Would you have time to sit down and speak to Martin Grey for me? From what you've been saying, it's unlikely he could have got his hands on the access codes to allow him to be involved with embezzling the money, but you might be able to get him to shed more light on exactly what happened on Saturday night. Ask him about his state of mind, now that it looks as though he might have lost his job. That way, when I get back, it should speed things up for me a bit. Is that too much bother for you?'

In fact, I was delighted to be asked. I'd been trying to think of ways in which I could grill Martin Grey without stepping on the lieutenant's toes. 'No problem. I'll enjoy doing it.'

20

TUESDAY MORNING

After Guido and his team had headed off, I sat in the cabin for a few minutes and considered my next steps. Part of me would have loved to be zooming across the bay with him – and I felt sure my four-legged friend would have loved it as well – but of course, my current remit was not arms smuggling but embezzlement. As far as the murder investigation was concerned, it was of course still possible that the perpetrator or perpetrators were to be found aboard the *Poseidon* or in the cells at the *Carabinieri* station, but, in the wake of the second death here on this yacht, it seemed ever more likely that both murders had been committed by one of the people around me now. In consequence, I couldn't help still having a keen desire to help root out the killer. As far as the missing millions were concerned, the first problem I faced was that, having been engaged to try to identify the perpetrator, I now had to report back to one of the two prime suspects. And the other one was dead.

Before going upstairs to speak to Edgar Beaumont, I wanted to sit down with Martin Grey, but first I needed to decide exactly what questions to throw at him. It occurred to me that I could give Oscar a quick run while I worked things out in my head, and the only place he could do that was back on dry land. I left the cabin and made my way towards the stern of the boat until I reached the stairs leading down to the watersports platform. Here I found two deckhands sitting on the side of one of the rubber dinghies that had been pulled up onto the deck.

I hadn't been involved in interviewing any of the crew, so I hastened to capitalise on this opportunity even though I knew this was unlikely to shed any light on the missing millions. I recognised Christopher immediately, but the woman beside him was unfamiliar to me. The badge on her chest identified her as Jeanne and I presumed that she must be the Frenchwoman mentioned by Guido as Heinrich Schiller's companion in Portofino last night. As such, this probably made her the last person to see him alive – apart from the murderer, of course. Christopher started to get to his feet when he saw me, but I waved him back to his place and took a seat on the side of the other dinghy opposite them both while Oscar wandered over to say hello.

'I just came out for some air. I've been interviewing some of your guests.' I didn't say in connection with what. The embezzlement was of course a closely guarded company secret so these two naturally assumed that I was involved with the murder investigation. Christopher was the first to ask about it.

'Have you made any progress? Jeanne and I've just been saying how creepy it is to think that we're on a boat with a murderer.'

'And a murderer who's maybe killed twice.' Jeanne's accent was noticeably French but she spoke English fluently. She was a fit-looking woman probably in her late twenties with a really short urchin cut that emphasised her no-nonsense look. I could well imagine her climbing to the top of a hundred-foot mast or diving over the stern to clear seaweed from a rudder. To be honest, I know very little about boats, so maybe nobody does those kinds of things these days, but she certainly looked an experienced sailor.

I shrugged. 'I'm sure the lieutenant's making progress but I don't really know how the investigation's going. I gather he's gone off somewhere now, so maybe he and his team will come back with a bit more information. I'm just on the periphery of the investigation really.'

Christopher caught my eye for a moment. 'Martin told me you were a private eye. Is that right?'

There was no point in denying it. 'That's right, I work out of Florence but I was only here on holiday, at least until the murder of Jerome Van der Groot got me involved.' It was interesting that the deckhand was on first-name terms with Martin Grey. As such, this probably made him better informed about the dynamics of the group than I had expected so I took advantage. 'I imagine Martin's as concerned as everybody else.'

Christopher nodded but I noticed a sour expression pass across the Frenchwoman's face. I was keen to see what might be behind it so I kept the conversation on Grey.

'He's very well known on British TV. Even I remember him and I've been living here in Italy for a couple of years now. I suppose you must meet lots of celebrities on your yacht.'

Christopher answered with another nod of the head but I noticed Jeanne roll her eyes. I waited until she looked across at me and then very gently queried her reaction to Grey's name.

'Would I be right in thinking that you aren't a fan of Mr Grey, Jeanne?'

She grimaced. 'You could say that. He's one of the guests, and so we have to treat them all with courtesy but, in return, would it hurt them to treat us with a bit of courtesy?'

I had a feeling I already knew what would be coming next but I asked all the same. 'Was he a bit of a pest?'

'A bit of a pest? He actually smacked me on my bottom and propositioned me.'

'What did you say to him when he did that?'

'There was a lot I wanted to say to him but I love my job so I just said nothing and reported it to Simon... the purser. Simon's a good guy but he knows the ethos here just as well as I do – the customer is always right. The words he used were, "Grin and bear it". Well, I certainly haven't been grinning and I've been making sure I stay clear of Martin Grey.'

'That sounds like a very sensible idea, and I can imagine your anger. I used to be in the police back in the UK, and smacking somebody's bottom would definitely be considered sexual assault. You could press charges against him if you wanted.' I saw her give me an expression that quite clearly said, *You must be joking*, and all I could do was give her a sympathetic look in return before continuing. 'I gather from your captain that relations between crew and guests are frowned on, and I can see why. Tell me, does any of it go on? I'm thinking in particular about this latest murder victim, Heinrich Schiller.'

I couldn't miss the way they both exchanged glances before the Frenchwoman answered. 'I liked Rick – that's what he preferred to be called, rather than his German name – but only in small doses. When he first joined the crew, he almost immediately tried it on with me and the other girls, and we all told him quite clearly to keep his hands to himself. In fairness, he did. I've never had any trouble with him since and I'm pretty sure it's the same for the others.'

I looked across at her companion. 'What about you, Christopher? How did you get on with him?'

I had to wait before he managed to compose his answer, and

there was an apologetic look on his face as he spoke. 'Look, I'm sorry he's dead, and it's awful that he died in such a gruesome way.' He caught my eye for a moment and I could see the anguish on his face. 'I was on anchor watch last night and when I did my rounds just before midnight, I found him lying just over there in a pool of blood.' His voice was choked and I could see that he was still in shock. And no wonder. 'He was curled up in a ball, stone dead, and even from a distance, I could see that his throat had been cut – well, slashed really. I've never seen a dead body before and it looked like a scene from a horror movie but, if I'm honest, I suppose it didn't really surprise me that much.'

'What, the fact that he was murdered?'

'Well, murder no, that's totally over the top, but he did have a habit of making himself unpopular. He was always finding reasons for coming on watch late or getting out of doing jobs, and a number of us have noticed things going missing. I've been convinced for some time that he's been stealing but, without catching him red-handed, there was nothing I could do. And if you speak to the captain, I'm sure she'll tell you about the trouble there's been over the past few months involving him and some of our female guests.'

I nodded. 'I had heard something about that but I'll go and speak to the captain again. Tell me, do either of you think he was carrying on with any of *this* group?' Again, I couldn't miss the exchange of looks between them. It was Christopher who answered first.

'I've not been aware of anything particular, apart from a running commentary from him about some of the women in their bikinis. He was only too willing to volunteer for lifeguard duty, but I'm quite sure that was just so he could be around the pool ogling the women.'

'But you don't think he was actually physically involved with anybody before his death?'

Christopher shook his head but Jeanne didn't look so sure. 'Like Chris, I haven't seen anything myself, but Maggie said something about seeing him sneaking around the guest cabins.'

'Maggie?'

'Maggie in Hospitality. She and Jess are responsible for general cleaning, laundry, that sort of thing.' She glanced at the watch on her wrist. 'If you want to speak to her, she'll probably be either in the laundry or in the saloon helping to get things ready for lunch.'

I glanced at my watch and saw that it was almost eleven o'clock. Oscar still needed a walk, so I decided to beg a lift back to Portofino in the launch and then come back a little later. Pre-lunch drinks yesterday had been at twelve forty-five or so and we had sat down to eat at one, so as long as I was back by noon, I reckoned I would be able to speak to the captain, Martin Grey and Edgar Beaumont without interfering with their meal schedule. As for me, after all the food I'd been eating in the last few days, I resolved to go back to Portofino after that for one of the excellent focaccia snacks Anna and I had had on the first day, rather than face another cordon bleu feast. I was sure Oscar would have disagreed with me on this, but I could already feel my belt a little tight around my waist and I knew Anna would notice when I saw her next.

When I asked for a lift, saying I just wanted to pop back to dry land for half an hour or so, Christopher made a helpful suggestion. 'Why don't you take one of these dinghies? It'll be lunchtime soon so we won't need it for an hour or two. Just make sure you don't leave it where it would be in the way of the ferry. They get very annoyed if you do that.'

He slid one of the dinghies back into the water and showed

me how to start the engine. Although this was all new to me, it wasn't exactly rocket science and I quickly got the hang of it. What was really interesting was to see how Oscar took to being in something a lot smaller than the launch and a lot nearer the water. I set off gently with him standing excitedly at the front, tail wagging, and I was just wondering whether I should clip him onto his lead in case he decided to go for a swim when the inevitable happened. He turned, glanced momentarily at me with a beaming canine smile on his hairy face and, before I could wag my finger at him and tell him no, he had leapt into the water.

I throttled back and managed to manoeuvre the dinghy alongside him. Trying to get him back into the boat without soaking myself in the process turned out to be an impossibility so in the end, I just chugged very gently into the port while he doggy-paddled happily alongside me, snorting every now and then and looking for all the world like a seal. It took almost ten minutes and I felt sure he would sleep well tonight as a result. It occurred to me that this had been from the *Regal Princess*'s current mooring close to the shore. It was just as well he hadn't pulled this trick where the yacht had been anchored on Saturday night. Even a healthy young dog like Oscar would have taken a long, long time and probably exhausted himself trying to swim almost a kilometre.

I guided him over to the far end of the promenade where a handful of fishing boats were moored up and he was able to exit the water without too much difficulty by walking up the old stone slipway. It was a bit slippery, with green weed below the water-line, but he manged fine. I was just hunting around for some-where to moor the boat when I heard a voice from the quay a metre above me.

'Buongiorno, Commissario.' It was Officer Solaro of the Coast-guard. Oscar recognised him immediately and headed over to him, tail wagging. I just had time to shout a warning so that Solaro could jump backwards to avoid being soaked as Oscar set about shaking himself violently, sending 'Eau de Labrador' all over the place, mercifully avoiding any passing tourists. The last thing I needed was a bill for a designer dress ruined by my dog trying to dry himself. I shouted an apology, but the young officer just gave me a smile.

'I'm fine, I know what dogs are like. If you're looking for somewhere to moor up, there's a ring just over there.' He pointed towards a massive iron ring set into the stone of the jetty and I chugged across to it and tied up. Getting out proved slightly tricky but Solaro very kindly bent down and gave me a helping hand.

'I didn't know you were a sailor, Signor Armstrong.'

'Call me Dan. Everybody does.' I gave him a rueful smile. 'I'm sure you can see that I'm not much of a sailor, but the guys on the *Regal Princess* told me driving a dinghy was dead easy. Unfortunately, they forgot to tell Oscar he was meant to stay in the boat.' We shook hands and I asked him if there was anything new on the investigation but, as it turned out, I probably knew more than he did. I gave him a brief summary of what had happened so far and queried why he hadn't gone off across the bay to check out the *Poseidon* as well. Now it was his turn to give me a rueful smile.

'The port captain came back from his trip to South Africa overnight and he's gone with Sara, my colleague, and the *Carabinieri* officers. The boss likes to be involved when something exciting's happening.' He glanced at Oscar. 'Your dog swims well. Maybe you should enter him for the *Miglio Blu*, the Blue Mile race. Hundreds of people take part every autumn in a swim along the coast between here and Santa Margherita.'

'A mile? That's way too far. No, I think a couple of hundred metres like today is more than enough. I wouldn't want to lose him.'

His expression became more serious. 'The lieutenant seems to think that the murderer is one of the people on the *Regal Princess*. Are you any nearer to finding out who it was?'

The two of us wandered over to an old stone bench against the wall beneath the cliffs of Castello Brown. There was nobody within earshot so I told him what I had so far.

'I have no concrete proof against anybody, but the way I see it, there are four possible motives at play here: either Van der Groot was killed by the person who's been stealing millions from the TV company – maybe the killer had even been in cahoots with Van der Groot himself – or he was killed by a furious TV personality who had just been sacked, or he was killed by a female actor who'd been forced to have sex with him and couldn't take it any longer. The fourth possibility is less likely and that's that it was done by somebody in the accounts department who discovered Van der Groot had stolen the money and killed him so as to avoid a scandal. However, I don't really think that one's credible.'

Paolo Solaro nodded. 'And what about the second murder? Was the deckhand killed because he knew too much?'

I nodded approvingly. 'That's pretty much the conclusion we've come to. The lieutenant said the man had a history of blackmail and extortion so we're increasingly confident that he must have seen something on Saturday night and he approached the murderer for money. Unfortunately for him, he ended up dead as a result.'

'What about this female actor you mentioned? Which one is she? The gorgeous redhead or the sexy blonde?'

I wasn't totally sure that his descriptions of Tamsin and Susie would have made it onto a formal case report but they were undoubtedly accurate. I smiled back at him. 'Susie Upton, the blonde. I'm not sure how convinced I am that she might have been a killer or, indeed, that she might have been trading sexual favours for promotion. As far as I can tell, that was maybe just a story put about by one of the other main suspects, Martin Grey. I don't know if you remember him.'

Solaro nodded. 'The mouthy one with the cheesy smile. Yes, I remember thinking he was a pain when we interviewed him. I'm not sure if I can see him as a killer, but I have to confess, I didn't really like him.' He caught my eye and said it before I could. 'And, yes, I know that doesn't make him a murderer, but there was just something very fake about him.'

'I feel very much the same way. Apparently, he and the first victim were both very drunk and very angry on Saturday night, so I suppose it might have led to murder. Without evidence, who knows?'

'And your other suspect, the one you said might have been fiddling the accounts. Was that the Schwarzenegger lookalike or the other guy, Edgar something French?'

I was impressed that the young officer was able to recall the people on the yacht without having to consult his notebook and I gave him a smile as I replied.

'That's the one: the older one, Edgar Beaumont. He's going through a nasty divorce at the moment and everybody tells me he badly needs money. That could have been a motive for embezzlement and he killed Van der Groot when he was found out. Like I say, what we need is evidence, hard evidence. The lieutenant said that they were taking fingerprints and DNA swabs this morning. You never know, we might get lucky. Whoever killed Heinrich Schiller, the deckhand, was careless enough to leave the murder weapon sticking in the body. It would be great if they also left their prints, allowing your forensics people to get a match.' I glanced at my watch. 'Right, I'm just going for a quick walk with Oscar and then I need to get back over to the yacht to interview Martin Grey. Wish me luck.'

21

TUESDAY MORNING

Oscar and I took a walk through the crowded streets and up the hill past the *Carabinieri* barracks where Maresciallo Veronese was for once missing on the terrace – no doubt across the bay at the *Poseidon*. As soon as we got away from the sea, the crowds began to thin and the narrow road very quickly reached an abrupt halt and an even narrower footpath continued up the hill ahead of us. It was very pleasant here in the trees but there wasn't really anywhere for Oscar to run, but at least he had the pleasure of marking virtually every single tree and gatepost he came to, thus indicating to other dogs that he now claimed control of the whole village. As we walked, I called Anna and got her as her train was arriving in Florence. She couldn't talk so I just told her everything was going well and that I would ring her this evening. She sounded quite happy and it was with a feeling of relief that I returned to the job in hand and headed back towards the harbour.

In the dinghy, I made sure that I kept hold of the end of Oscar's lead. He had almost dried out completely in the hot July sunshine and I certainly didn't want him to leap overboard and get soaked all over again. The trip out to the yacht through the multitude of moored boats took only three or four minutes, although I had a moment of concern when the ferry loomed up dead ahead of me, looking huge from where I was sitting. Fortunately, I managed to take avoiding action and stay well clear, and the remainder of the brief voyage was uneventful. The view back towards Portofino with its faded yellow, orange and pink houses highlighted against the backdrop of dense deep green vegetation on the surrounding hills was delightful. Shame about the crowds... and two murders.

I found Martin Grey at the pool, doing a determined and stylish front crawl against the counter-current swimming jet. I waited several minutes until he stopped swimming and noticed me. The expression on his face wasn't exactly welcoming but he swam over to the ladder and climbed out.

'Good morning, Chief Inspector.'

'Good morning, Mr Grey, and it's ex-chief inspector nowadays. I wonder if I could have a word with you in private.'

For a fraction of a second, I thought I saw what might have been a look of insecurity on his face before he summoned the cheesy grin that Officer Solaro had noted. He looked around and indicated a couple of sun loungers at the end of the pool. 'We seem to have the deck to ourselves at the moment, so how about over there?'

I followed him across and we both sat down in the sun, Oscar positioning himself in the shade of my body on the opposite side from Grey, who sat back and gave me an expansive smile that looked almost genuine. 'How can I help?'

I decided to play down my suspicions for the moment. 'Lieutenant Bertoletti has had to go off. There's been a potentially important development that might result in the apprehension of Jerome Van der Groot's killer. In the meantime, he's asked me to speak to one or two people here on the yacht. I don't have many questions so I won't take up too much of your time.'

The smile stayed firmly on his face as he nodded. 'Fire away. I'll be only too happy to give you any help I can.' He looked and sounded cheerful but, of course, he spent his career looking like that so it didn't necessarily mean anything but, maybe, I told myself, I was just being too cynical. My ex-wife often accused me of this and she was probably right. Doing my best to stifle any feelings of mistrust, I started on the questions.

'Have you heard that I'm investigating the disappearance of a considerable sum of money from the company's accounts?'

'Yes, indeed, but I doubt whether I'll be able to help. I'm afraid I'm terrible with figures.' He gave me what could probably have been described as a cheeky grin. 'All I know is that I've got six fingers on each hand, but that's as far as my maths goes.'

I duly smiled back. 'Don't worry, I'm sure you aren't involved in anything like that. Apart from any other considerations, only a limited number of people have all the access codes and passwords. What I was wondering was whether you can think of anybody in the accounts department or elsewhere in the company who might have been in urgent need of money. Anything you tell me will be in the strictest confidence.'

He took his time before replying and, at first, he repeated what the others had already told me. 'I'm afraid poor old Edgar is going through the mill at the moment with a divorce, and it would appear that his wife's lawyers are intent on taking him to the cleaners. I would think he would love to get his hands on some extra cash but I'm not sure I see him as a thief.' He caught my eye for a moment. 'But brass is brass, isn't it? What is it they say – "Money doesn't buy happiness, but it makes unhappiness a lot more comfortable"? Who knows, maybe he did dip his fingers in the till.'

'Anybody else?'

'The only other person is Susie. She spends money like water and she seems to have a different outfit every day. And I'm not talking cheap stuff either. If it doesn't have a designer label, Ms Upton isn't interested.'

Considering the clothes I had seen *him* wearing and the fact that his swimming shorts had Burberry emblazoned on the front of them, I had a feeling this might be the pot calling the kettle black, but I pressed him all the same. 'So you think Susie might be on the lookout for money?'

'Definitely. She seems to throw herself at every millionaire we meet. I heard recently she was working her way through the Manchester United football team. I've heard her described as the good time had by all.' Even if I hadn't already been warned that he enjoyed spreading libellous allegations about his colleague, the petulant note in his voice was a clear indication of jealousy. And jealousy, as thirty years in the murder squad had taught me, can be a powerful motive for murder.

'Thank you. I'll relay that to the lieutenant. The other thing he wanted me to ask you was exactly what happened on Saturday night immediately before Jerome Van der Groot was murdered. I believe you and he were involved in an argument.'

This time, the cheesy smile did slip. 'Not so much an argument as a bloody lynching. Are you familiar with the expression "kangaroo court", Mr Armstrong? In my case, it was very public humiliation in front of my colleagues. As soon as we get back to the UK, I intend to speak to my lawyer about this totally unacceptable and disrespectful treatment. Miserable old sod! Would you believe Jerome had the gall to accuse me of betraying company secrets to another TV company, and I found myself summarily dismissed?' He glared at me and I got a brief glimpse of a more visceral Martin Grey beneath the jolly professional veneer. 'Sacked, me? Me, the instantly recognisable and much-loved public face of the company? Of course I'm sorry Jerome's dead, but I think the old man must have been going doolally.' He caught my eye again. 'Is the lieutenant absolutely certain that it wasn't suicide? It wouldn't surprise me.'

In spite of his protestations, I distinctly got the impression that the death of the CEO hadn't saddened him in the slightest. Ignoring the fact that he had described the victim – who had been barely a handful of years older than me – as 'old', I decided to stick with obfuscation. 'I'm not really sure of the facts. Certainly the *Carabinieri* are treating it as murder. Tell me, is it true that Jerome Van der Groot wanted to give your job to Susie Upton?'

His perfectly tanned face suddenly turned a very unhealthy puce colour. 'As if she could take on the role of host for the biggest-grossing game show on UK television! Bloody ridiculous! As I say, I reckon Jerome was losing it. His health hasn't been that great recently, so maybe something was going wrong in his brain.' He then spat out a colourful selection of unprintable expletives to reinforce his contention that Van der Groot had been insane, and even Oscar looked up in amazement.

'So it's not true that you were talking to another TV company?'

'I talk to lots of people and I have a whole heap of friends, some very good friends, in a number of different media companies.' He thumped his fist on the table for good measure. 'Was Jerome really trying to tell me that I can't even choose my own bloody friends?' His outrage was only too clear to hear and I could well imagine how an excess of alcohol could have led to actual physical assault on Saturday night, although murder still seemed excessive retaliation even for a narcissist like Martin Grey.

'Returning to Susie Upton for a moment, what do you think of a rumour I've heard that she was involved with Jerome Van der Groot, maybe trading sexual favours in order to get on in the company?'

I was interested to hear none of the backtracking he'd demonstrated when asked the same question by the lieutenant, but maybe that was because he was already visibly furious. 'Of course she was, anybody could see it, the little slag! How else did she manage to do so well? That's why he was going to give her my job. What a miserable little...' The list of invective he then went on to level at Susie would have scandalised an East End docker and I could sense the passion – no doubt unrequited – below the surface. And unrequited passion can be a powerful motivator.

'Until somebody murdered him.' I deliberately let a more sinister note enter my voice and after a second or two, a new expression appeared on his face. This time, it wasn't so much anger as uncertainty, and I saw him go straight into damage limitation mode – in fairness, remarkably fluently.

'Yeah, you're right, and like I said, it's very sad.' He didn't sound it. 'It's particularly sad for me because I wanted the satisfaction of seeing him hauled up before an employment tribunal for his shameful treatment of me.' He looked across at me and gave me a look of great sincerity, his eyes trained right on mine. 'Murder is a terrible thing.' I waited for another litany of swear-words, but this time, I waited in vain.

He might well have been a good comedian and a successful game-show host, but, as an actor, he lacked sincerity. Filing away this lack of sympathy for his deceased employer, I nodded. 'It certainly is.' I got to my feet and Oscar immediately did the same. 'Anyway, thank you for your time. I need to go and speak to the captain now. Sorry to drag you away from your exercise.'

He gave me a generous smile – one that might well have been tinged with relief – and dived neatly into the pool.

As I climbed the stairs to the bridge, I reviewed the conversation with Grey. One thing was for sure: his choice of vocabulary meant that he would never have made it into the Oxford Union Debating Society, but, more significantly, I found it interesting that, when asked, he had had no hesitation at pointing the finger at both Edgar Beaumont and Susie Upton. Whether this was just because of antipathy towards them or to deflect suspicion from himself remained to be seen. Certainly, from what he'd told me, he'd had a deep and lasting loathing for the first victim. Deep enough to have made him resort to murder?

I found the captain up on the bridge, deep in discussion with a man in a smart, white shirt with gold braid on the epaulettes. Tamsin had pointed him out to me the previous day as the first officer, sort of a deputy captain, but we hadn't spoken yet. He was probably no older than my daughter, in his early or maybe mid-thirties, and he was the first to look up when Oscar and I came in. As my arrival interrupted their conversation, I was quick to hold up an apologetic hand. 'I'm sorry if I've come at a bad time. I can come back. It's not a problem.'

The captain beckoned to me and we all shook hands. 'Not at all. Do you know Timothy, my first officer? We've just been discussing how we're going to reschedule parts of this week's cruise in view of the fact that we've been stuck here for days. Have you any idea when the *Carabinieri* will let us leave?'

I shook my head. 'I'm sorry, but I haven't. I know the lieutenant's gone across to a boatyard in Lavagna today where he's hoping to unearth something that might help him solve this case. He'll probably be calling back here a bit later on this afternoon, so you can ask him yourself.'

'Thank you, I will. How can I help you now?'

'It's about the murder of Heinrich Schiller. I've been hearing rumours about your having had to speak to him in the past about fraternisation, or more, with guests on previous trips. Is that correct?'

She nodded. 'Yes, I'm afraid so. Rick wasn't one of our successes. He was sent to me by our head office in Genoa at a time when we were desperate to fill a vacancy, but I've been keeping an eye out for a replacement ever since. Apart from him having an unhealthy interest in our female guests, I've recently been hearing more serious allegations about possible theft.' She caught my eye for a moment. 'I'm appalled that he's been murdered, but it wouldn't surprise me if his death wasn't just a random killing.'

'In what way?' Although I had a pretty good idea I knew what the answer was going to be.

'I'm not aware of him being involved with any of the guests currently on the *Regal Princess*, but it wouldn't totally surprise me if we were to discover that he'd been carrying on with one of them, and this might have aroused jealousy or worse.'

'But you have no idea whether he might have been carrying on with someone?'

This time, the first officer answered. 'One of the housekeeping staff mentioned something this morning but, since Rick's now dead, I didn't pay much attention. I think she said she'd seen him hanging around the guest accommodation.'

I immediately picked up on what he had said. 'Thank you, I've heard that rumour as well. I believe I have to speak to a woman called Maggie. Does that sound right?'

The first officer nodded. 'Maggie's been with us for several seasons now and she knows more about what goes on in the ship than anybody on board. At this time of day, you'll probably find her in the kitchen or in the saloon, preparing for lunch.'

22

TUESDAY LATE MORNING

I found Maggie in the saloon, skilfully folding freshly laundered napkins into fish shapes. She was probably in her forties and she had a friendly face. She was wearing the same regulation blue polo shirt and shorts as the other crewmembers and I spotted her name badge straight away. I went over to her and gave her a friendly smile. Oscar also trotted up to her and gave her bare knee a nudge with his nose and she looked up from her work and smiled back at both of us.

'Hello. You're with the police, aren't you?'

I didn't enlighten her as to my precise role here. 'My name's Dan Armstrong. I wonder if I could have a quick word. It's about the deckhand who was murdered last night.' She nodded and I looked around. For now, we were the only people in the saloon so I got straight to the point. 'I've just been talking to the first officer and he said you were mentioning something this morning about Rick Schiller being seen around the guest accommodation. Is that correct?'

She nodded. 'Yes, that was yesterday morning, just after ten. I was surprised to see him for two reasons: first, deckhands aren't supposed to visit the guest accommodation and, second, seeing as he'd been on anchor watch the previous night, I would have expected him to have been in bed, catching up on his sleep.' She had a lovely, singsong Welsh accent.

'Would you be able to tell me if he spoke to anybody or if you think he'd been visiting one of the guests in their cabin?'

'I can't, I'm afraid. All I can tell you is that he was right at the far end of the corridor and there were no guests in sight. As soon as he saw me, he came hurrying past and disappeared. He didn't speak to me and I could tell he knew he shouldn't have been there. If he'd been visiting somebody in a cabin, I imagine it must have been one of the last two: that would be Ocean Spray to port or High Tide to starboard.' Seeing the expression on my face, she explained. 'The company think it more romantic not to give the cabins numbers, but the fancy names cause all sorts of confusion.'

I gave up trying to remember whether starboard was left and port right, or the other way round, and asked one or two other questions, but it soon became clear that this was all she'd seen, so I thanked her and left her to her napkins. A quick trip to the purser's office give me the names of the occupants of the two cabins at the end of that corridor and they turned out to be Susie Upton and Martin Grey. This, I told myself, was potentially significant. I needed time to think things through before reporting back to Edgar Beaumont, so Oscar and I walked down to the pool deck and found it completely empty. Presumably people were either not in the mood for a swim or they were back in their cabins getting ready for lunch.

I wagged my finger at Oscar, warning him under no circumstances to go for a swim, and he grudgingly settled down beside me when I took a seat at a table in the shade. Less than a minute later, one of the hospitality staff appeared and asked me if I'd like a drink. I gladly ordered an espresso and asked if she could find a bowl of water for Oscar. While waiting for her to bring our drinks, I thought back on what I'd just learned. If our blackmail theory was correct, which of the two comedians had Schiller been visiting? If his purpose had been blackmail and he had been visiting Martin Grey, I presumed it must have been in relation to the murder of Jerome Van der Groot. If Schiller had been visiting Susie Upton, this might have been for the same reason or maybe something as simple as a close encounter with the sexy actress. Even though Susie had said that Schiller hadn't been her type, Louise had said that she was no saint after all.

My musings were interrupted by the return of the waitress with, not only my coffee and a bowl of water for Oscar, but also a handful of biscuits for him. Before handing them over, she asked if it was all right to give them to him, and I swear I saw him nod before I did. When it comes to food, my Labrador displays remarkable comprehension skills.

Less than a minute after she'd left, we were joined by the familiar figure of Neil Vaughan.

'Hello, Mr Armstrong, can I join you?'

I pushed out a chair and he sat down opposite me. He gave the deck a full 360-degree survey before leaning towards me until our heads were almost touching. When he spoke, it was in a whisper. 'I was wondering how your investigation's coming along. Any progress?'

I decided I had nothing to lose by being honest with him. 'Without proof, it's almost impossible, but I suppose my gut feeling is that the person embezzling all that money was either Jerome Van der Groot or Edgar Beaumont.'

He nodded a couple of times and then leant even closer to me. His voice was so low, I had to struggle to hear what he said next. 'I think I've found something that might help. In fact, I know

I have.' In response to my immediate expression of interest, he elaborated. 'I've been back through each of the suspect bank transfers over the last twelve months, and in each case, there can be no doubt that they were all signed off by Edgar, not Jerome, and certainly not by Adam or Louise.'

I sat back and took a sip of my coffee. So it was looking very much as if we had found our thief. The question was whether Edgar Beaumont would also turn out to be a *murderer*.

Any further conversation was interrupted by the sight of an orange shape speeding across the water towards us, leaving a long wake of white water behind it. I immediately recognised it as the Coastguard launch and as it approached, I could see Lieutenant Guido Bertoletti standing in the cockpit with Maresciallo Veronese beside him. The boat slowed when it reached the *Regal Princess* and disappeared below us to land at the watersports deck. A minute later, there was the sound of feet on the stairs and both *Carabinieri* officers appeared, followed by the Coastguard captain and another officer. From the smiles on their faces, it was clear that things had been going well, and I couldn't wait to hear how well.

'Have you caught the gunrunners?'

Guido came across and sat down alongside me. Neil Vaughan, realising he was encroaching on police business, jumped to his feet and tactfully disappeared up the stairs towards the saloon. The other officers sat down and Guido gave me the news.

'Game, set and match. What a bunch of amateurs! Not only did we find a couple of shipping manifests in a bin on the boat and clear evidence of where the cases of arms had been stored in the front hold, we tracked the two men to a hotel in Lavagna, where we found them sunning themselves by the pool. Even better, when we got the manager to open the safe in their room, we found a hundred and fifty thousand euros in cash.' By now, he was positively beaming. 'So we've got them and, hopefully, by following the paper trail, we should be able to roll up the whole gang.'

'What about the murder of Jerome Van der Groot? What did they have to say about him?'

His smile faded. 'Nothing, absolutely nothing. Just like Mario Fortunato, they deny ever seeing the man and vehemently deny having murdered anyone. What about here? Any progress on the embezzlement?'

I outlined what I'd just heard from Neil Vaughan and the lieutenant's smile returned. 'Excellent. Beaumont steals the money and then when his boss finds out, Beaumont murders him and then subsequently kills the deckhand who saw him do it. Maybe we've cracked the arms-smuggling ring and solved the double murder in the same afternoon. I think we should go and have a serious talk to Mr Beaumont, don't you?'

'I certainly do and, if I'm not treading on your toes, I'd love to sit in on the interview.'

'Of course you can, Dan. And do ask as many questions as you like.'

'Thank you very much but, before we do that, I need to tell you what I've learnt about two of the other suspects.'

I went on to tell him how Martin Grey had acknowledged how angry he'd been on Saturday night after effectively being fired and how he'd also pointed the finger at Susie Upton because of her extravagant taste in clothes and how he definitely believed she and Van der Groot had had a relationship. I suggested that this relationship might have soured to the extent that she decided to commit murder, although I still couldn't see Susie as a killer. Guido listened intently before passing judgement.

'Let's see what Beaumont says when we hit him with the information that we believe him to be the person behind the theft of the millions. If he still continues to deny killing either victim and we believe him, then it looks like we've got two other very strong candidates for Van der Groot's murder. Well done, Dan.'

I called the waitress and asked her if she knew where Edgar Beaumont might be. She replied with the news that he was sitting in the saloon having a glass of Scotch. The way she said it gave the impression that this was a not unfamiliar occurrence. Rather than all troop upstairs together, Guido and I left the other officers sitting at the table and went up to confront Beaumont. When we told him we'd like to speak to him in private, he drained his glass and led us to his cabin once more. He immediately headed for the tray of drinks and poured himself another generous glass of Scotch before sitting down opposite us and enquiring how he could help. Guido didn't mince his words.

'Edgar Beaumont, I'm now in possession of proof that you have defrauded your company of over two million pounds and you will be charged accordingly.' Ignoring the stunned expression that appeared on Beaumont's face, the lieutenant continued in the same harsh vein. 'I now put it to you that your crime was discovered by your former boss, Jerome Van der Groot and, in order to prevent him from going to the authorities, you murdered him and then subsequently murdered Heinrich Schiller, one of the deckhands on this yacht, who threatened to expose you.'

He didn't end on a question. He didn't need to. As he'd been speaking, all the colour had drained away from Beaumont's face and I saw him swallow his whole glass of whisky in two big mouthfuls. There was silence for almost half a minute before he managed to regain the power of speech.

'You say you have proof that I've embezzled that money?'

The lieutenant nodded. 'Yes, and it's irrefutable.'

I thought this was exaggerating what Vaughan had said, but Beaumont appeared to accept it at face value. He looked down at his empty glass longingly before setting it on the coffee table in front of him and putting his hands together almost as if in prayer. I saw him take a big breath before he started speaking, his voice hoarse and his demeanour downcast.

'I've been afraid of this ever since Jerome was murdered. Yes, it's perfectly true that I stole the money from the company and, like I told Jerome, I'm genuinely ashamed of what I did. I wasn't thinking straight. I've had money problems, big money problems, and it was the only solution I could think of at the time.'

He stopped for breath and I picked him up on something he'd just said. 'You told Jerome Van der Groot you were ashamed of stealing the money? When did that happen?'

He answered automatically, his eyes still on his empty glass. 'The end of April when he approached me about it. He had a printout of all the different transfers and we both knew that he'd got me dead to rights.' He looked up and I could see that his eyes were red-rimmed. 'People didn't like Jerome, but he was a good man, a generous man. He told me that if I paid the money back, he wouldn't inform the authorities, and I could take early retirement without anybody ever knowing.'

Remembering what Mr Muscle had told me, I queried this. 'My understanding is that no monies have ever been received back from you. Certainly they don't appear in the books.'

'That was Jerome's idea, to avoid giving away that I'd done it. He opened a separate account and I've been paying into it for the last three months, gradually selling or mortgaging my assets in order to do so. I can give you the account number; it's with our same bank. For the record, that account currently holds in excess of one and a half million pounds. By the end of this year, I promised him I would finish paying everything back, and I will.'

'I'm sure you can see, Mr Beaumont, how this could prove to be a powerful motive for murder.' The lieutenant was still sounding aggressive, although I had a feeling Beaumont had been telling the truth. 'Until a minute ago, you were under the impression that only you and Jerome Van der Groot knew that you're a thief.' I saw Beaumont wince as he heard the last word of the sentence and as Guido continued, his already pathetic expression grew even more bleak. 'What better way to rid yourself of the burden of repaying so much money than to murder the only person who knew what you'd done?'

'No, no, that's impossible. I admit that I took the money and I've told you I'm paying it back, but there's absolutely no way I would ever commit murder.' He shook his head so forcefully, the table in front of him shook. 'I beg you to believe me. I am not and I never could be a murderer.'

23

TUESDAY LUNCHTIME

The lieutenant and I left Beaumont to his whisky bottle and headed outside, looking for somewhere to talk in private. We found this on the very top deck. I had never been up to this sun deck before and saw that it was actually on the roof of the captain's bridge with far-reaching views in all directions. From here, we could look down into a fishing boat as it chugged past and see the collection of lobster pots and nets strewn about in it. More interestingly, Guido caught my arm and pointed to what I had just assumed to be the wake of the boat, but which in fact was soon revealed to contain a pod of half a dozen dolphins, following the fishermen towards the open sea. It was an idyllic scene and the contrast with the reprehensible behaviour here on the *Regal Princess* was all the more stark in comparison. Guido appeared to be thinking along the same lines.

'Why people can't just enjoy life as they find it without stealing and killing, I'll never know.' He turned towards me. 'What's your opinion of Mr Beaumont? It sounded to me like he was telling the truth.'

I nodded in agreement. 'Assuming there really is a secret account into which he's been repaying the money – and Neil Vaughan should easily be able to check that for you – I think we have to accept his story about the embezzlement and the deal with Van der Groot to repay it. As for his involvement in murder, like you, I tend to believe him as far as that's concerned as well. Surely, if he was going to murder Van der Groot, he would have done it back in April when the embezzlement was first discovered. He has no alibi for Saturday night or, indeed, last night, but then not many of the guests here have. Of course, if he's not our murderer, then who is?'

Before Guido could answer, his phone started ringing and he had a short conversation before turning back to me with an expression of triumph on his face. 'That was the lab. They've been able to find a match with the partial prints on the handle of the knife found sticking into Schiller's heart. Feel like making a guess?'

It was with a certain degree of confidence that I nodded and offered my choice of culprit. 'Martin Grey. Am I right?'

To my considerable surprise, he shook his head. 'No, it appears that the fingerprints match those of Susie Upton.'

'Susie Upton, really?' In spite of my suspicions, this still came as a shock.

'Yes indeed, Dan, we have our murderer! The way I see it, she's been trading sexual favours with her boss for some time until she finally cracked and couldn't take it any more. She murdered Van der Groot on Saturday and then when Schiller started blackmailing her, she killed him last night.'

He was beaming with success and I couldn't blame him. After all, he'd managed to solve the gunrunning case and the double murders in a remarkably short space of time. Or had he? The trouble was that I still found it hard to believe that Susie could be our murderer, but the fingerprint evidence was certainly compelling. I nodded a couple of times before adding a word of caution.

'That's excellent news, but it still doesn't answer the question of how she managed to murder him, dump the body and the dinghy somewhere close to the coast and then get back to the *Regal Princess* without being seen or heard. How definite were the Coastguard about the whole currents thing? Isn't there a possibility that the murder might have been committed here on the yacht and maybe the wind helped push the body and the dinghy onto the coast just past Portofino?'

He shook his head, but the triumphant smile remained on his lips. 'No, I've just been through that again with the port captain now that he's returned from South Africa, and he confirms what the others had already said. Yes, the murder might have taken place here on board but, considering that on Saturday night, the yacht was moored a lot further out, there's no doubt that the body and the dinghy could only have ended up where they did if they'd been abandoned much closer in. Susie Upton must have seized the opportunity to offer to go with him back to port, but then murdered him partway. As for how she then got back here, I reckon we've managed to find the answer to that question.'

'Really?'

'She swam back.'

Seeing the expression on my face, he went on to explain and it confirmed my impression of him as an excellent and thorough detective. 'I got my people to check the social-media background of our main suspects and they discovered a series of photos on Susie Upton's Instagram feed showing her taking part in a number of open-water swimming races. One of these was a two-mile swim around some Welsh island with an unpronounceable name. In comparison, seven or eight hundred metres in our nice, warm Ligurian sea must have been easy for somebody like her.'

I gave myself a mental ticking-off. Of course I had read that swimming was one of her hobbies, and I hadn't thought to check whether it was of the swimming-pool variety or long distance. So, it looked as though we really had caught our murderer, although I still found it hard to believe.

We hurried back down the stairs again to where Maresciallo Veronese and the port captain were waiting and broke the news to them, resulting in smiles all round. After that, it all happened very fast. The three officers disappeared into the yacht to find and arrest our murderer while I stayed outside with Oscar, still – in spite of the evidence – not totally convinced of her guilt. A few minutes later, Susie was brought out in handcuffs – although I thought that a little excessive – and the group headed for the Coastguard vessel moored at the stern of the *Regal Princess*. As she passed, Oscar stood up and wagged his tail, and she caught my eye for a moment, her expression a mixture of disbelief and dismay.

'Dan, you've got to help me. They've accused me of murder, of two murders. I didn't do it. You've got to believe me. I didn't do any of it.' Before she could say anything else, the little group disappeared from view down the steps and less than a minute later, I saw the orange Coastguard boat pull away and head for the shore.

My eyes were still on the boat as it entered the harbour when I had two surprise visitors. These were the two comedians, Doug Kingsley and Billy Webster. Kingsley had obviously had a shave and a shower since I had last seen him and he was wearing a fresh T-shirt, this one sporting a photo of King Charles with ridiculously large ears holding his fist in the air in triumph. Beneath it was the word *FINALLY!* His corpulent companion was still wearing last night's T-shirt, but he looked far more animated then earlier on. They were carrying three pint mugs of beer and I wondered idly, not for the first time, whether this was bottled or if the yacht provided beer on draught. I had a feeling that, on a luxury vessel like this, draught beer was all part of the service. Whether they had brought enough to satisfy the appetite of a bunch of British comedians was another matter.

Doug Kingsley set a pint mug down in front of me and pulled up a chair. Oscar stood up and wandered over to say hello to them but it was clear from the start that they'd come to see me. Billy Webster was the first to speak – after wiping beer froth off his upper lip.

'It's a bloody stitch-up. Susie's innocent. There's no way she could ever have killed anybody – no way, mate, no way at all.'

Kingsley nodded in agreement. 'There's only one person on this boat who could possibly have murdered Jerome and that's Martin.' He sounded convinced but I reminded myself that relations between him and Grey had been strained – to say the least – so his opinion was to be treated with caution. I picked up my beer glass and took a refreshing sip.

'Thanks for the beer, guys. Very welcome. What makes you so sure Susie didn't do it? The lieutenant's convinced that she was having an affair – probably against her better judgement – with Jerome Van der Groot and when she couldn't take it any more, she just snapped and killed him.'

Billy Webster gave me a highly sceptical look. 'Pull the other one, mate. She was no more having an affair with Jerome than I'm likely to give up beer any time soon.' To reinforce his point, he swallowed half of the contents of his glass in a couple of gulps.

I took another, considerably smaller, sip of my beer and queried what Doug Kingsley had just said. 'So you don't think it was Susie, but why do you think it was Grey?'

'Because on Saturday night, Jerome hit Martin where it really hurts – and I'm not just talking about his wallet. He told Martin he was fired, out on his ear, and that hit the pretentious little git's self-esteem. Martin thinks he's the best thing since sliced bread and everybody else is a plonker compared to him. You should have seen the two of them on Saturday night. Jerome was livid, angrier than I think I've ever seen him, but Martin was apoplectic.'

'And you think he went off and killed Van der Groot as a result?'

'I don't think it, I'm *sure* of it.'

'Well, if he's the murderer, explain this to me: the Coastguard have established that Van der Groot's body must have been dumped in the water much closer into the shore than where you were moored on Saturday night. The same applies to the dinghy being set adrift. So, if Grey was in the dinghy with Van der Groot's body before he dumped it in the water, how did he get rid of the dinghy and the body and then get back here to the *Regal Princess*?' As I asked the question, a bell began ringing in my head. If Susie had been capable of swimming eight hundred metres, then, if I remembered right, so had Martin Grey. I pulled out my phone and checked his Facebook posts for the last year again and came across the photos I'd seen of him competing in no fewer than four triathlons. Another quick check under 'triathlon' told me that most races included a swim of at least a mile. I took another, much bigger, swig of beer and put this suggestion to the two comedians. Doug Kingsley was the first to respond.

'You're right. He spends a lot of time in the pool, swimming against that current thing, and when we were over in Sardinia, he swam across the bay and back. That was a good long way.' He picked up his glass and banged it hard against Billy's, spilling some of it onto Oscar's nose, which was currently resting on the big man's knee. As a result, Oscar spent the next minute or two licking his lips appreciatively. Doug Kingsley sounded euphoric. 'Cheers, Bill, we've nailed him.'

As the idea gradually grew and took hold in my head, I realised that Martin Grey could indeed have committed Saturday night's murder and swum back to the yacht just as well as Susie Upton. The problem we had was that *her* fingerprints, not his, were on the knife found sticking into the German deckhand's body. Unless...

Leaving my beer, I jumped to my feet and ran up three flights of stairs to the rooftop sun deck followed by an excited Oscar. Fortunately, as before, it was empty. I pulled out my phone and called Guido Bertoletti. He answered immediately and I didn't waste any time. 'Guido, the partial prints on that steak knife, what does partial mean? Were they smudged or what?'

If he was surprised at the question, his voice didn't show it. 'The people at the lab said that they were indeed smudged; discernible but smudged. Why, what are you thinking?'

'On Saturday night, Martin Grey was quite clearly furious with Jerome Van der Groot, but he was equally furious with Susie Upton because she was taking over his job from him. What about this scenario? Let's assume he kills Van der Groot, piles the body into the dinghy and heads off into the night, trying to distance himself from the scene of the crime. When he's far enough away, he jettisons the corpse and the bloodstained dinghy and then swims back to the yacht just like Susie Upton might have done. I'm sure you'll find that your people who were checking the social-media entries for the suspects will have noticed that Grey was keen on doing triathlons. As such, he could easily have managed to swim seven or eight hundred metres.'

I heard Guido have a brief conversation with somebody his end before he came back on the line. 'Yes, he definitely did triathlons, so it could have been him, but what about the second victim and the steak knife? Fingerprints are fingerprints.'

'I'm still trying to work it out, but maybe it went something like this: Grey is seen murdering Van der Groot on Saturday night by Schiller, who subsequently approaches Grey for money in return for keeping quiet. Grey decides to kill the man rather than pay up, but he sees this as the perfect opportunity to get even with the woman who's usurped his position. What if he helps himself to the knife she's been using at dinner that evening, picking it up with a napkin or a handkerchief, which would account for the smudging of her prints? Let's face it, we've both been wondering how Schiller's murderer could have been so careless as to leave the murder weapon behind, instead of just throwing it over the side. Also, although it would have been patently obvious that the German was dead or dying after his throat had been cut, why stab him in the heart? Because, that way, Grey knew he would leave the murder weapon with Susie Upton's incriminating prints on it and, hopefully, by so doing would be able to rid himself of her just as he'd rid himself of Van der Groot. What do you think?'

'It's certainly credible, but just about the only proof we have in this case are Susie Upton's fingerprints on the murder weapon. How do we pin it on Martin Grey?'

'You're right; it isn't going to be easy. We either need to fool him or to frighten him into confessing. He's a pretty tough character, so frightening him isn't going to be easy, but I need to think about how we could fool him into admitting he did it.'

'Well, one thing's for sure, I agree that I definitely need to talk to him again. Susie Upton's now safely locked up, although she hasn't stopped protesting her innocence. It won't do her any harm to sit in a cell for a bit before I question her properly. Give me ten minutes to finish the paperwork and I'll come back out to the *Regal Princess* where we can have a talk, just the two of us.'

'Don't worry. I'll borrow a dinghy and come up to the barracks to talk to you. That way, we know nobody's listening in. Just make sure the captain doesn't decide to sail away now that Susie Upton's been arrested. The more I think about it, the more I believe she isn't our murderer.'

24

TUESDAY AFTERNOON

On my way to the *Carabinieri* barracks, I bought myself another of the lovely cheesy focaccia sandwiches from the little bakery by the harbour and shared it with Oscar as I fought my way through the crowds. When I reached Piazza della Libertà, I was pleased and relieved to see my van still there and free from parking tickets.

Maresciallo Veronese was back in his usual spot on the terrace and he gave me a big smile. 'You might be amused to hear that we received a call from a Sergeant Rossi of the Rapallo police this morning telling us about a visit he'd received from a random Englishman on Sunday, claiming to know the identity of the one-eyed man we found floating in the sea. He said the man sounded very vague. Nice of him to let us know, wasn't it?'

I smiled back at him. 'And only forty-eight hours late. Is that fairly standard?'

'For Pietro Rossi, yes. I was at school with him and let's just say that he wasn't the sharpest pencil in the box. Anyway, come on in. The lieutenant's waiting.'

He led me inside and I found the lieutenant in his office,

finishing writing something by hand. He waved me into a seat opposite him.

'*Ciao*, Dan, any bright ideas?'

I had spent the last fifteen minutes thinking hard. 'Like I said on the phone, I think our only options are to frighten him or to fool him, and Grey doesn't strike me as the sort of guy who's going to be easy to frighten.'

'My feelings entirely. As far as trying to fool him is concerned, I reckon he's also a pretty smart character, so that isn't going to be easy either. If we go in saying that we've discovered CCTV footage, or a witness has come forward claiming to have seen him on Saturday night or last night, he's going to ask for proof and, of course, we don't have any.'

These same thoughts had been going through my head as well. I racked my brains and dredged up a memory from the past. 'There's something I remember that worked about ten years ago. Whether it still works today remains to be seen. I had a similar situation where I strongly suspected a known drug dealer of being responsible for the death of a young woman with some dodgy cocaine mixed with a very nasty drug called levasimole, but I didn't have anything concrete on him. In desperation, I found a little plastic bag, filled it with washing powder, and waved it in front of him, saying we'd found it in his house. In fact we'd turned his house upside down without finding anything, but he took one look at the bag and immediately admitted the whole thing.' I looked across at Guido. 'That time, I got very lucky. It's unlikely it'll work twice but I can't think of anything better.'

'But a bag of washing powder isn't going to cut it this time.'

'No, but...' A sudden thought came to me. 'My involvement in this case all started because of a conversation I overheard in the gents' toilet in a restaurant in Lucca. I'm pretty sure Beaumont was one of the voices, but I haven't been able to pin down the identity of the other, in spite of listening to all the men in the GreyratTV group on the yacht. It's just occurred to me that there's one other voice that I haven't checked.' I saw the quizzical expression on Guido's face and explained. 'It's the voice of the first murder victim himself, Jerome Van der Groot. Maybe Beaumont was talking to *Van der Groot* back there in Lucca, and the man they were talking about was Martin Grey. I wonder...'

I pulled out my phone and started searching the Internet. In fact, it didn't take me more than a minute to locate an interview with Jerome Van der Groot on YouTube. I switched to speaker mode, turned up the volume and the voice that filled the lieutenant's office was unmistakably the voice of the second man I'd heard in Lucca. I gave it a few more seconds but there could be no doubt about it so I turned off the recording and looked across at Guido.

'There's no doubt about it: the two voices I heard belonged to Beaumont and Van der Groot, and I'm sure they must have been talking about Martin Grey. Presumably, evidence of his passing on secrets to their rivals had only just emerged.'

'Well, I'm glad you've got that sorted, although I fear it won't help us much with trying to squeeze a confession out of Grey.'

'Or will it?' I was thinking hard. 'The situation we have at the moment with Edgar Beaumont is that I imagine he's sitting on the yacht wondering whether he's going to be arrested and thrown into an Italian jail for embezzlement. Assuming he's already paid well over half the money back, you know and I know that he'd be unlikely to face anything other than a civil lawsuit if – and it's a big *if* – anybody in the company decides to press charges against him, but *he* maybe doesn't know that yet. If you speak nicely to him, I have a feeling he might be prepared to do you a favour in return for you leaving the affair of the missing monies in the hands of Neil Vaughan and the company.'

'What sort of favour? We can't just start making up phoney evidence. That would be entrapment.'

I nodded. 'Of course, but with Beaumont's help, you might be able to rattle Grey. How about getting Beaumont to recreate the conversation that I heard, for Grey's benefit? Everybody agrees that Grey's a narcissist and if we get Beaumont to repeat and maybe slightly embellish some of the insulting things that Jerome Van der Groot said about him and his treachery, maybe it might push him over the edge.' I caught his eye for a moment. 'It's flimsy, but that's all I've got. What about you? Can you think of any better way?'

'Nothing springs to mind but I think you're right: Martin Grey's fatal flaw is his ego. If we can seriously damage that, then he might start talking.'

* * *

Officer Solaro took Guido, Veronese and me back out to the *Regal Princess*, and on the way, we did our best to refine our admittedly shaky plan. First things first, we had to speak to Edgar Beaumont. When we got there, we found him still in his cabin and I couldn't help noticing that the level of whisky in the bottle behind him had dropped considerably in the course of the morning. He must have been well used to it because he was still sounding reasonably lucid in spite of his alcohol intake. As agreed, I was the first to speak this time.

'Mr Beaumont, I now know that the conversation I overheard in that restaurant in Lucca on Friday night was between you and Jerome Van der Groot. Why did you deny having such a conversation when the lieutenant queried it with you?'

He looked up, bleary-eyed, but his brain still functioning. 'I panicked. The lieutenant asked me if I'd been threatening to harm somebody at the restaurant and I was afraid that if I said yes, he might have considered me a suspect for the murder.' He gave us both a pleading look. 'I haven't murdered anybody, please believe me.'

'We do believe you, but we're trying to establish who the real murderer was. There can be no question now that it was definitely somebody here on this boat. If *you* didn't do it, who do you think might have done it?'

He looked puzzled. 'But I thought you'd arrested Susie? Not that I believe for a moment that she could possibly be a murderer.'

The lieutenant took over. 'I have indeed arrested Susie Upton, but we're still investigating all possible leads. If, as you say, she isn't the murderer, then who do you think that might have been?'

There was a long pause before Beaumont answered, and I almost thought he was about to fall asleep before he suddenly rallied and looked up. 'I can still hardly believe it – even of him – but there's only one person here on the yacht who might have had reason to wish Jerome dead and that's Martin, Martin Grey. Whether he really did murder Jerome or not, I have no idea, and I still find it hard to believe that any of my colleagues could kill anybody, but you asked me, and that's my answer.'

I exchanged glances with the lieutenant and then asked a question of my own. 'Can you remember what you were both saying about Mr Grey back there in Lucca? Presumably you'd just found out that he'd been talking to your competitors.'

'We were both appalled and Jerome was furious. He said a lot of very uncomplimentary things about Martin and threatened to sack him, if not strangle him, for what he done.' He glanced up. 'Not that he would have strangled anybody. It was just a figure of speech, but he was hopping mad.'

'If you can remember some of the uncomplimentary things

that Jerome Van der Groot said about Mr Grey, would you be prepared to repeat them to Grey's face? We'd very much like to see how he reacts when he discovers just how low his boss's opinion of him was.'

Beaumont snorted. 'Not just his boss. I also thought his behaviour was despicable and it was just the tip of the iceberg as far as he's concerned. I've been saying for some time that the company would be much better off without him.'

The lieutenant nodded. 'So if we call him in here, would you be prepared to repeat some of the accusations so we can watch his reaction?'

Beaumont sat bolt upright and nodded in return. 'I'd be only too happy.'

Maresciallo Veronese disappeared out of the door and returned a couple of minutes later with Martin Grey. Guido invited him to sit down and told him he would be recording this conversation. There was an insolent smirk on Grey's face – the sort that made me feel like wanting to give him a slap – as he helped himself to a shot of Beaumont's Scotch before sitting down opposite the lieutenant. He was wearing yet another designer polo shirt and a pair of cargo shorts – the ones with pockets on the sides of the thighs – and, as usual, not a single hair on his head was out of place. He smiled unctuously at Guido.

'May I be one of the first to offer you my congratulations, Lieutenant. Excellent work in catching a very dangerous criminal. The fact that we can all sleep soundly in our beds tonight is down to you.' He held up the glass of Scotch towards the lieutenant and then took a big mouthful. Guido remained unimpressed as he switched on the voice recorder.

'Mr Grey, we have some supplementary questions we would like to put to you. My companion here, Mr Armstrong, happened to overhear a conversation that took place on Friday night in

Lucca between Mr Beaumont and the late Mr Jerome Van der Groot. The two of them were clearly furious and the object of their anger was you. Are you aware of that?'

The insolent smile stayed on Grey's face. 'I always love it when people talk about me. No such thing as bad publicity, after all.'

The lieutenant shook his head. 'You may change your mind about that when you hear what they were saying. Mr Beaumont, could you tell us what Mr Van der Groot said about Mr Grey, please?'

I was pleasantly surprised to see Beaumont looking positively bullish. His tolerance of alcohol was impressive. If I'd drunk half a bottle of Scotch in the space of a few hours, I'd probably have been hanging over the side of the yacht being violently sick. 'I can't remember everything Jerome said and most of it was unprintable, but I'll certainly give you some of the highlights.' He subjected Grey to a scornful stare. 'He said you were a slimeball, a self-obsessed narcissist, and that he wouldn't trust you as far as he could throw you. He said if he had the opportunity to throw you off a cliff, he would do so with delight. I would add to that that I would have been equally delighted to give him a hand in doing so. The sooner you're out of GreyratTV, the better.' Realising what he'd said, he glanced at the lieutenant for a moment. 'We wouldn't really have pushed him off a cliff, but we were both feeling very bitter.'

As the insults came pouring out, I kept a close eye on Grey. At first, he kept the smile on his face, but with each new insult I could see it was getting harder and harder for him to maintain the charade of serenity. He was sitting across the coffee table from us, his hands drumming nervously on his thighs. For now, he was unable to make any retort because Beaumont was still in full flight and I could see that the head of Accounts was enjoying himself now, no doubt getting a lot of bottled-up resentment out of his system.

'He said you were a liability and he said you were incompetent. You might be interested to know that even before word of your treachery had reached us, Jerome and I had been engaged in serious discussions about replacing you. We only want good, committed, competent people working for the company, and you qualify on none of these counts. Compared to all our other presenters and performers, you excel in only one area: the number of complaints we receive about you, not just about your warped sense of humour and your foul language, but your ignorance.' At the sound of this word, Grey clearly gave up any attempt to feign a lack of interest, and I could see that Beaumont was on a roll. 'Remind me to show you the ratings one of these days. You come out bottom of all our presenters – after all, a quiz-show host who's unaware that the capital of Spain is Madrid doesn't deserve to be running a quiz.' Finally, Beaumont delivered the *coup de grâce*. 'In comparison to you, Susie is a goddess. I remember Jerome saying quite clearly that you aren't even qualified to clean her shoes for her.'

Grey jumped to his feet but Veronese laid a large hand on his shoulder and pushed him back into his seat. Grey shot him a dirty look and then returned his attention to Beaumont. He was positively spitting with rage and I knew that this was our best chance of getting him to incriminate himself. The lieutenant was obviously thinking along the exact same lines because he suddenly looked across at Grey and raised his voice.

'How does this make you feel, Mr Grey? Angry? Angry enough to commit murder?'

Grey looked back at him and there was a sneering tone to his voice as he replied. 'Yes, of course it makes me angry because it's untrue, just a pack of lies!' He was almost shouting now.

'And what about when Rick Schiller, the deckhand, tried to blackmail you? Did that make you angry as well? Angry enough to murder him as well?'

'I don't know what you're talking about. I haven't murdered anybody. The idea of picking up a steak knife and stabbing somebody is unthinkable.'

A sudden hush fell over the cabin as the lieutenant and I exchanged glances. After a few seconds, the lieutenant looked back across the table at Martin Grey. When he spoke, it was with a lower, less urgent voice, but his words cut through the silence with solemn power.

'How do you know that the victims were killed with a steak knife? The only people who know that are my colleagues in the *Carabinieri*, my friend Mr Armstrong, our forensic laboratory and the purser, who was sworn to secrecy.'

Too late, Grey realised the mistake he'd made. He started to backtrack, blustering that it was common knowledge when we all knew for a fact that it wasn't. There was now sweat beading on his brow and the sound of his hands drumming on his thighs was loud enough to rouse Oscar. Unexpectedly, I saw my dog get to his feet and walk slowly across to Grey's side. He's normally a pretty good judge of character and I was vaguely surprised that he was showing interest in this unsavoury character, but then he did something very strange. Instead of poking the man with his nose or rubbing up against his bare leg, he sat down, raised a paw, and started scratching at the man's shorts. Grey swatted him away irritably and it was only as I saw his hand disappear into the side pocket of his shorts that the penny dropped. There was something in there and I felt sure I knew what it was.

I jumped to my feet and threw myself across the coffee table to grab Grey by the right hand before it came back out of his pocket. As I did so, I shouted to a surprised *Maresciallo* Veronese.

'Grab his other hand. I think he's armed.'

While Oscar and the other two men looked on in surprise, Veronese and I wrestled with Grey until we had him firmly under control. When both of his arms were firmly secured behind his back, I reached into the side pocket of his shorts and retrieved the object whose outline both Oscar and I had spotted.

It was a steak knife.

There was stunned silence for a few seconds before Guido spoke for all of us. 'What were you hoping to do with that, Mr Grey? Were you going to murder all of us as well? After all, you've already killed two people, so why not make it half a dozen? You thought you'd hit on the perfect plan, didn't you? You decided to murder the boss who'd said such terrible things about you and straight after that, you managed to cast the blame onto the one person in the company you know is able to run rings around you in terms of professionalism, intellect, and charisma.'

Finally realising that the game was up, Grey belched forth a stream of foul language – during which he helpfully admitted both murders – aimed principally at Beaumont and Susie, but the lieutenant and I also received a mention, but neither of us minded. We had our killer and all the swear words in the world weren't going to stop him going to jail for a very long time.

25

TUESDAY AFTERNOON

More officers arrived and Martin Grey was marched off the *Regal Princess* in handcuffs, while Guido went through to the saloon and announced to all the guests and crew that they had nothing more to fear. The captain insisted on opening several bottles of champagne, but I limited myself to just one glass because the next thing on my agenda was to drive back to Anna in Florence. Billy Webster gave me a bear hug that threatened to crack my ribs and Tamsin and Louise gave me somewhat more restrained hugs and kisses. The same boat that conveyed the murderer to the harbour also brought back a very relieved and a very emotional Susie Upton, who for some reason decided to smother me in kisses when she saw me.

Needless to say, Oscar was not excluded from the festivities and he looked remarkably happy to be on the receiving end of hugs and kisses of his own. I still hadn't really had time to think through his intervention back in Beaumont's cabin. Maybe he'd just been trying to tell me that it was lunchtime and that he was hungry as usual. To that end, he had felt that directing my attention to a steak knife would be the best non-verbal way of communication. Alternatively, could it really be that my dog was developing into an accomplished detective in his own right? Either way, I knew that we owed him, and his reward didn't take long to arrive.

A few minutes later, his happiness swelled – along with his stomach – when he was brought a large helping of what looked like fillet steak with the compliments of the chef and the sous-chef. The blissful expression on his face as he hoovered it up was a sight to behold and I, for one, didn't begrudge him a single mouthful.

When the *Carabinieri* officers and I finally left the yacht, we could hear the powerful engines already being started up. The GreyratTV cruise was back on course and I hoped it would prove to be far less eventful than the past few days. I phoned Anna from the boat and left a message on her answer phone saying that I hoped to be in Florence by early evening.

Back on dry land, I headed straight back to my van. As I passed the little handbag shop, I hesitated and glanced in the window. Maresciallo Veronese, noting my interest, produced an unexpected piece of information.

'This shop belongs to my sister-in-law. She makes a fortune out of charging silly prices to silly people.'

I grinned at him. 'One of those people is my girlfriend – although she's far from silly – but there's no way I can afford to buy her one of these.'

He and the lieutenant exchanged glances and then, without hesitation, caught hold of my arms and dragged me into the shop. A cheery woman came over to greet both officers with kisses and to shake my hand.

'*Ciao*, Giovanna, my friend wants to buy a handbag for his girlfriend.' Veronese caught hold of her arm and pointed across at me. 'He's a hotshot detective from England who deserves the very,

very best price you can possibly manage. Which bag did you want, *Commissario*?'

I pointed it out to him, and his sister-in-law went across to the window to retrieve it. She handed it to me and, seeing me gulp when I handled the price tag, she then proceeded to astound me by naming a price that was less than half of what it said on the label. I made a weak attempt to object but the deal was very quickly done and the precious bag was put in an equally flashy carrier bag for me. But the generosity didn't stop there. After a brief exchange between the three Italians, Giovanna disappeared into the stockroom and re-emerged with a beautiful leather dog collar with Gucci emblazoned across it. Guido held it out for Oscar to sniff and added his own thanks.

'This is the very least I can do for the two of you. God knows what carnage that crazy man could have wreaked with a knife in a confined space. Look after him well, Dan; he's a treasure.'

Oscar was busy scratching his ear at the time and he didn't react. Besides, he already knew he was a very good dog.

Guido dropped the collar into the carrier bag, waved away my further protests, and accompanied me back to the van. When we got there, I shook hands with the *maresciallo* and was about to offer my hand to Guido when he grabbed me and gave me a hug and a grin.

'Thanks, *Commissario*. If there's ever anything I can do for you, you have my number. Come back and see us.'

As I drove back along the tortuous coast road towards Rapallo, I reflected that I was leaving, not only one of the most picturesque little villages I had ever visited, but also a number of good friends. I glanced in the rear-view mirror at the black nose resting on the seat back and addressed myself to my dog.

'Nice people, Oscar, shame it took two murders for us to get to know them.'

For a moment, I swear he nodded in agreement before disappearing from sight. There was a heavy thump and a heartfelt sigh as he settled down for three hours' sleep, no doubt filled, not only with dreams of swims in the sea and squirrels, but now also of fillet steak and designer collars. I hoped his brief spell in the millionaires' playground wouldn't go to his head but, when all's said and done, he's worth it.

ACKNOWLEDGEMENTS

Warmest thanks to Emily Ruston, my lovely editor at the marvellous Boldwood Books, as well as to everybody there, in particular the ever-hawkeyed Sue Smith and Emily Reader for ensuring that it makes sense. Special thanks to the talented Simon Mattacks for producing the audio version of the book. Listening to him is like listening to Dan himself. Thanks also to my good friends John Smith, for accompanying me to Portofino, and John Dearden, for his patient and helpful input.

ABOUT THE AUTHOR

T. A. Williams is the author of The Armstrong and Oscar Cozy Mystery Series, cosy crime stories set in his beloved Italy, featuring the adventures of DCI Armstrong and his labrador Oscar.

Trevor lives in Devon with his Italian wife.

Sign up to T. A. Williams' mailing list here for news, competitions and updates on future books.

Visit T. A. Williams' website: http://www.tawilliamsbooks.com

Follow T. A. Williams' on social media:

x.com/TAWilliamsBooks

facebook.com/TrevorWilliamsBooks

ALSO BY T. A. WILLIAMS

The Armstrong and Oscar Cozy Mystery Series

Murder in Tuscany

Murder in Chianti

Murder in Florence

Murder in Siena

Murder at the Matterhorn

Murder at the Leaning Tower

Murder on the Italian Riviera

Murder in Portofino

Poison
& Pens

POISON & PENS IS THE HOME OF
COZY MYSTERIES SO POUR YOURSELF
A CUP OF TEA & GET SLEUTHING!

DISCOVER PAGE-TURNING NOVELS FROM
YOUR FAVOURITE AUTHORS &
MEET NEW FRIENDS

JOIN OUR
FACEBOOK GROUP

BIT.LYPOISONANDPENSFB

SIGN UP TO OUR
NEWSLETTER

BIT.LY/POISONANDPENSNEWS

Boldwⓞod

Boldwood Books is an award-winning fiction publishing company seeking out the best stories from around the world.

Find out more at www.boldwoodbooks.com

Join our reader community for brilliant books, competitions and offers!

Follow us
@BoldwoodBooks
@TheBoldBookClub

Sign up to our weekly deals newsletter

https://bit.ly/BoldwoodBNewsletter

Printed in Great Britain
by Amazon

45869488R00136